YULETIDE GEMS

A REGENCY NOVELLA DUET

GRACE BURROWES

CHRSTI CALDWELL

WORTH MORE THAN RUBIES

By Grace Burrowes

DEDICATION

Worth More than Rubies by Grace Burrowes

Dedicated to the fierce little tigers of every species, and to the librarians who read to them!

CHAPTER ONE

"Must you be so gracious to every dowager, beldame, and debutante we pass?" Tertius Dundee, eleventh Duke of Dunfallon, kept his voice down. A peer did not shout on a public walkway, particularly when he was determined to elude the notice of the ladies.

"Yes, I must," Nicholas Haddonfield, Earl of Bellefonte, replied. "My governess pounded gentlemanly deportment into my hard little head before I graced the schoolroom, and the ladies enjoy my overtures. Besides, Yuletide approaches, and the season enhances my already-abundant good cheer."

"You can afford good cheer," Dunfallon retorted. "You're married."

"And happily so, thank the Deity and my darling countess." Bellefonte tipped his hat *again* and beamed his signature smile at a pair of widows swaddled in fur muffs and wool scarves. Because his lordship stood over six and a half feet tall and sported a head of shining blond curls, his gallantry was like a beacon across Mayfair, summoning the admiring glances of any female with eyes to behold him.

"Remind me," Dunfallon said, "that the next time we meet for breakfast at the club, we arrive separately."

"Nonsense. A brisk stroll works up the appetite."

"Blast ye, Bellefonte, don't ye dare even think—"

This time, the earl made a sweeping gesture out of removing his hat before a roving band of well-dressed young ladies.

"Enjoy your shopping!" he called. "Remember that I have been a very good boy this year!"

A chorus of tittering and simpering followed from the young women, their chaperones, and the maids trailing after them. Across the street, a petite female attired in a white velvet cloak gawked at the spectacle Bellefonte created. Her older companion, sensibly attired in blue, smiled indulgently.

"What sort of fool wears a white cloak in London?" Bellefonte asked, settling his hat onto his head, then taking it off again and tipping it to the pair across the street. "The fabric will be gray before she's bought her first pair of dancing slippers."

The day was brisk but sunny. A shiver nonetheless passed over Dunfallon's nape. "That wee princess is Miss Minerva Peasegill, accompanied by her mama. Miss Peasegill turned down three proposals during the Season and two during the Little Season, to hear her mama tell it. Stop lollygagging and get on wi' ye."

"She's quite pretty," Bellefonte said, budging not one inch, "if you like the delicate porcelain look. Still, white isn't very practical. I like a practical woman. My countess, for example—"

"Move your lordly arse, Bellefonte, or s'help me, I'll... God have mercy, they're coming this way."

Dunfallon's best hope lay in the fact that Bellefonte, being as tall as a lighthouse, would hold the ladies' attention. Dunfallon himself could steal away unseen if he moved with the purpose and stealth of a border reiver beneath a quarter moon.

The chronic congestion of London's fashionable streets prevented Miss Peasegill and her mama from charging across the thoroughfare. Dunfallon took half a moment to assess the surrounds.

If he ducked into a shop, the ladies might well follow. If he simply loped off down the walkway, they would also give chase, hallooing and you-hooing like hounds on the scent.

Where was a gentlemen's club when a duke needed safety from the matrimonial press-gang?

His gaze lit on a modest two-story building tucked between a coffee shop and a milliner's. The windows displayed neither gloves, nor boots, nor fans. No porters loitered outside prepared to bear purchases home for any shoppers.

A solicitor's establishment, perhaps, or... The sign on the lamp-post swung in the chilly breeze: *W. Bart. St. Lending Library. All welcome.*

"Excuse me," Dunfallon said. "Find another companion for breakfast, Bellefonte. Please delay the ladies as long as you can."

Bellefonte's smile became less genial and more piratical. "They'll ambush you in the churchyard, at the house parties, and at the Yuletide open houses. Mistletoe was invented by spinsters, you know."

"Or by clever bachelors, among whom I hope to number for a good many years." Dunfallon moved off with the pedestrians thronging the walkway. By the time he'd reached the lending library, Miss Peasegill's signature "Halloo! Halloo, my lord!" was ringing out behind him.

My lord, not *Your Grace,* meaning Dunfallon had avoided capture—this time.

The library, thank the blessed powers, was open. Dunfallon slipped inside with the same relief he'd felt when he'd dodged past French patrols and Spanish bandits. He remained by the doorway, a trickle of shame blending with his relief.

Miss Peasegill was merely a young lady in search of a tiara. She'd been raised with pursuit of that sole objective in mind, and now she had a handful of months left to achieve her goal. If she failed and ended up wedded to some cit's spotty son, she would be forever classed among the unfortunates who *did not take.*

Dunfallon well knew how it felt to be judged inadequate. He

considered returning to Bellefonte's side, but the sheer abundance of books on display caught his eye. As the second ducal spare, he'd learned to appreciate the company of books. His old tutor, MacAlpin, believed that a boy who read widely was a boy well armed against life's challenges.

Papa had thought that a boy absorbed with books was a boy who never gave his father any trouble, which for the first sixteen years of Dunfallon's life had been *his* sole ambition.

Windows two stories tall filled the library with light, and the air was gently scented with leather and lemon oil. A double-sided hearth took up the center of the main room. A fat white cat lounged on the mantel, and a mezzanine level ringed the premises on three sides. Book shelves lined the walls and stood in rows on the opposite side of the hearth. The fourth side of the upper level looked to be some sort of enclosed office, or perhaps a room for literary rarities.

A second fireplace was set against the back wall, and a pair of older gents nodded in wing chairs before the blaze. One of them had a lapful of knitting. The other drowsed under the open pages of a newspaper.

The library had an air of peace and repose, precisely the sort of refuge Dunfallon sought. Not as dark and sniffy as a gentlemen's club, not as elegant as the ducal town house. Just right for a bachelor seeking respite from marital doom.

A woman emerged from between two bookcases. She held a large bound tome and was attired from head to foot in gray, save for a sprig of prickly holly pinned to her lapel. No cap, dark hair tidily bunned at her nape, and only the slightest of welcoming smiles.

The very best sort of woman, one who looked to have no use for tiaras or dukes. Pretty green eyes, though, and a direct gaze.

"Good morning. I am Miss Emerald Armstrong. Welcome to West Bartholomew Street Lending Library."

"Miss Armstrong." Dunfallon's bow would have been the envy of Bellefonte's adoring throng. "A pleasant day to ye."

"Are you Mrs. MacInnes's nephew? If so, Mr. Dunn, you are

somewhat overdressed for the occasion. You can start on the sweeping and make up in vigor what you lack in punctuality. The children will be here at nine of the clock, and you'll want to haul up several buckets of coal before they arrive. They offer to help, you see, and then the job takes four times as long because a deal of hand-washing becomes necessary. Dirty hands and library books are a bad combination."

Her voice was precise and laced with a brisk hint of humor. She apparently looked forward to the arrival of the children, and for that alone, Dunfallon decided to do a bit of sweeping. That and the certain knowledge that Miss Peasegill would tarry on the walkway with Lord Bellefonte until spring, given half a chance.

"And where would the broom be, Miss Armstrong?"

"Come," she said, setting the book on a table. "I'll show you around, and if you have questions, you must ask. A library is a temple to the curious mind, according to my late father, and we cannot find answers if we don't ask questions."

She might have been quoting old MacAlpin. Dunfallon hung his cloak on a peg and followed the lady down a curving set of steps into a whitewashed half basement serving as a sort of parlor. The hearth along the back wall crackled with a merry blaze, and sunken windows added more light.

"The cleaning supplies are kept here," she said, opening a tall cupboard. "The coal chute is through that door. Mind you wipe your feet before you go upstairs. We send over to the chop shop for a noon-ing, and I told your aunt that we can provide you a meal in return for your labors. Nothing fancy, but one does not work at one's best without sustenance. You are free to leave after the midday meal, or you may use West Bart's as your study. I cannot promise quiet, but we do keep the place warm, and we have a Welsh Bible you can consult."

"A Welsh Bible?" Who was this Mr. Dunn, and why would he need a Welsh Bible? "Miss Armstrong, I'm afraid there's been a slight misunderstanding."

She bustled up the curving steps. "No misunderstanding. Your aunt has arranged a curate's post in Swansea for you, but you don't speak the language. If you work here on Monday, Wednesday, and Friday mornings, you may use our Welsh primers and Bible to learn something of Welsh in the afternoons. Come spring, I will not have spent the coldest months hauling coal and sweeping mud, for a pleasant change, and you will be somewhat better prepared for your first post."

"First impressions do matter," Dunfallon said, "but there really has—"

The front door swung open. "Miss Emmie! I'm here!" A dirty little boy beamed great good cheer at the librarian while letting in a gust of frigid air.

"And I'm that glad to see you, Caspar," Miss Armstrong replied. "Please do close the door and moderate your volume. You are the first to arrive, so you will choose our story."

"Who's that?" Caspar turned hostile perusal on Dunfallon. "Ain't seen him afore. Did he remember to wipe 'em great big feet a' his?"

"Dunn—Mr. Dunn, at your service." Did one bow to a cheeky boy? Dunfallon supposed not, because nobody had bowed to him when he'd been a cheeky boy. "I'm to assist Miss Armstrong with general duties as assigned, and yes, I did most conscientiously wipe my feet."

"Ye're a dogsbody for Miss?" Caspar asked as Miss Armstrong took the boy's cap from his head. "Lucky bloke. I'll show you how to sweep the hearth if you like. I know what story I want."

Miss Armstrong slapped the cap against the nearest bookcase, sending a cloud of dust wafting across the morning sunbeams.

"You'll want one of Mr. Dingle's tales," she said. "Winter is bearing down hard, so I suspect you want the one about the hot soup and the icy bridge."

"That story makes me hungry," Caspar said, "but 'em's clever kittens, Miss Armstrong. I always like to hear the stories about the clever kittens. They're my favorites."

More children arrived, and Tertius Dane MacManus MacTavish Dundee, eleventh Duke of Dunfallon, ducked down the steps and busied himself hauling up eight buckets of coal—as much as the coal bins would hold. He then swept the library from top to bottom under Caspar's careful supervision.

Caspar abandoned him for the dusting portion of the program— thank the celestial intercessors—because the time had come for Miss Armstrong to read *The Tale of the Icy Bridge*. A dozen ill-clothed and malodorous urchins listened raptly to her rendering of the story, as did the fat white cat dozing on her lap.

As did one reluctantly fascinated duke.

"I'da skated across the creek," Mary Smith said when Emmie finished reading the story. "Found me some skates and shot across the ice afore it could break."

"I'da watched you fall in and get trapped until you drowned," Ralphie Patterson retorted. "And I woun'ta fished you out because I know better 'n to try to cross new ice."

Mary shoved him with her elbow. "You don't know nuffink, Rotten Ralph." She was small but scrappy, and her comment served to start a discussion—not an argument—of why the author had made the choices he had.

Emmie tried to gently hint at themes such as mitigating risk when risks were unavoidable, sticking together in hard times, and using ingenuity to solve problems. The clever kittens had poured hot soup from their flasks onto the rickety, icy bridge, melting patches of ice step by step and making a safe path home.

First, they had considered the riskier courses—hopping from one piece of ice to the next, spending the night in the open far from home while hoping the ice would be frozen in the morning, asking passing strangers for aid—but then they'd lit on the scheme with the hot soup and found their way back to their loving mama.

For the duration of the story, Mr. Dunn had silently wielded his broom and then a feather duster amid the shelving on the main floor. He moved quietly for such a big man, and he worked steadily. His attire would have been more appropriate for lounging away the morning at some elegant club, but his work ethic was that of an ambitious under-footman.

The children begged for a second story, and Emmie, of course, refused. She made them wait for their daily story, made them read, practice penmanship, and study simple sums. If she yielded to their clamoring for another story, the whole day would turn into an endless story hour.

Can't have that.

"You mustn't blame them for trying," Mr. Dunn said when Emmie reshelved the book. "You have a way with a story."

"Mr. Dingle has the way with a story," she said. "The children love his kittens, and what they love, they can learn from. Do you enjoy fiction, Mr. Dunn?"

He paused in his dusting. "As a lad, I did."

"But you're for the church now," Emmie said, bracing herself for the usual excuses. "Fiction puts fanciful notions into heads that should be filled with only pious or patriotic thoughts. Fiction is a waste of money the public can ill afford to spend on books. Fiction is the first step on the road to idleness and sloth."

"As bad as all that?" he asked. "You make a good story sound like the literary version of blue ruin."

Mr. Dunn was tall, broad-shouldered, and spoke with a soft burr that had been more in evidence when he'd first arrived. His face was not precisely handsome, but it was attractive in a rugged, blue-eyed way, as was his slightly unruly chestnut hair. His physiognomy was fierce, for all his dapper attire. Fierce and, at the moment, lit with humor.

"The situation is worse than that," Emmie said. "Writing fiction provides a few women a means of earning their own coin without scrubbing floors or having babies. When men publish, they are authors. When women publish, they are scribblers." She held up a hand, lest Dunn launch into a sermon about Eve's fall. "I blaspheme, I know, but midday approaches, and one wants to stay on schedule. Idleness, sloth, and gluttony are on the program for the afternoon."

He gestured at her with the duster. "You write stories, I'm guessing."

Drat and damnation. For one instant, Emmie was tempted to confide in him, but no. Her ambitions were her own, and they were private. Just because a fellow was capable of doing some housework didn't mean he could be trusted.

"I publish an advice column, another literary frolic permitted to the ladies. I do believe you have dusted West Bart's Lending to within an inch of its life. Might you pop out to the chop shop? I grow a bit peckish."

She wanted him off the premises, even temporarily. She'd expected Mrs. MacInnes's nephew to be an anemic scholar better suited to reorganizing biographies than hauling coal. One look at the specimen before her, and Emmie's heart had rejoiced.

This man could *work*, and work hard. A fine quality in any fellow, but he was also a noticing sort of person—as little Caspar could be noticing—and that was not as laudable a gift.

"Will your order at the chop shop be waiting?" he asked, brushing past Emmie and continuing to the front door.

"Soup and sandwiches," she said, following him, "and hot cider. That is the usual midday fare here. If you need something more substantial, then the pub at the corner serves a good meat pie. We have an account at both places."

How did an aspiring curate come by that lovely, piney scent? How did he afford such a fine wool coat? Perhaps Mrs. MacInnes doted on this particular nephew, though she had an army of them. Perhaps Mr. Dunn was the family black sheep, and he faced banishment to Wales for having overstepped the bounds of propriety once too often.

"Sweeping and dusting are more taxing than they look," he said, swirling a beautiful merino cloak over his shoulders, "but I will make do with the usual. What about the children?"

"They have their bread and butter, Mr. Dunn, courtesy of Lady Bellefonte's generosity. The library directors begrudge them even that. Some of the children will stay for most of the day simply because it's warm here. Others will embark on honest scholarship to pass the time. The older boys will be about their begging, lest they get a beating when they go home."

"They beg?" Clearly, Mr. Dunn disapproved of begging.

"Yuletide approaches. Folk are more generous. Caspar and his friends would be fools to pass up such an opportunity. For most of them, the options are beg, steal, or starve."

Mr. Dunn set a fine beaver hat onto his head and stood by the front door, looking as if he wanted to offer a disagreeable comment.

"Off you go," Emmie said, waving her hand. "The shop is on the corner, and they will be very busy if you wait much longer."

He withdrew a supple pair of gloves from a pocket. "I want to know about those stories you write."

"I do not write stories."

"You are spinning a fiction at this very moment, Miss Armstrong. I'm away to the North Pole."

He had his hand on the door latch, the picture of a gentlemanly pulchritude. Emmie was relieved to see him on his way—truly, she was—when he turned back to her.

"Have you been a good girl this year, Miss Armstrong?"

"A saint," she said, though what sort of question was that?

"A saint who fibs," Mr. Dunn muttered. "Perhaps there's hope for me."

With that, he was gone, leaving a soft, cedary aroma lingering in the air.

CHAPTER TWO

Lemon verbena was a scent worn by governesses and maiden aunties, but on Miss Armstrong, the fragrance was... beguiling. Dunfallon liked using the most precise and vivid prose to convey a concept, and that fanciful modifier came easily to his unfanciful mind.

Beguiling, like the hint of humor in her voice even when she scolded a naughty child, or like the understated affection in her touch with the same miscreant. What sort of stories did she write, and why was she so protective of them?

He marched through the foot traffic on the walkway, bemused by the combination of tart, sweet, and spicy that characterized both the lady and her chosen fragrance. Miss Armstrong's father had apparently been a scholar. Perhaps that explained her bookish inclinations.

Dunfallon wanted to read the stories she'd written. That was only fair, given how the morning had progressed. Would her tales, too, feature the exploits of intrepid feline youngsters, as Mr. Dingle's tales did? Or perhaps Miss Armstrong reserved her talent for plucky damsels and swashbuckling pirate captains?

When was the last time I read such a yarn? Stayed up half the night on the high seas, muttering imprecations at a literary dastard?

Cheering on my heroes and wishing the story would never end? When was the last time I whiled away an hour with a tall tale as a cat purred contentedly in my lap?

"Not for years, laddie," Dunfallon muttered as he opened the chop shop door for a woman trying to keep hold of a toddler with one hand and manage a cloth sack with the other.

"Thankee, sir!" the child piped as the mother sent Dunfallon a harried smile.

Dunfallon paid for his own food rather than add to the library's account and accepted a largish box of comestibles that savored of good beef broth and fresh bread. Plain fare that nonetheless reminded him that he was hungry.

A duke wasn't often permitted to partake of plain fare, but then, dukes didn't typically spend the morning lugging buckets of coal or wielding a broom under the tutelage of an eight-year-old drill sergeant.

The box in Dunfallon's hands meant that despite his height and fine tailoring, he earned no second glances from fine ladies. Gentlemen kept their hands free, the better to assist any damsels who encountered difficulties mincing between shops.

He carried his booty past a chorus of young men yodeling some old hymn appropriate to the season. A batch of slacking apprentices no doubt, earning the odd coin with their noise.

Dunfallon was soon back at the library and dragooned into buttering slice after slice of warm bread. Miss Armstrong passed the food out, and if a patron's little paws had yet to be washed, he or she was directed to remedy the oversight before Miss surrendered the goods. The two old gents before the fire roused themselves to partake as well, and both of them subjected Dunfallon to a visual inspection.

"You ain't like no curate I ever seen," white-haired Mr. Pettibone opined, tearing off a bite of bread and stuffing it into his mouth. "Curates is young and skinny and perpetually afflicted with the horn colic."

"Met a lot of curates at sea, did you, Petty?" bald Mr. Bevins asked, dipping his bread into his cider. His voice carried a West Indies lilt, and his dark eyes twinkled with humor.

"We had chaplains," Pettibone replied, gesturing with his bread, "same as you did in the artillery. Chaplains be like curates."

An argument ensued of much greater vigor than the subject warranted, which—judging from Miss Armstrong's smile—was the usual case with Petty and Bevins when they weren't napping.

"Come have your soup, Mr. Dunn," she said, "before it grows cold. Hot food tastes better in chipper weather, don't you think?"

"Compared to the Trossachs this time of year, London is balmy, or so every loyal Scotsman would have you believe."

"Then I would like to see the Trossachs in winter. I usually take my meal upstairs. On the occasion of your first day with us, you are welcome to join me."

Meaning on subsequent days, Dunfallon's company would not be needed. The sheer novelty of a limited welcome was refreshing—or something. That a librarian's vocabulary included a pronoun akin to the royal *we* also caught Dunfallon's ear.

"Upstairs with *us*, then." He accepted a tray from Miss Armstrong, then paused at the foot of the steps when the boy Caspar caught his eye.

The lad wasn't merely skinny, he was gaunt, and London's weather was far from balmy. Dunfallon passed over a sandwich, put a finger to his lips, and followed Miss Armstrong to the mezzanine.

She led him into the little room he'd supposed was secure storage for valuable books.

And perhaps it was. The back wall consisted of shelves crammed with venerable tomes, while the outer wall featured a pair of French doors that let in what light was to be had at midday. A well-stuffed sofa lined the inside wall, a low table before it and a worn green quilt draped over the back.

The parlor stove next to the French doors made the space cozy, and a battered desk in the corner suggested pretensions to office functions.

"I nap here when I'm supposed to be penning overdue notices," Miss Armstrong said. "You are sworn to secrecy."

"You should have had me bring some coal up." Dunfallon set the tray on the table. "I've never done so much hauling and portering in my life as I have in this one morning." And he'd never realized that so simple a thing as keeping his hands free—for balance on icy walkways, for defense, to thwart ambitious pick-pockets—was a privilege.

"You'll step and fetch aplenty as a curate," Miss Armstrong observed, taking a seat on the sofa unassisted. "If your congregation is small, the elders and committeemen will work you half to death."

As a duke's extra spare, Dunfallon had expected to join the diplomatic ranks, though the church had also been a possibility, and he'd thus been appropriately educated. For him, though, there would have been no mending walls, repairing roofs, or carrying parcels for the spinster aunts on market day.

He would have been groomed for a bishopric or the deanship of a cathedral, God help him.

"I lack a true vocation," he said, "though I seem to be managing the stepping and fetching adequately. Might I sit?"

"Please. We don't stand on ceremony at West Bart's. If you wait for me to invite you to sit, and I wait for you to hold all the doors, we will both do a great deal of pointless standing about. Why is there only one sandwich on this tray? If I have told Caspar once, I have told him a thousand times, he must set a proper—"

"Haud yer wheesht, missy. I gave the lad my sandwich." Dunfallon lowered himself to the sofa, careful to sit a good eighteen inches from Miss Armstrong. When she'd said they did not stand on ceremony at the library, she'd spoken the truth. The door was firmly closed, and they were alone behind it, meaning Miss Armstrong could, in theory, force Dunfallon to offer for her.

Except that she never would. How Dunfallon knew this, he could not say. Something to do with the swish of her skirts as she patrolled her demesne or the relish in her voice when she spoke the villain's part of a story. Miss Armstrong did not aspire to wear a tiara, which made her quite the puzzle.

What *did* she aspire to?

"If you do not long to become a vicar," Miss Armstrong said, ladling him a bowl of steaming soup from the crock on the tray, "then what are your ambitions? You are clearly well educated, your aunt is a fixture in polite society, and you have some means." She brushed a glance over the gold pin securing his cravat.

To remain a bachelor was a petty, if sincere, aspiration. Dunfallon surprised himself by giving an older, more honest reply.

"I once upon a time longed to be a writer, but my family had no patience with that nonsense. I went for a soldier after I'd drunk my way through university, and the transition to the military wasn't as difficult as you might think. I'm at somewhat of a crossroads."

She passed him a spoon. "How fortunate you are, to be at a cross-roads. Women do not find themselves at that happy location. Our paths are laid out for us—the good path, the better path, and the best path, though the wrong path also beckons. For what we are about to receive, we are exceedingly grateful."

And for the outspoken company. "Amen." Dunfallon took a taste of delicious beef barley soup.

"You doubtless think I am ridiculous for lamenting the limitations of my gender," Miss Armstrong said, serving her own portion, "but you have the requisite masculine adornments to do as you please with your life."

Did she refer to his *testicles*? "Adornments?"

"*Mister* before your name, a top hat upon your handsome head, a very fine walking stick with which to smite your foes or to attack hapless hedges if you're cup-shot. The accoutrements of your gender are many and well recognized."

"Do you dislike being female, Miss Armstrong?"

She sent him a look that conveyed something like disgust—with him. Despair, impatience, distaste?

"I am pleased enough to be female, considering the alternatives, but if you are a woman, you are to keep yourself to dull and chaste paths until you can snag the attention of some eligible man. You are to be attractive, but not flirtatious. Have interesting conversation, but no controversial opinions. Find your waltzing partner's every bleating and bloviation fascinating and his execrable dancing delightful. You are, in fact, to perfect the art of lying to a man so skillfully that he thinks himself in love with you."

When Dunfallon would have replied, she waved her spoon at him. "And if a lady is so very, very fortunate as to become some fellow's unpaid housekeeper, clerk, shopgirl, seamstress, governess, cook, gardener, or manager of same, her reward will be the duties of mistress without any of the mistress's freedoms or remuneration. Instead, it shall be her greatest joy to bring forth her children in pain and perhaps survive the ordeal the first half-dozen times or so."

Miss Armstrong held out half the remaining sandwich to him. "Would you trade your lot for mine?"

Dunfallon thought of Miss Peasegill gaily hallooing after him as if she'd spotted Reynard breaking for his covert. Had that been a deception on her part?

He would ponder that possibility later. "What of the fellow's devotion to you, Miss Armstrong? His determination to provide well for you and to raise a family with you in a home full of love and laughter? What of his loyalty when you are sickly and out of sorts, his good cheer in the face of life's vicissitudes? What of his companionship and hard work and affection?"

Now, where had that sermon come from, considering that bachelorhood loomed as the most precious jewel in Dunfallon's hoard?

Miss Armstrong picked up her half of the sandwich. "You describe marriage to a paragon, and he does not exist, Mr. Dunn. My mother died trying to give my father an heir, and when Mama was barely cold in the ground, Papa married a much younger woman. Step-mama promptly presented Papa with a healthy son, suggesting..."

She took a bite of her sandwich, though Dunfallon could finish the thought easily enough: Suggesting her dear papa's grief had been summarily eclipsed by his desire for male progeny.

"I'm sorry," Dunfallon said, though he was apologizing for what amounted to a sacred duty among aristocratic men—men with standing whose daughters did not become librarians. Such men were to perpetuate the male line at all costs, to ensure the family's wealth remained in the family.

Even families without titles needed sons to manage the land and coin—or the shop—for future generations, and in titled families... Titled families preferred to have so many sons that they numbered them rather than named them.

"I am spoiling your appetite with my sour opinions," Miss Armstrong said. "I do apologize."

"Just the opposite." Dunfallon had finished his soup and started on his half sandwich. "You are honest and articulate, so I will do my best to return the compliment. Do you suppose men like being misled, manipulated, and viewed as prize stags to be brought down by the most skilled markswoman, who then resents her stag for indulging in one of the few true pleasures of married life—pleasures that are supposed to be shared, unless he's a complete bungler?"

"Do you believe," he went on, "that a husband delights in carrying responsibility for the welfare of an entire household, despite being as frail and mortal as the next fellow? Do you suppose those bachelors you disdain never tire of the duty waltzes and duty musicales and duty escorts and duty house parties?"

He should not have mentioned that bit about shared pleasure, but Miss Armstrong looked intrigued rather than appalled.

"You raise valid questions, Mr. Dunn. I suppose debating skills are much prized among aspiring clergy." She took another bite of her sandwich. Miss Armstrong enjoyed a healthy appetite and didn't lace herself too tightly to indulge it.

"I was never aspiring clergy," Dunfallon said. "I am not exactly aspiring clergy now. I was a bookish fellow with an outspoken distrust of authority, as most true scholars are apt to be. My teachers despaired of me, but they also knew to cram my head full of the ideas of men far more astute than I could hope to be."

"Of *men?*" She might have been referring to a particularly unattractive class of insect.

"I read Mrs. Radcliffe and Mrs. Burney too. Whacking great tales of adventure and social drama. Silly sometimes, too—sideways satire —but that's part of the joy of a good story."

Miss Armstrong set down her sandwich and bestowed on Dunfallon a smile of such delighted sweetness that had she shot him in the bum with an arrow, he could not have been more astonished. When she smiled like that, Miss Armstrong barreled right past *beguiling* and galloped into the nearer reaches of *fascinating*.

The slight detachment that she carried around like a banner when executing her librarian's duties was exchanged for the pennant of the prettiest lady in the shire, the most warmhearted, intelligent, alluring, unexpected...

God have mercy, he wasn't the only one dissembling. Miss Emerald Armstrong wasn't what she appeared to be, not at all, and that pleased Dunfallon as spirited debate, hot soup, and bachelor freedoms never had.

"Which of Mrs. Burney's is your favorite?" she asked, scooting a few inches closer. "Everybody prefers *Evelina*, but where would *Pride and Prejudice* be without *Cecilia?*"

"Ah, but are we sure that *Pride and Prejudice* was written by 'a lady'?"

Miss Armstrong went off into flights, about Mrs. Burney's gift for satire being perfected by the later author into delicate irony, and the female perspective enlightening both, and on and on she held forth.

As she did so, Dunfallon added a few other descriptors to the list he was curating on Miss Armstrong's behalf. She was lovely, a general term that seldom graced his vocabulary unless his family's whisky was under discussion. She was astute, able to connect seemingly distant points of logic that were, in fact, related.

And she was—despite the spinster attire, tidy bun, and firm

command of unruly urchins—intellectually and morally passionate.

"I'm off on my rounds," she said after dining on *Waverly's* bones at length. "I must make the weekly trek returning books that were borrowed from our sister libraries and mistakenly surrendered here. You are welcome to bide in this office as long as you please. You will be back on Friday, won't you?"

Before this nooning, Dunfallon had been fashioning a polite epistle about an enjoyable morning, a regrettable if puzzling misunderstanding, and best wishes for the library—along with a bank draft. Dukes were much given to conveying their parting sentiments with bank drafts.

Besides, he had much to see to. December always meant a mountain of reports from the stewards, debts to settle, charities to fund, and family correspondence on top of the usual mountain of business mail, in addition to social obligations that featured various strengths of bad punch.

The clerks and under-stewards were in particular want of supervision in December, to say nothing of the household staff, who'd spend the month sampling recipes for wassail left to their own devices.

And yet, where parting sentiments should have resided, Dunfallon instead felt a nagging reluctance to leave. Miss Armstrong also had much to see to—a building to look after, children underfoot, thousands of books to keep track of. Who assisted her with any of it?

He'd spied an oil can in the cupboard downstairs, and any number of hinges, hasps, and door latches on the premises would benefit from its use. She needed at least two spare buckets of coal for her parlor stove, and this office could use a thorough dusting too.

"What is on the agenda for Friday?" he asked. The deadly sin of lust—for books, of course—came to mind.

"After our story, the children and I will decorate the library for the holidays. We'll hang cloved oranges in the windows, though I daresay we'll eat some oranges as well. We'll put up wreaths and greenery outside and wrap red ribbon on the banisters. The pensioners will help, too, of course, but I'd hate to ask them to climb the ladders. The smaller children will make snowflakes of old paper, and we hang those in the windows too."

How dreadfully... appealing. The library would be full of mayhem and fun, the opposite of a gentlemen's club. At the library, nobody would be inebriated or boasting of last night's wagers and conquests. Nobody would be crying into his imported brandy about parsimonious uncles or jealous mistresses.

"I will be here Friday," Dunfallon said, getting to his feet, "and if we are through with our repast, I'll take the dishes back to the chop house."

"That would be appreciated. When I return from my rounds, I have a half-dozen overdue notices to write, and I've put them off too long as it is. I hate asking a patron to surrender a book if they are still truly enjoying it."

She rose, and Dunfallon realized he'd not only volunteered for more porter's duty, but he was being dismissed by a busy woman who thought he was some sort of clergy-in-training.

"I don't want to be a curate." He didn't much want to be a duke either.

"Then don't be." She patted his arm, much the way she might have patted Caspar's head. "What would you rather be instead?"

He owed her the truth, and yet... His Grace of Dunfallon would not be welcome back on Friday, nor permitted a private repast with the lady librarian. He would have no opportunity to lug coal up two flights of stairs for Emmie Armstrong, or to oil every hinge and lock in the library for her.

"You ask about my aspirations. I have always wanted to be a pirate king. Until Friday, Miss Armstrong, and my thanks for a delightful meal."

He bowed—catching another whiff of lemon verbena—then collected the tray and saw himself out. Maybe aspiring curates did not bow to opinionated librarians, but dukes certainly did, as did pirate kings.

"Mr. Dunn reads Mrs. Burney, and he could debate the gender of *Pride and Prejudice*'s author," Emmie said. "Not lecture me, my lady, but rather, engage in honest and good-natured *debate*."

The discussion *had* been good-natured, though Mr. Dunn's voice —a growling bass-baritone—imbued his discourse with more ferocity than the speaker likely intended.

Leah, Countess of Bellefonte, sniffed the orange in her hand, then added it to the basket on the potting table. "You do not mean to tell me that Mr. Dunn respected your opinions, Emmie? One of Nicholas's most endearing features is that he listens to me and to the children. He maintains that a smart man will also listen to his horse, and to his siblings if they deign to bestow advice. I've caught him in conversation with the pantry mouser too."

Lord and Lady Bellefonte had a horde of siblings between them, a growing brood of children, and a veritable regiment of nieces and nephews. His lordship was built on Viking proportions, and his good humor was on a scale with the rest of him. Emmie had found the earl more than once playing hide-and-seek with his children—and his countess—in this very conservatory.

"Lord Bellefonte accepts counsel from his sisters?"

"Nicholas adores his family," Lady Bellefonte replied, adding more oranges to the basket. "He and I would not be married but for a promise he made to his late father. Nicholas is an earl—that cannot be helped—but he is first and foremost the head of our family."

"And a firm advocate for the traditional kissing bough, apparently," Emmie said, eyeing a second basket brimming with greenery and topped with bunches of mistletoe.

"Oh, that, too, and never leave the gingerbread unguarded around him."

"His lordship sounds like certain small boys I know." And not like Mr. Dunn, who'd given Caspar his sandwich. A gentleman should be charitable, but that he would *notice* Caspar's hunger was unusual. Of all the boys, Caspar was the most proud and the worst at begging.

"Nicholas does not put on airs," her ladyship said, sniffing another orange, "for which—among many other traits—I treasure him." Her ladyship's smile was cat-in-the-cream-pot pleased. "Where did I...? Ah, here they are." She pried the cork off a large glass jar, sniffed, then sealed it up again and banged the cork down with her fist. "You need not look so puzzled, Emmie. Good men abound. They aren't all like Hercules Flynn."

The fragrance of cloves wafted on the humid air of the conservatory. "*Lord* Hercules," Emmie muttered. "Even when we were engaged, he did not give me leave to drop his honorific." He'd been all too happy to drop his breeches, though.

"Lord Hercules will not be at our open house, Emmie. My guest lists never include him." Her ladyship stashed the cloves among the pine boughs and mistletoe. "Nor do they include Lady Hercules."

"She and I are quite civil." Emmie collected spools of red and green ribbon from the table and added them to the basket of oranges. "More than civil, in fact. I feel sorry for her. Hercules set me aside because his present wife had the larger dowry. All of Society knows this, but worse, the lady herself knows it. I gather her family didn't allow her much choice, given that Lord Hercules's family is titled."

"And I," Lady Bellefonte said, passing over a spool of gold ribbon, "like many others, think you had a narrow escape. Lord Hercules is intemperate."

He wagered, he drank, he dueled. Standard behavior for a marquess's spare. "He has never read an entire book, not even *Tom Jones*. When he told me that—boasted of it—I knew I was making a mistake."

"Precisely." Her ladyship shook out a red and green plaid cloth and folded it over the oranges and ribbon. "Lord Hercules was wrong for you, and engagements often dissolve when finances come under discussion. All that is behind you, and this year, you must come to my open house."

Some traitorous, lonely part of Emmie wanted to attend. "That would be unwise, my lady. Lord Hercules won't impose himself on the household, but he has many friends, and some of his friends have wives and sisters. I do not care to once again be referred to as The Face That Launched a Thousand Sips."

"Lord Hercules was sipping deeply before he became engaged to you. Make no mistake about that."

"He was drunk when he asked leave to court me." Emmie had never told anybody that. Had never put into words the despair that had enveloped her when she'd realized how much fortification Hercules had indulged in before embarking on their courtship. "He smelled of cheap perfume too."

Her ladyship ceased fussing with a second plaid cloth and wrapped Emmie in a quick, fierce hug. "A very narrow escape, then. Your freedom is worth whatever petty gossip followed from his defection."

Emmie moved away, took up the second cloth, and folded it atop the greenery. "My brother has barely spoken to me since. Ambrose said if his best friend wasn't good enough for me, then I clearly had no need of a brother either."

"Oh dear. Shall I have a word with your muddle-headed sibling? You were not the one to cry off, except in the technical sense."

Lady Bellefonte meant well, but she had never encountered the stubbornness of a young man trying to don the confident air of an effective patriarch.

"Hercules insinuated that I was impossible to court, and Ambrose believed his old school chum rather than listen to me. I cannot prove what Hercules asked of me in confidence, and I have my competence." *And my books.* "Thank God I am enough of a fossil that Ambrose cannot interfere with my funds."

"You are a woman of independent means and to be envied. I am a woman with an open house that you should attend."

Why did Mr. Dingle's cozy little tales about intrepid kittens never feature a feline who dreaded Society? A young lady mouser who'd been the butt of gossip and mean toasts? One whose name had appeared in the betting books and whose only sibling refused to speak with her?

Probably because such a tale could not be turned about with a brilliant flash of ingenuity and some good luck, and Mr. Dingle's tales always ended happily.

"Say you'll come, Emmie." Lady Bellefonte made the invitation a command rather than a wheedle. Perhaps in this household, Lord Bellefonte did all the wheedling. What an odd thought.

"You can bring along this Mr. Dunn," her ladyship went on, "if an escort is the problem."

"I would rather not attend, my lady. Holiday punch can bring out the friendly overtures from the bachelors."

"And from the chaperones and footmen and even the curates. That is part of the appeal of the season, but if you fear the friendly overtures, allow me to put your worries to rest. Nicholas has invited Dunfallon, and with the duke in the room, nobody will notice you."

"*His Grace* of Dunfallon?" Some unwritten law required social pariahs to read the Society pages. West Bart's Lending subscribed to three weeklies and two dailies, and Dunfallon's name appeared in them all. If he drove out with a marquess's daughter, that was remarked. If he stood up with a duke's niece, that was observed. If a young lady and her widowed mama joined him at the opera, that was speculated upon.

How much of the duke's socializing fell under Mr. Dunn's "duty" category?

"The very one," Lady Bellefonte replied. "His Grace of Don't Fall For Him, the most eligible bachelor in the realm. The soldier-statesman, pride of Scotland, and despair of the matchmakers. He's not a bad sort, really, though his humor tends to be understated. Dunfallon is the dour Highlander, while Nicholas is Merry Olde to the life. They are nonetheless fast friends and have been for years."

Perhaps Dunfallon, for all his wealth and standing, found the holidays trying too. "His Grace doubtless needs friends. He lost two older brothers, from what I've read." The first had been given a Christian name—the same name as all the previous Dukes of Dunfallon. Kenneth, or Callum, or Camden. Something resoundingly Scottish. The spare had been Secondus and the current duke... Tertius? What a sorry lot of names to impose on baby boys.

"Those of us who need friends are often the last to accept friendly invitations," Lady Bellefonte said. "Let's enjoy a spot of tea, and I'll have the footmen take these baskets over to West Bart's. I'll do East Bart's tomorrow, though they don't seem to take their decorating as seriously as West Bart's does."

Because East Bart's did not welcome every urchin, pensioner, or stray cat through its doors. "East Bart's has a different set of patrons, but we are all devoted to reading for pleasure and improvement, and we all appreciate your support, my lady."

Emmie owed much to Lady Bellefonte, and her ladyship had never expected anything other than a well-run library in return.

"I am happy to support the libraries," she said. "Books were one of few comforts I had growing up, and all of my children are avid readers. Let us repair to a cozy sitting room, my dear. A conservatory in winter always feels a little stuffy to me, though winter is precisely when a conservatory is most useful."

Emmie allowed herself to be gently herded along to an elegant, light-filled parlor done up in blue, cream, and gold. She indulged in two cups of hot, sweet tea and an assortment of fruit tarts—why did fruit taste especially wonderful in winter?—and waited for her ladyship to renew the invitation to the open house.

That renewed invitation did not come, which was fortunate. Emmie was happy among her books, with her urchins and pensioners and the occasional bluestocking, spinster, or widow. Lady Bellefonte managed the library's directors, and that left Emmie free to run the premises.

"What is he like, this curate?" Her ladyship asked when the tray had been removed and the fire built up. "How old is he?"

Mr. Dunn was like... Scotland. Imposing, lovely, more complicated than his attractive features suggested, and more vigorous than a curate should be.

Also more expensively dressed.

More opinionated.

Taller, as exponents of generations of wealth tended to be tall.

"He is no boy," Emmie replied, because her ladyship expected an answer. "Old for a curate, but then, good posts are hard to come by these days. Well-read, articulate, not one to speak for the pleasure of hearing himself declaim. Has a luscious burr and a mind both curious and confident. Not without humor, though far from silly."

"You like him."

"I... do." Emmie's admission was laced with puzzlement. She had found Lord Hercules likable at first. He and his many friends excelled at being likable, while they insulted a lady behind her back. "Mr. Dunn is a hard worker, and he doesn't put on airs."

He also didn't fit the description of a curate in many significant particulars, and that turned Emmie's liking ever so slightly cautious.

"And he argues with you over novels and politics," Lady Bellefonte observed.

"Yes," Emmie said. "Well, no. Not argues. We debate, we discuss, we agree on some issues and differ on others. Hours after he's left the premises, I'm still pondering the points he made and thinking of the clever ripostes I should have offered him when I had the chance."

Talk wandered from there to books, to her ladyship's vast family, to recipes for punch, and by the time Emmie had returned to the library, the enormous baskets were already waiting in her office. When she unwrapped the greenery to set it out on the balcony, she found heaps more mistletoe atop the pine boughs than she recalled Lady Bellefonte packing.

Lady Bellefonte had made some sort of mistake, clearly.

Or had she? East Bart's had no use for mistletoe, though perhaps West Bart's did.

CHAPTER THREE

"Why don't the kittens ever fight?"

Young Caspar posed that question to Dunfallon after Friday's story hour had descended into bickering refereed by Miss Armstrong. Dunfallon had made sure to get the coal hauled up from the cellar before the reading had begun and had dusted the downstairs while Miss Armstrong once again regaled London's aspiring pickpockets with a tale of Mr. Dingle's four intrepid kittens.

"I'm sure the kittens aired their occasional differences, as most siblings do. Pass me that orange."

Caspar's assistance had been inflicted on Dunfallon's efforts to hang the cloved oranges. Some of the oranges resembled dyspeptic hedgehogs, with cloves mashed into them willy-nilly. A few had aspirations to symmetry. Little Mary Smith, whom Miss Armstrong had described as a reluctant reader, had taken the better part of an hour to carefully adorn her orange, and all the while, Dunfallon suspected she'd rather have been eating it.

Caspar tossed him the orange. "I don't mean, why don't the kittens spat and tiff? I mean, why don't they fight, like when that mean man put 'em in a sack? They should have clawed his face off and bit his fingers and pissed on his shoes." Caspar took a few swipes at the air, his hands hooked like claws. He hissed for good measure and—perhaps the boy had thespian capabilities—backed up to the nearest bookshelf and wiggled his skinny backside, tomcat-fashion.

Dunfallon tied off the orange and tried not to laugh. "Often, fighting makes a situation worse. The fellow who tried to kidnap the kittens might have taken to hurling rocks at them as they fled if they'd chosen your tactics. Another orange, please."

Caspar tossed over another specimen, this one still a bit green on one side. The best of the lot had been reserved for snacks later in the morning.

"I tried to cover the green bits with ribbon, but the ribbon kept sliding around."

Dunfallon came down the ladder, an awkward undertaking while holding an orange. "We can do some rearranging," he said, pushing the ribbon one direction, pinning it with cloves, and hiding the unripe area. "Is that better?"

"Now it's lopsided. You didn't move the ribbon on t'other side."

"My tutor claimed the artistic temperament abhors compromise."

More fiddling ensued, with Caspar providing detailed directions and the occasional insult—"Don't you know nuffink?"—as Dunfallon attempted to obey his commanding officer. When Miss Armstrong came by on an inspection tour, Caspar was pressed against Dunfallon's arm, holding forth about the orange having to hang straight, while Dunfallon attempted to fashion a bow out of the dangling ribbon.

"Are we having a council of war?" she asked.

"We are," Dunfallon replied as Caspar straightened. "We've been battling crooked, unripe fruit unfit for holiday duty. This specimen," —he held up Caspar's orange—"has been brought to rights, but it was a very near thing."

"The results are lovely," Miss Armstrong said. "Let's hang it on my office door."

"That un's mine." Caspar had acquired the swagger of a royal herald.

"I suspected it was. Tie some gold ribbon around the bow and fasten your magnificent orange to my door latch, would you?"

Caspar snatched the fruit from Dunfallon with the skill of a cutpurse and was off across the library.

Dunfallon watched him go, a pang of something like sadness accompanying the boy's departure.

"Caspar asked why Mr. Dingle's kittens never fight their way out of difficulties," Dunfallon said. "I hadn't much of an answer for him. He's so damned skinny under those too-big clothes. If he weren't a fighter, he'd probably be dead."

"Mr. Dingle must be an interesting character." Miss Armstrong took up a perch on a lower rung of the ladder. "His stories are so... The children are inspired by them. That Caspar would put the query to you—about solving his problems with his fists—shows that the boy has been rethinking some assumptions."

What a picture she made, at her ease against the ladder, the morning sun catching the glints of gold ribbon on the oranges hung in the window above her, and the fresh scent of cloves warming the old library.

"Did Mr. Dingle do the boy any favors by throwing tactics that have served so well into a questionable light?" Dunfallon asked.

"Yes." Miss Armstrong was off her ladder and marching toward him, skirts swishing. "Yes, he did, and I wish dear old Mr. Dingle would come out of retirement and write more stories, though I suspect Dingle is a missus. The kittens found their way home because they stuck together and used their heads. Hammerhead—the supposedly slow one—had the strength and courage to climb the trees and look for landmarks. Jewel, who loves books, remembered which landmarks were near home from the maps their mama had shown her."

Miss Armstrong picked up an orange and hefted it as if warming up for a rousing game of cricket.

"When,"—she shook the orange at him—"is cooperation in the face of troubles a bad idea? The children often leave here in pairs and trios since we started reading Mr. Dingle's collection. They are safer that way. Some of them aspire to writing stories of their own, and thus they are paying better attention to their reading lessons. Mary hasn't exactly developed the vocabulary of a barrister, but she has learned to write her name."

Miss Armstrong finished this tirade standing barely six inches from the toes of Dunfallon's boots. Lemon verbena begged to be sniffed at closer range even than that. Dunfallon instead plucked the orange from her, bent down, and spoke softly.

"Wellington tried cooperating with the Spanish loyalists, and the Spanish Bonapartists laughed all the way to the safety of the hills. Some Scots tried cooperating with the English, and all that did was cost the rest of us our Parliament, our dignity, and the right to farm our ancestral lands. Cooperation can be a very bad idea indeed." He'd taken some rhetorical license with history and hoped she'd correct him.

Miss Armstrong brushed at a streak of dust on his sleeve. "One must choose collaborators carefully. Perhaps Mr. Dingle should have included that caveat. Did you serve in Spain?"

Dunfallon had the oddest urge to hold still, like a cat who, having once been petted, refuses to budge until all hope of another caress is lost.

"Aye, I served, if you can call mud, death, gore, and bad rations serving."

"I did wonder why you're still a curate," she said, backing up a step. "They tend to be youngish. The oranges look very nice."

Dunfallon hung the last orange from the window latch, which upset the careful symmetry of Caspar's design. "I'm oldish?"

"You are not a boy, just as I am not a girl." Miss Armstrong took to studying plain fruit decorated for the holidays. "I rather like that you aren't a boy."

"You like ordering me around." And Dunfallon, oddly enough,

enjoyed doing her bidding. He'd been distracted as he'd plowed through yesterday's ream of correspondence, wondering how Miss Armstrong was managing at the library without a ducal dogsbody to step and fetch for her.

"Oh, I *adore* ordering you about," she said. "You take on your tasks as if they matter."

Those tasks mattered to him because they mattered to her. "Miss Armstrong, you will put me to the blush."

"As if one could. We have need of the ladder elsewhere."

Something about that request brought out a subtle diffidence in the usually forthright Miss Armstrong. "You are ready to hang the mistletoe. If you think I will permit you to climb this ladder when I am on hand to be ordered about, you are very much mistaken."

"Mr. Bevins and Mr. Pettibone are happy to assist."

"They will be happy to argue with one another about the proper approach to climbing a ladder, where the damned stuff should hang, how the bow should be tied on each bundle, and how one properly holds a ladder still. They will ignore your advice, while I will heed it to the letter." Dunfallon hefted the ladder and gestured with one hand. "Lay on, Macduff."

Miss Armstrong led the way. "'And damned be him that first cries, "Hold, enough!"'" Are we fighting to the death over some greenery, Mr. Dunn?"

"Of course not. We will cooperate to see the job done, miss, as any self-respecting pair of kittens would."

Her shoulders twitched as she wound her way between bookshelves. "You are not a kitten, Mr. Dunn."

"Glad you noticed, Miss Armstrong." Dunfallon smiled at her resolute and retreating form, even as part of him had embarked on a mental lecture straight out of old MacAlpin's vast repertoire: *Laddie, what the hell are ye aboot?*

While Dunfallon pondered the answer, he set up the ladder by the front door. Pettibone and Bevins launched into their opening salvos, and little Mary Smith dragged a chair in the direction of the grandfather clock beneath the mezzanine.

Miss Armstrong uncovered a basket overflowing with mistletoe. "I left the pine swags on my balcony. We can hang them outside when Mr. Dunn joins us again on Monday." She shot him the merest hint of a questioning glance.

"Wild unicorns couldn't keep me away, Miss Armstrong."

She selected a kissing bough from among the pile in the basket. "We'll hang the mistletoe, and then Mr. Dunn can fetch the nooning. Perhaps, Mr. Pettibone and Mr. Bevins, you might take turns holding the ladder?"

If Dunfallon waited for the combatants to sort out who held the ladder first, he would be fetching the nooning on Doomsday Eve.

"Perhaps Mr. Bevins might investigate what the fair Mary is attempting to do to the hands of the grandfather clock," Dunfallon said. "My guess is, she's famished for an orange and moving the minute hand ahead accordingly."

"She don't have the clock key," Bevins said. "Miss keeps the key in the office."

"The girl might have a penknife," Pettibone retorted. "A pick or two, a hairpin. Them old clocks ain't the vault at the Bank o' England."

"You two had best go see," Miss Armstrong said. "That grandfather clock was donated by Mrs. Oldbach, and I wouldn't want it to come to any harm."

Both old men shuffled off, and Dunfallon appropriated Miss Armstrong's beribboned bundle of leaves and white berries. "Where shall I hang this? Speak now or forever hold your mistletoe."

"Below Dr. Johnson's portrait," Miss Armstrong said, "and another below His Majesty's."

Miss Armstrong brought strategy to her deployment of mistletoe. By hanging the bundles from the mezzanine, she ringed the library with festive greenery and also made avoiding unwanted encounters easy.

"We have several boughs left," Dunfallon said. "Shall we add a few bunches to the usual locations?"

"I don't care for mistletoe ambushes," Miss Armstrong said. "If we hang it from the chandelier in the foyer, or over the reading chairs, somebody could be taken by surprise."

Somebody had ambushed *her*, apparently, and a few of Dunfallon's more wayward thoughts slunk off to the far corners of his imagination to be replaced by distaste. Mistletoe was a bit of holiday silliness, not an excuse to impose advances on the unwilling.

"I can offer the extra to the chop shop," he said, "and they can share with their patrons."

"A good suggestion, and it must be getting time for our nooning, though I haven't heard the clock chime." Miss Armstrong looked askance in the direction of the grandfather clock. "Perhaps it needs winding."

"I suspect it needs repairing. I saw Ralph Patterson pushing the hands forward earlier, and he probably broke the mechanism. Mary might have been thinking to fix what Ralph put wrong. According to that clock, it's still a quarter past ten."

"And Ralphie is nowhere to be seen," Miss Armstrong said. "I fear you are right, and if we don't pick up our order at the chop shop on time, they will sell it to other customers."

Dunfallon passed her his pocket watch. "It's barely past noon. I'll have a look at the clock when I get back. Keep hold of my timepiece for now and see what has detained Caspar abovestairs."

She flipped open his watch—Uncle Quintus had given it to him upon the occasion of his departure for university—and pretended to puzzle over the inscription. "I do believe you are attempting to order me about, Mr. Dunn."

"The lad's probably fallen asleep on your sofa, but he might also have found a book to interest him. I'd be curious to know which volume could hold his fancy."

That lure was too much for Miss Armstrong to refuse. She snapped the watch closed and bustled off. Dunfallon grabbed his cloak and the basket holding the remaining bunches of mistletoe. He earned the merriest of smiles from passersby on his way to the chop shop, and before he'd arrived, he had an answer to the question that had plagued him earlier.

Laddie, what the hell are ye about?

"I'm falling in love," he muttered, handing a few mistletoe bouquets to a flower girl on the corner. "I'm finally falling in love."

"Two inches t' the right," Bevins called from the left side of the ladder.

"To the left," Petty retorted from the other side. "Are ye blind as well as deef, old Bevvy?"

Mr. Dunn left the pine wreath right where he'd tied it and came down the ladder. "Miss Armstrong says the wreath goes where I hung it, and there it shall stay. I daresay if you gentlemen had the benefit of her central vantage point, and not slightly to either side, you'd agree with me."

Emmie watched two old soldiers decide whether to continue the skirmish or accept the dignified retreat Mr. Dunn had offered them.

"Mr. Dunn is correct," she said. "If we stand off to the side, our perspective is different than if we're standing at the center of a view. Shall we see what mayhem the children have wrought while we've been hanging our greenery?"

In point of fact, Mr. Dunn had done the hanging of the greenery, while Emmie had watched him and wondered how so mundane a task, when done competently, could be attractive. He'd scampered up and down the ladder, sometimes holding string or twine between his teeth. He'd draped the swagging with perfect symmetry and had known exactly where a dash of red or gold ribbon should go.

And—wonders abide!—he'd heeded Emmie's suggestion to hang a double length of swagging over the main door. The library had never looked so festive, and Emmie had never felt so muddled.

"I'm for a warm fire," Mr. Dunn said, hefting the ladder before custody of same could also provoke debate. "Unless somebody reads those hooligans a story, rebellion and more clock tampering are bound to ensue."

Bevins squinted up at the largest wreath, which hung precisely at the center of the pine roping gracing the library's façade. "Ralphie apologized about the clock. He didn't mean any harm."

"The little varmint busted an auntie-cue," Petty retorted. "If Dunn hadn't a-knowed how to tinker it back into service, Mrs. O woulda had the lad walk the plank."

"No, she would not," Mr. Dunn replied, his burr acquiring a hint of a growl, "because nobody would peach on our Ralph unless the tattletale wanted to answer to me and to Miss Armstrong, who will soon begin shivering due to our lack of gallantry. Besides, Ralph assisted me with the repairs, so he has atoned for his misplaced curiosity. Further recriminations would only injure the lad's dignity."

Emmie could imagine that voice castigating the Regent for his financial excesses, or preaching forgiveness to the Archbishop of Canterbury. One did not ignore such a voice, nor the message it conveyed.

She was soon heating the pot of cider over the fire, while the children were assembling on the sofas and chairs nearest the hearth.

"You might toss in a bit of this." Mr. Dunn withdrew a corked glass jar from his pocket.

Emmie took a whiff. "Mulling spices. These come dear, Mr. Dunn."

"Because they are potent. A pinch or two will liven up the brew, and spices lose their pungency if they're not used."

The scent was delicious, evoking every sweet, warm, wonderful holiday memory from Emmie's childhood. "A pinch or two."

He took the bottle from her, upended about a quarter of the contents into his palm, rubbed his hands together, then dumped the spices into the pot of cider.

"My pinches are larger than yours," he said, while Emmie

goggled at his extravagance, "in proportion to my hands. What tale will you regale us with today?"

Perhaps his heart was larger than hers. The children had never had mulled cider before—and probably never would again.

"Mr. Dingle's *The Ferocious Tigers of Hyde Park.*"

Mr. Dunn lifted Aristotle down from the mantel and scratched the cat gently about the nape. "A stirring tale of noise and mischief masquerading as ingenuity. The juvenile horde will be riveted."

The cat began to purr.

"He'll get hair all over your fine coat." Burgundy today, and though his cravat lacked lace and the pin securing it was merely amber, he would still be the best dressed curate ever to rusticate in Wales.

"The better to keep me warm when the snow starts." Mr. Dunn set the cat back on the mantel with a final scratch to his shoulders. "Cats are generous like that, as are horses and dogs."

Emmie went to what was now referred to as the "orange window." The rich scent of cloves wafted from the dangling fruit, and the bright decorations contrasted starkly with the leaden sky beyond.

"I am not fond of snow," she said. "When I was a child, snow was great fun. My brother and I would go sledding, or rather, the footmen would be tasked with hauling us around on the toboggan, then sending us on a flying pass down from the orchard, before they had to drag the thing back up the hill again. I never realized that snow for most people is nothing but hard work or a day in the shop that sees no custom."

Mr. Dunn stood behind Emmie, close enough that she felt his warmth, felt his height and strength.

Won't you please hold me? The wish came from nowhere, with the power of a well-aimed blow. *Hold me and keep me warm and let me rest in your embrace.*

"A good snow can also give us an excuse to rest for a day or two," Mr. Dunn said. "To be still and at peace, reading a good book, playing a hand of cards with family, instead of forever racketing about from one task to the next. Snow has its charms, and unless I miss my guess, we're in for a sample of them before the day is through."

Emmie faced him, rather than stand mooning at the oranges and wishing for the impossible. "How is it you know Mr. Dingle's tales so well?"

"Nieces," he said, gaze on the portrait of the Bard that held pride of place over the dramas and comedies. "I have an older sister, and she is the mother of three young ladies, though I apply that term in its most euphemistic sense. They are half grown now—they were mere toddlers last week—and I did my avuncular duty by them."

A chant began from the children by the hearth. "Sto-ry... sto-ry... sto-ry..."

"What is your Christian name, Mr. Dunn?"

He glowered at the children, who fell silent. "My friends call me Dane."

One of those pauses ensued, where the conversation might have gone in a friendlier, even daring direction.

I would be honored, Miss Armstrong, if you'd allow me the privilege of familiar address under appropriate circumstances. In the rarefied social circles Emmie had been raised in, such a request might well presage courting aspirations.

Might I have leave to use that name on informal occasions, Mr. Dunn? In those same, stupid circles, asking such a question labeled a woman as forward, a hoyden, or—for the fortunate, beautiful, and well-dowered few—an original.

No bold overtures ensued, and Emmie was both disappointed and relieved. A fellow who seemed too good to be true was too good to be true, and Mr. Dunn was... lovely.

He was also scowling at the front door. "You have a caller."

Mrs. Oldbach, swathed in a black cape and scarf and carrying a bright red muffler, stood near the front desk. She clutched a walking stick, the head of which had been carved to resemble an eagle. She and her raptor both appeared to peruse the library with regal disdain.

"She must have heard about the clock," Emmie said, dredging up a welcoming smile. "I suspect Bevins of currying favor with her underfootmen over darts."

"That's the dreaded Mrs. Oldbach?"

"She drops in from time to time, though never to borrow a book." The children were squirming in their seats, and Caspar was glaring daggers at Mrs. Oldbach. Even Aristotle, perched on the mantel, looked displeased to see her.

Mr. Dunn bent near enough that Emmie caught his cedary scent. "I'll read the tale for the day, miss. You go charm the gorgon." He patted Emmie's shoulder—a comforting stroke—and moved over to the hearth. "Cease yer fearful din, ye heathens and hooligans, and lend me thine ears."

The children fell silent, and Mrs. Oldbach left off casting dubious glances at the mistletoe. Mr. Dunn set the storybook on the seat to the left of the fireplace, where the meager light from the windows would fall over his right shoulder.

"I'm told we're to learn about tigers in Hyde Park today, though I've never heard such a silly notion in all my life. Who is to turn pages for me?"

Emmie had never thought to use a page turner. Mary Smith— who scorned reading in all its guises—held up her hand. "I can turn yer pages, Mr. Dunn."

"And who will help serve the cider?" Every hand shot up, and Emmie realized that Mr. Dunn had engineered a display of helpful, cheerful behavior from the children for Mrs. Oldbach's benefit.

Or for Emmie's?

She hustled over to the door and greeted Mrs. Oldbach with all the warmth and jollity due any gorgon. Mrs. O, a spry, white-haired veteran of Mayfair's most ferocious whist tournaments, allowed that the library was looking *quite* festive, but of course she did not limit herself to pleasantries.

"Who is that fellow wrangling the infantry?"

"Mr. Dunn, a curate-in-training who needs a place for some quiet scholarship prior to assuming a post in Wales." Though as to that, he had yet to use the library for any scholarship at all.

Mrs. Oldbach snorted. "If he's come here for peace and quiet, he has a taste for martyrdom. Good-looking for a martyr, but then, some of 'em are. You will attend my holiday tea, of course?"

Oh, not this. Please, not this. "I've sent my regrets, I'm afraid."

"Again." Mrs. Oldbach imbued a single word with toboggan-loads of reproach. "You flit about all day here with the literary riffraff and that lot,"—she sniffed in the direction of Mr. Bevins and Mr. Pettibone—"and decline the prospect of a genteel holiday tea. Your mother would despair of you."

The cider had been distributed without a single mug spilling, and Mr. Dunn took the reading chair. He beckoned Mary, and she—the most accomplished pugilist among the younger patrons—scrambled into his lap and positively preened.

Aristotle moved three entire feet along the mantel to sit closer to Mr. Dunn.

"You have to start with 'once upon a time,'" Ralph said. "That how all Mr. Dingle's stories start, because that's what he wrote."

A chorus of "Stow it, Ralph" and "Hush, you big looby" followed in annoyed undertones.

"*The Ferocious Tigers of Hyde Park* by Mr. Christopher Dingle," Mr. Dunn began. "Dedicated to fierce little tigers of every species."

"What's 'at mean?" Caspar called. "What's a spee-she's?"

"Good question," Mr. Dunn replied, while Mary turned the page. "Save it for after the story, and that's where we'll begin our discussion."

"Now comes 'once upon a time,'" Ralph bellowed.

"So it does," Mr. Dunn said. "Thank you, Mary. Now, attend me, my geniuses and prodigies, for our story begins... 'Once upon a time, there were four little kittens. Hammerhead, Mark, Luke, and Jewel. They lived in old Londontown with their dear mama, and though they were good little kittens—or ever tried to be—their mama was forever begging them not to make..."' He paused dramatically and sent his audience a look. "'*So... much... noise.*'"

The children had joined in on those last words, and Emmie nearly forgot Mrs. Oldbach was standing at her elbow. "This is how a story should be read," she murmured. "Like a pub song or a prayer."

"And the look on your face frequently characterizes young women suffering the pangs of romance," Mrs. Oldbach retorted. "Wherever you found him, if you let that fellow disappear into the wilds of Wales, you have tarried too long on the literary battlefields, Miss Armstrong. I see my clock continues to function quite well, so perhaps rumors of vandalism here at the library were greatly exaggerated."

"I would tolerate no mischief at West Bart's Lending, ma'am. I hope you know that."

Mrs. Oldbach muttered something about the folly of the young and, with a *thump* of her walking stick, went on her way.

Emmie, by contrast, pulled up a stool between the bookshelves, took a lean against the biographies, and let herself be swept away by the ferocious tigers of Hyde Park.

CHAPTER FOUR

"I'd kiss ye awake, but this is a library rather than an enchanted castle, and I've no wish to get m' face slapped."

Miss Armstrong did not at first reply to Dunfallon's observation. She instead nuzzled a copy of Boswell's *Life of Samuel Johnson* and sighed. The field marshal, decorating authority, diplomat-in-chief, and literary ambassadress of West Bart's Lending had apparently been felled by that unstoppable force, holiday fatigue.

Dunfallon crouched down to be at eye level with her as she dozed upon her stool. "Miss Armstrong, are ye being coy?" She could not be coy if her good name depended upon it, of that he was certain.

She opened her eyes, and that smile started up again. The one that conveyed joy merely to behold a fellow, though confusion filled her gaze in the next moment. "Mr. Dunn?"

"You fell asleep despite my most stirring rendition of Dingle's tale. The tigers of West Bart's Lending decided to let you rest. Truly we are in the season of miracles, because the little blighters whispered through the whole discussion and even thereafter when we played the map game. Your patrons know St. Giles intimately, but have little familiarity with Mayfair. Bevvy and Petty suspended bickering in honor of your slumbers too."

She blinked, she yawned, she stretched. Miss Armstrong was apparently not one of those obnoxious people who rose all cheery and full of chatter.

"Gracious. How long have I... I still have your pocket watch." She fished it from the folds of her skirt. Flipped it open and stared. "I slept for nearly *two hours*. Mr. Dunn, how could you?"

He offered her a hand, and she allowed him to assist her to her feet—another miracle. "How could I not? If you fall asleep at midday in the midst of my best rendition of tigers, then you have been deprived of sleep. Make a habit of that, and lung fever will find you, or worse."

"Where are the children?"

"I sent them home early, due to the snow, but fear not, they got their nooning." Dunfallon had ordered them proper beef pasties from the corner pub, baked potatoes from the chop shop, and shortbread from the bakery in aid of their continued good behavior—and their survival.

"Snow." Miss Armstrong went to the orange window and gazed out upon a street bathed in the icy blue shadows created by fresh snow falling as an early twilight descended. "So dreary. I worry about the children in weather like this."

"I worry about you. Do you walk home without an escort?"

"Of course. The distance is all of two streets, and I'm not some duchess to be ferried about by a coach and four."

For the hundredth time, Dunfallon's conscience bellowed at him that now would be a good moment to clear up that little misconception about his station in life. And for the hundredth time, his heart bellowed in response that Miss Emerald Armstrong would never again look upon him with that special smile, much less permit him to set foot in her kingdom.

"And if you *were* a duchess?" he asked.

She crossed to the hearth and began poking at the coals. "I'd support libraries, and look after children, and look after my duke, too, though maybe those fellows don't need much looking after."

"Suppose not." Dukes were supposed to do the looking after—of their families, the Regent, the Church, the realm, the occasional armed battalion, and—on some fine day—their duchesses.

Dunfallon had snuffed the sconces around the library, save for one by the front door and another by the main desk. Miss Armstrong was thus illuminated mostly by the fire in the hearth, and the shadows gave her features a pensive cast.

"I've been invited to a holiday open house," she said. "I'm genteel enough to make up numbers, and Lady Bellefonte is kind. Lord Bellefonte's a good sort too. Her ladyship says His Grace of Don't Fall For Him will be there."

"I beg your pardon?" Even as he posed the question, Dunfallon knew to whom she alluded. He'd accepted Bellefonte's invitation because his lordship was like a great mayfly, buzzing persistently on the topic of Yuletide cheer and Lady Bellefonte's much-prized invitations.

"Dunfallon will be there," Miss Armstrong said. "The Scottish duke, the most eligible bachelor in the realm. Has pots of money, great good looks, *and* a Highland castle or three. Lady Bellefonte says he also has a sense of humor, though I doubt that's truly the case."

She heaped half a scoop of coal on the flames and watched the fire catch on the fresh fuel.

"Why can't a duke appreciate the occasional jest?" A jest being a very different matter from willfully deceiving a lovely woman.

"Dunfallon was the extra spare," she said. "Lost a brother to the proverbial stupid—tragic—accident and another to consumption. His Grace was sent off to Spain to participate in that protracted tragedy, and he fought at Waterloo as well. Then he was packed off to Vienna for all the conferring and waltzing. Such a lot of duty, and one wonders... I am rambling. This happens when one's imagination is allowed to flourish."

What the hell, what the bedamned *hell*, did she wonder about His Grace of Dunfallon?

"Do you want to go to this open house?" Dunfallon asked, taking a seat on the raised hearth.

"No, but Lady Bellefonte is a devoted library patron and a friend. I should attend."

Bloody hell. "Not if you don't want to." It was again on the tip of his tongue to confess. *I am Dunfallon, and I would love to see you there,* when Miss Armstrong set aside the poker and sat back on a hassock.

"If a duke," she said, "who is probably lonely, overworked, too serious for his own good, and homesick for his castle, can bestir himself to attend, I ought to as well. The tattle rags suggest Dunfallon has been hounded by the matchmakers ever since he put off mourning years ago, from the ballrooms to the house parties to the Little Season. I'll be at the open house, if only to offer Dunfallon silent moral support and to guard the gingerbread from Lord Bellefonte's predations. Lady Bellefonte doesn't mind that her husband snitches, but he's a corrupting influence on the children when they are trying especially hard to be good."

The sensible, ducal part of Dunfallon's mind wondered what all this sympathy for His Grace was in aid of, but another part—the purely masculine part who was homesick and tired and dreading the loss of his library privileges—was all too aware that he was alone, in fading light, with a woman whom he esteemed.

"Why should Dunfallon deserve your moral support?"

She exchanged a look with Aristotle, whose shining eyes gave his shadowed form a supernatural cast.

"I know what it is to be the butt of gossip, Mr. Dunn, to feel speculative gazes on me everywhere and unkind whispers coming from all corners. I suspect part of the reason our officers did so well in Spain is because they'd trained not on the playing fields of Eton, but in the ballrooms and on the bridle paths of Mayfair."

"We did *so well* because Napoleon stretched his resources too thin, and the Spaniards excelled at guerrilla warfare. Then too, Wellington was effective at getting his army provisioned, and he was shrewd as hell in battle."

"You do not express yourself as a curate, Mr. Dunn."

"I'm not a curate."

"Not yet, but I do wonder if you kiss like one."

Thoughts of confession guttered like a candle in a stiff breeze of astonishment. "I beg your pardon?"

"Earlier, you said you considered waking me with a kiss—I did not dream that. But you declined to avail yourself of the opportunity."

The fire was warm at Dunfallon's back, and outside, darkness was falling in earnest. The library was uncharacteristically quiet, but for the crackle of the fire and a contented rumbling from the cat on the mantel.

"I don't impose kisses on sleeping beauties. I offer them to ladies who are awake enough to appreciate and reciprocate my efforts." *There ye go again, not sounding like a curate.*

"Are you offering to kiss me, Mr. Dunn?"

"My friends call me Dane."

"My friends call me foolish. I prefer the peace and predictability of my library over getting back on the social horse, but earlier today..."

He waited while she seemed to come to some decision.

"Earlier today, I suffered the fiercest wish to be closer to you. This is doubtless more foolishness on my part."

Of all the things she might have said... "Why?"

"Why is it foolish?"

"It's not foolish, but why closer *to me*? I'm woefully blunt. In my sister's opinion, I lack patience. I am in want of social polish, and my burr is too much in evidence when I'm annoyed or amused." Or, apparently, sharing confidences with pretty librarians.

Miss Armstrong cradled his jaw against the warmth of her palm. "Whoever called you impatient hasn't seen you waiting while Mary fumbles to turn yet another page, hasn't seen you explaining to

Caspar the definition of 'species,' and hasn't seen you listening when Ralph states the obvious and hopes he sounds clever. You are the soul of patience when you referee endless rounds of the map game, making certain the children begin to learn their street names. You have the social agility to manage Bevins and Petty's bickering, and your burr is perfect for rendering the growling of a tiger."

"And these attributes you perceive in me, they attract you?"

She brushed his hair back from his brow. "They do."

Between mentally begging her to repeat the caress and lecturing himself not to make a complicated situation worse, Dunfallon was blessed with an insight.

Miss Peasegill and her ilk could pursue only the Dunfallon tiara, because they had not bothered to acquaint themselves with the man who could offer it to them. They had not paid attention to the subtle effect of mood on his burr. They had not wondered if he liked animals or disdained to allow them into his domiciles. They had never inquired about his literary tastes.

To them, those aspects of the *man* were irrelevant beside the shining wealth and consequence of the *duke*.

To Emmie Armstrong, the ducal trappings probably wouldn't matter all that much even if she knew of them. This conclusion caused such a lightness in Dunfallon's heart that he knelt beside the lady's hassock and took her hand.

"Might you kiss me, Miss Armstrong?"

"Emmie. My friends call me Emmie. If I kiss you, it has nothing to do with mistletoe, Mr. Dunn."

"Dane. Please call me Dane."

"Dane."

She pressed her lips gently to his mouth, and he was lost.

In Emmie's opinion, no institution on earth matched a good library for gratification of human needs. Libraries reverenced knowledge as cathedrals reverenced spirituality. Libraries gave physical shelter to their patrons, while library books fed the imagination, the intellect, and the heart.

Emmie had been born for the library the same way some men were born for the military or the Church, though it had taken Lord Hercules's perfidy to bring that truth home to her.

A new truth came to Emmie on the scent of mulling spices and cloved oranges: She had also been born to kiss Dane.

He didn't pull her hair or nibble or mash himself against her or do any of those other obnoxious things Lord Hercules had apparently believed must attend a kiss. She tasted Dane, he tasted her back, gently, respectfully. When he slid his hands into her hair, she caught a whiff of cinnamon and nutmeg, and that brought to mind the image of those hands—strong, competent—crushing spices for the children's delectation.

His kisses, like those spices, warmed her, as did the heat of his body when he shifted closer. His arms came around her, and Emmie was enfolded in pleasure.

Such a relief, to be held, to be cherished. A burden fell away, of both loneliness and despair.

"I sometimes think," she said, rubbing her cheek against Dane's lapel, "that spinsters become eccentric because nobody touches them —some spinsters. They float through society like ghosts, with never a hug, never a cuddle, and they cling to their pets and their tipple because they begin to doubt themselves to be real."

He cradled the back of her head against his palm, the fit of his body against Emmie's a perfect delight.

"Soldiers experience the same thing. Nothing but marching, grumbling, bad rations, and fighting. No softness, no joy, unless it's the joy of killing more of the enemy than he killed of ours. The laughter is bitter, the sleep exhausted and plagued with nightmares. I suspect the enlisted men sometimes took to brawling for the reason you allude to—to assure themselves that they were real, that they still inhabited the world of trees, sky, and bruised knuckles."

Emmie adored that Dane's mind ranged over myriad topics and experiences, that his thinking roamed freely in any direction, uninhibited by prejudice or propriety.

And merciful hosts, he knew how to hold a lady. "What of curates?" she asked, closing her eyes. "Do they long for human warmth?"

He resumed kissing her, and the tenor of his addresses became more passionate, though no less respectful. He invited, he suggested, he never demanded.

And that, Emmie learned, could be frustrating when she herself was tempted to demand—that his hand travel the last few inches to settle over her breast, that he shift to the side so she might explore him more intimately, that he scoop her into his arms and carry her up to the sofa in the office, there to...

To what?

"Emmie Armstrong, ye are no spinster." He'd all but rumbled those words against her hair, his embrace preventing her from seeing his face.

"And you are no curate."

He eased back enough that she could see his smile. "And God be thanked for that mercy. I am one kiss away from importuning you for favors I have not earned, and I don't want to let you go."

"Kissing agrees with you," she said, smoothing his hair where her fingers had previously disarranged it. "You look younger, more mischievous." And more handsome.

He shifted back to sit on the raised hearth, kissed her fingers, and took hold of her hand. "While you look like every holiday gift a grown man doesn't admit he longs for, and yet, I can already see you back on the job, sorting, labeling, and arranging thoughts in your mental library."

He traced a finger down the center of her forehead, and Emmie's middle went fluttery. "I worried," she said. "I should not have."

"Worried?"

Perhaps libraries, when darkened and quiet, also took on some qualities of the confessional. "I worried that Lord Hercules tossed me aside not because my dowry was the smaller of the two on offer, but because of... me."

She leaned forward, though she couldn't quite close the space between them. Her cheeks flamed, with anger rather than humiliation.

"This lordling was in the running for your hand?" Dane asked. "And he offered for another with a larger dowry?"

She wanted to leave the tale there, which was bad enough, but this was Dane, and she owed him the rest of it.

"We were engaged, and the lawyers were working out the settlements. Engagement means..."

"That you allowed him the liberties I will spend the rest of the night dreaming of, and that you might well have conceived his child." Dane rested his forehead against Emmie's. "Go on."

Hercules hadn't even asked about the possibility of a child. "He told me we wouldn't suit and that he was setting me free, and he would graciously allow me to put it about that I'd tossed him aside."

"Meaning you took all the blame for his fickleness and greed."

"And I have been hiding at West Bart's Lending ever since. I am done with Society, with the gossip and snide whispers. I am through with all eyes latching upon me as I descend into a ballroom, knowing that everybody hopes I'll stumble."

He straightened. "You are prodigiously honest, Miss Armstrong, but was it truly that bad? The gossips favor fresh game, and even the most wicked scandals eventually become old news."

In for a penny... "My own brother thinks I abandoned his dear old school chum nearly at the altar, and Lord Hercules has not set him straight. Ambrose and I haven't spoken much since. I bide here in Town as a nominal companion to my auntie. She had no use for Lord Hercules and tells me I need to come out of self-imposed exile. I thought I'd take up traveling on the Continent in the spring, rather than face the Mayfair whirl again. Auntie can be as stubborn as Ambrose can."

She hadn't told anybody that last bit, about traveling. Not even Lady Bellefonte.

"You'd admit defeat because of one titled bungler?"

Emmie withdrew her hand from his. "He didn't merely bungle, Dane. I allowed him *liberties*. Need I provide you a map with all the quadrants labeled? Society draws certain conclusions when an engagement is broken, and those conclusions do not redound to a lady's credit."

He studied her by the flickering firelight, and in the dancing shadows, Emmie saw reflected generations of Highland warriors. Fierce, shrewd, brave, and vigorous.

"That's not the problem, is it?" he asked softly. "The problem isn't the gossip—if you were engaged to a lordling, gossip was a fact of your life before the engagement ended. The problem is, he made you doubt yourself. Doubt your desirability *and* your worth."

Emmie rose, rather than face that patient, insightful gaze.

"His lordship bragged about never reading a single book," she said, pacing before the hearth. "Then he'd rut on me, and when he was done, he'd pat my cheek and tell me that I'd learn to please him eventually and not to worry, because he was a patient man, and even a bluestocking antidote had her charms."

She came to a halt with her back to her audience. "He should have been trying to please *me*, shouldn't he? I have yet to find the library book that deals with such matters, but I'm almost sure—after kissing you—that Hercules was the bumbler, not I."

"'Bumbler' is too kind a term to describe his disregard for your feelings." Dane spoke from immediately behind Emmie. "He is an ass, meaning no disrespect to the worthy donkeys of the world. A jackanapes, a niddering poltroon." He added something harsh in Gaelic.

"What does that mean?"

"Coward."

The word—a judgment when Dane uttered it—reverberated in the library's quiet. "You think Lord Hercules is a *coward*?"

"And a sneak. If the truth had come out—that he'd tossed you aside for the greater fortune—do you believe the young lady in possession of that greater fortune would have had him?"

Emmie turned slowly. "She barely had a say in the matter. Lord Hercules is the son of a marquess. Her family wanted that connection."

"If they can look that high, then they can also afford to have a care for the young man's sense of honor. You were betrayed, Emerald Armstrong, and I can assure you, with every ounce of masculine instinct in me, that there is nothing whatsoever amiss with your desirability or your worth."

His burr had become very pronounced, the r's rolling, the t's acquiring knifepoints. Outside, darkness had fallen, and the snow was piling up apace.

You were betrayed. Those three words articulated a wrong Emmie hadn't been able to name, and Dane had spoken them with towering confidence in his conclusion.

"You have given me much to think about, sir." He'd also made Emmie smile, for no reason she could name. "I don't suppose you'd allow me to ravish you on the sofa in the office?"

She wanted to ravish him out of simple desire—she knew enough to put a name to those feelings—but also a little bit because of that doubt he'd mentioned. The doubt that plagued her every time she contemplated another social outing, the doubt that followed her to the churchyard, the same doubt that had her staring at her wardrobe and trying different styles for her hair.

"That sofa," Dane said, "is too short if you want to ravish me properly, and no, I will not allow you to make the attempt anyway. If and when we become more intimate, we will have a comfortable bed, comestibles to keep up our strength between bouts of passion, and a clear understanding of our mutual expectations."

Emmie wasn't sure what all that meant, but she did grasp that Dane wasn't scandalized. He was... He was contemplating those further intimacies and how they might best be enjoyed.

And he had a point.

Mr. Dunn, the supposed curate bound for Wales, had little in common with Dane, the passionate kisser and honorable lover. The two somehow had to be reconciled, and the hour for that exercise had not come.

"Then I suppose your ravishment will have to wait." Emmie patted his chest.

"As will yours."

She wanted to whoop with glee at that riposte. Instead, she kissed his cheek. "If you'll bank the fires, I'll lock up."

"I locked up an hour ago. I will see you home before the snow gets any deeper. I also told the children that the library was likely to be closed tomorrow, or would at least open a couple hours late."

"Getting airs above your station, Mr. Dunn?"

He took up the poker, studied it, and aimed a wicked smile at her. "I'm getting all manner of ideas, so please fetch your cloak, ye wee besom, lest ye drive a poor laddie daft."

Emmie bundled up, and when Dane offered his arm on the walkway, she took it. The journey home, while short, took some effort in snow half a foot deep. Dane passed her his walking stick, which also made the going easier, and when she would have handed it back at Auntie's front door, he insisted she keep it.

"I'll come by the library on Wednesday morning," he said. "You can return it to me then, and we will sort out some more complicated matters that I'm incapable of tackling just now."

He bowed correctly over her hand—the wretch—and then went whistling on his way. Emmie watched him long enough to wonder what he'd look like in a kilt, then slipped into the house.

She'd never been a *wee besom* before. She preferred it to her former status as Lord Hercules's castoff. Preferred it enormously, and she would count the hours until she and Dane could resume tackling complicated matters—or tackling each other—on Wednesday.

～

"What the 'ell you think you're doing, Mr. Dunn?" The voice belonged to a pint-sized wraith in a jacket too long for his height and too thin for the elements. "I seen you in the library with Miss Armstrong, and she ain't your missus, and you ain't a curate, and you'd best start explaining, or I will kick you where you don't never want to be kicked."

Caspar emerged from the shadows between two town houses, his tone bristling with banked violence even though his teeth chattered.

"Good God, lad." Dunfallon wrapped his scarf around that skinny neck, making sure to cover the boy's ears. "You are a more than decent tracker. Do you always see the lady home?"

"We take turns. I take the most turns, like when it's raining or snowing. The older boys have business to be about, and the little 'uns should stay outta the wet."

"The older boys go begging?"

Caspar took to rearranging the scarf. "Some beg."

Meaning some others got up to housebreaking, picking pockets, or worse. What was a boy to do when his options were crime, humiliation, or starvation?

"Come with me," Dunfallon said, setting off at a modest pace in deference to Caspar's shorter legs.

Caspar stayed right where he was, a dark shape against an increasingly thick curtain of gray. "I don't go nowheres wif men who got nasty ideas."

"You are safe with me, lad. Besides, if you are to properly berate me for taking liberties with Miss Armstrong, you'd best wait until your teeth stop chattering."

"Be-rate. Is that like to 'rip up at'?"

"Exactly like. Now come along, and I promise to feed you a decent supper while you castigate me. Were you waiting outside the whole time Miss Armstrong and I tarried at the library?"

"Aye. She sometimes gets to readin' after she locks up. I sneak in the coal chute if that happens because Miss Emmie can read for *hours*. Then she pikes off and I have to climb out the basement window to catch her. You shouldn't have been kissing her with the drapes open."

In point of fact, the lady had been kissing Dunfallon. "I should not have been kissing her at all."

"Because she thinks you're a curate?"

"How do you know I'm not? I have the education for it." Dunfallon asked the question out of curiosity, rather than any intent to argue. If Caspar had come to that conclusion, Emmie probably had as well.

She's Miss Armstrong to you, laddie.

"You ain't a curate because you don't talk curate-ish. Petty says a curate is allus thankin' the Lord for what can't be helped—like the weather or a key fitting the lock it was made for. You cuss in Scottish. My mum says my da was Scottish, though I never knew 'im. Bevvy says you don't walk like a curate, as if headin' off to the chop shop was some kinda crusade. You don't kiss like no curate neither."

"Your own observation, I take it."

"I got eyes, and you and Miss was goin' to town right in front of the fire. This scarf smells like Christmas."

Such longing imbued that last pronouncement. Dunfallon paused on a street corner. No wheeled traffic braved the snow and darkness, and the porch lights made only small orbs of gold in the vast gloom. London was for once still, and the quiet was profound.

Dunfallon was not about to lose sight of the boy in weather like this, but neither could he take him to the ducal residence or to his apartment at the Albany. The staff was discreet, but not *that* discreet. Then too, darling sister Amy had her spies among them.

"I'm not a curate. I'm a peer."

"A fancy lord?"

"After a fashion. Miss Armstrong has no use for peers, and an innocent mistake on her part meant I could find refuge in the library, so I allowed her error to go uncorrected."

Caspar sneezed twice and, of all things, produced a wrinkled, grubby handkerchief with which to wipe his nose.

"You're right she don't care for fancy lords, Your Toffship, but she got no use at all for liars."

"In the normal course, I'm not given to mendacity." Dunfallon chose a direction, and Caspar came along without argument.

"How you do talk, Lord Dogsbody. You thought about kissing her, and so you read us a story, and that made her think about kissing you."

"Is that how it was?" Dunfallon had read the children a story out of necessity, not because he'd been trying to impress Emmie. "She liked my storytelling?"

"She likes all Mr. Dingle's stories, and you made a proper job of the tigers. Me and the lads have used the tigers' rig to make it sound like we're a gang when it's only three of us."

"You growl and wave your tails in the undergrowth, then dash off a few paces and do the same again until the enemy thinks they're outnumbered by enormous carnivores?"

"And we use different voices, like Dingle's tiger kittens, and we sound like we're eight fellers instead of three, and that's a lot of fists and teeth and boots. I call to the others, 'Get out your knives, lads, one for each hand! Benny, keep that cudgel handy! Mack, we'll need your peashooter!' I sound like Ma when I say it, and Ma in a temper would scare Wellington hisself. Bevvy says Miss wrote those stories for us. Petty don't argue with him."

"And when Petty and Bevvy don't argue about a conclusion, it must be holy writ." Dunfallon turned another corner, and his destination came into view.

"Miss Emmie is smart enough to have written 'em stories, and Petty and Bevvy agreed you wasn't a curate."

"And they were right. I'd appreciate it if you'd allow me to choose the time and place of my confession to Miss Armstrong."

For confess, he would, and go shopping for a ring directly thereafter. One didn't allow the next Duchess of Dunfallon to pass up her tiara over a minor misunderstanding.

CHAPTER FIVE

"These are for the children," Lady Bellefonte said. "I'd thought to save them until Christmas, but with this weather, indoor entertainment seemed the better idea."

Her footman set a box of wood-framed slates on the library's reception desk. The slates were new and of the type used in schoolrooms.

"This was very kind of you," Emmie replied. "I've been requesting slates from the directors for two years, and they remind me that the library is not a select academy."

"But your library is a place of learning, my dear, and slates can be used to practice drawing, penmanship, sums, and much else that stands a child in good stead. Besides, I am giving these to the children rather than to West Bart's Lending. If the children choose to leave their slates here for safekeeping, that is none of the directors' business."

"I suppose not." They shared a conspiratorial smile that included more than a dash of determination.

The front door opened, and Emmie knew without looking who

had arrived. The very air changed when Dane was on hand, and not simply because of his luscious scent.

"You are late, Mr. Dunn," she said and ruined the scold entirely with a welcoming smile. "I have errands for you, sir. Lady Bellefonte, may I make known to you Mr. Dane Dunn, late of Perthshire, by way of the Peninsula. Mr. Dunn is on his way to a curate's post in Wales come spring."

The footman, whose job entailed hours of silence and miles of discretion, made a snorting noise.

Lady Bellefonte's dark brows rose, and Dane looked as if he were one of Mr. Dingle's kittens facing the mastiff with the cocklebur in his ear. Nowhere to run, no help in sight.

"Mr.... Dunn." Her ladyship held out a hand for him to bow over, and he complied.

"My lady, a pleasure."

A silence blossomed, with Lady Bellefonte sending Dane the sorts of looks she probably reserved for her husband when he led the children on a gingerbread-snitching raid.

"Mr. Dunn," Emmie said, "if you take the slates up to my office, then nip over to the stationer's for some ribbon, we can wrap them for the children later this morning."

Lady Bellefonte made a shooing motion with her gloved hand. "Do as you are told, *Mr. Dunn*. Run along."

He hefted the box of slates and made for the steps.

Lady Bellefonte watched him go with a gimlet eye. "Emmie, that man is no curate."

"I have suspected as much, and he's all but admitted the same. I'm hoping he'll explain himself without my having to drag it out of him."

"He had better have the best explanation in the history of explanations." Her ladyship's gaze roamed over the rows of bookshelves, the cheery hearth, and Aristotle batting gently at a low-hanging orange. "You have built something lovely here, Emmie. One could hardly see to read for all the grime on the windows before you took

West Bart's in hand. Mr. Dunn had best not be trifling with you, or my Nicholas will have a very pointed discussion with him."

"He's not trifling with me," Emmie said, "and I'm not trifling with him either."

Some of the starch went out of her ladyship's posture. "So that's the way of it? Nicholas said you simply needed time, and he's very intuitive about these things. I will see you and *Mr. Dunn* at my open house."

She swanned off, the footman in tow, though he cast a dubious glance in the direction of Emmie's office as he held the door for the countess.

Emmie's progress toward the steps was impeded by Mary, who stood on the bottom stair as if she'd taken her regular shift guarding the gates of hell.

"Will Mr. Dunn read us the story today, miss?" She imbued her words with characteristic truculence, and yet, Emmie heard the hope lurking in the child's question too.

"He is a gifted storyteller, isn't he?"

"Will he?"

"I shall ask him to. Do you happen to know where Caspar is?"

"Caspar has a proper job. A serious, proper job. He'll be a groom or maybe a footman, if he don't muck it up." She sidled around Emmie and scampered off a few paces. "I'll miss him, though he was always winning the map game. He oughtn't to do a bunk on his mates, but a proper job... Mr. Dunn found him honest work, and it pays. We're happy for him, though I'll miss him."

She went over to the window seat, picked up Aristotle, and stood gazing at the oranges with all the dignity of a miniature bereaved queen.

"I'll miss him too," Emmie said softly. She mentally added Caspar's change of circumstances to the growing heap of matters Mr. Dunn had to explain. When she reached her office, the door was closed, the better to keep in the heat, of course. Rather than knock, she sailed in and found Dane seated at her desk.

Reading her story notebook.

"What do you think you're doing?" she snapped.

He rose, looking not the least bit self-conscious. "Admiring your work. You left the notebook out on the blotter for anybody to see."

Emmie snatched up her stories and hugged them to her chest. "Then you should have realized these are rough drafts and not for public consumption."

He came around the desk, in no hurry at all, and for reasons known only to unrepentant snoops, he looked even taller and more serious than ever.

"If these are your rough drafts, then your polished work should fetch you a very tidy sum. You studied the female satirists and went them one better. I would never have thought to use the jaundiced wit of the typical adolescent to illuminate society's foibles."

Despite her dismay and upset, Emmie grasped that her writing was being complimented. "People dismiss schoolgirls one week and want to marry them off to the nearest eligible the next. Boys are supposed to be translating Caesar in May and taking up arms for England in June. In my experience, young people are very keen judges of society. Then they finish growing up and succumb to the weight of propriety. They become disappointed and..."

"Bitter?" he asked, standing close enough that Emmie could see the gold flecks in his blue eyes. "Retiring? Cautious? Circumspect?"

"They lose their innocence and make pacts with the demons of expedience." As Lord Hercules had chosen the expedient bride. Had Dane not peeked at her stories, she might have been able to leave the conversation there, but he had peeked, and she was upset, and he was most of the reason.

"Did you lie to me about your name out of expedience?" she asked.

Dane took a step back. "I assume Lady Bellefonte put you wise?"

"Why, no, she did not. You've been telling me yourself."

"Does this have to do with my diction and dress?"

"Only in part." Emmie stepped around him, slid her copybook

into the middle drawer, and closed it quite firmly. "A curate might well be a younger son of a genteel family, and unruly spares are sent off to the countryside on repairing leases all the time. You, however, failed to make use of the library's Welsh resources. Didn't sign them out, didn't even bother learning where we shelve them."

He smiled slightly. "I was too busy lugging coal and fetching soup."

"You told me on several occasions that you are not a curate, and I believed you. You also have a gold watch inscribed from 'Uncle Quint, to the best of the lot as he prepares to battle the forces of ignorance.' I assumed that was a gift given when you went off to university, and it is an exceptionally fine timepiece. "

"Too fine for a man who has taken a vow of poverty?"

"No, but too fine and too dear to you to be casually lent to a librarian, and you have yet to ask for it back." She dug the watch out of her pocket, where it had been a comforting weight, like a happy secret or the memory of a precious kiss.

"You lent me your walking stick as well," Emmie went on. "You are generous with fine things, and all that aside, I stopped by East Bart's Lending to return some books that had been erroneously left here. I spotted a new fellow at East Bart's, who was reshelving biographies. He's neither Scottish, nor charming, nor patient with the patrons—the real Mr. Dunn, I now suspect. He also apparently has little sense of direction, but when he showed up at a Bartholomew Street library, willing to work in exchange for use of their Welsh resources, they doubtless obliged him with a mountain of reshelving.

"At the time I barely noted his presence in passing, but now... This is the misunderstanding you alluded to when first we met, isn't it? This is why you were late on the first day, but never thereafter. Why Bevins and Petty watch you the way Aristotle would watch an industrious mouse. I've seen the puzzle pieces and when I put them together, I see that you cannot be some younger son in disgrace or a sartorially inclined churchman."

Though part of her had wanted him to be. Part of her had wanted those puzzle pieces to make a simple, pleasing picture with only a few minor rough edges. Another part of her had been waiting for the disappointment.

Dane ran a hand through his hair. "My old tutor warned me that effective deception was not in my gift. I did wonder what had become of the real Mr. Dunn. You kissed me without knowing my name?"

"Your name is Dane, and you are about to tell me the rest of it. Besides, I've seen you reading to the children. I know who you are."

"You could not possibly. When did you stop by East Bart's?"

"The day you showed up on my doorstep, overly fashionable and insufficiently curious about the Welsh language." Also too handsome, too robust, too much at home among a vast collection of books.

He studied her, perhaps as he'd studied battle maps in Spain—he would not have lied about that part. His gaze suggested he was noting details, cataloging facts, and developing contingency plans.

"Might we sit?" he asked.

"You will tell me why you dissembled?"

"I shall."

"And what's become of Caspar?"

He gestured to the sofa, and Emmie took a seat. "Does nothing escape your notice, Miss Armstrong?"

"At West Bart's Lending, very little. One learns to be vigilant about what matters."

He looked around the room, an office teetering between cozy and shabby. His head nearly brushed the crossbeams, and Emmie was acutely aware of his recent remark regarding the limitations of the sofa.

Dane made her an elegant bow. "Dunfallon, at your service, as in His Grace of. The first part—my title—shouldn't matter in the least, but the at-your-service part is what I hope you'll take to heart."

Emmie was very glad she was sitting down, because that was not the admission she'd been expecting. Not at all. "You're *Dunfallon*?"

"I have that honor."

"And *you* read my stories?" The *Duke of Dunfallon* had swept and dusted her library, hauled her coal, and... kissed her? The Duke of Dunfallon had tramped to the chop shop and back like some under-footman?

"I completed one tale in its entirety, and I would dearly like to read more."

Emmie absently patted the place beside her. She'd been prepared for him to be a younger son, a spare, an impecunious society bachelor with a need to avoid dunning creditors, possibly even an heir kicking his heels while trading on his expectations... but *Dunfallon?*

Gracious, merciful, everlasting, almighty kittens. Emmie mentally re-shelved some conclusions and dusted off others. The notion that a peer of the realm, a duke, a war hero, had been Caspar's pupil regarding the serious matter of how to clean out a hearth...

When the shock wore off, Emmie might find the situation humorous—provided His Grace was honest about the rest of it, because he might be a duke, but he was also far more than that.

"It's only fair that you read my stories," she said slowly, "seeing as *I've read so many of yours.*"

He dropped onto the sofa without ceremony. "Explain yourself. Please."

If nothing else had convinced her of the truth of his confessions, that note of command in his voice would have. Dane... Dunfallon, rather, was accustomed to being obeyed, but Emmie wondered if he was accustomed to being understood, much less appreciated.

All things considered, Emmie appeared to be adjusting fairly well to having a duke as her adoring swain. Dunfallon could not make the same claim for himself regarding her latest revelation.

Nobody had accused him of writing the kitten stories, and he'd stopped worrying that anybody ever would.

"You are Christopher Dingle," she said. "That was the secret I hoped you'd confide in me."

"And how did you divine that near impossibility?" He sounded as testy as old MacAlpin when the indigestion plagued him.

"In a sense, Aristotle told me." Emmie took up a green brocade pillow and fiddled with its tassels. "He will tolerate affection from the children when they are having a low moment, but he doesn't like men. Bevvy and Petty have never been allowed to so much as pat his head. He has hissed at my brother."

She clearly approved of the cat for that rudeness. "I like animals," Dunfallon said. "That does not prove I could pen a few silly stories for children."

Emmie stroked the tassel she'd been twiddling. "I wish you could hear the difference between how I read Mr. Dingle's stories and how you read them. The children noted it at once. You didn't need Mary to keep up with the page turning, because you knew every word by heart."

Dunfallon felt the same rising anxiety he'd experienced in Spain when the sound of French war drums had grown ever closer on the day of battle.

He hadn't run then, and he wasn't about to run now. "I told you, I have nieces. I've read them Dingle's whole collection, as well as Aesop, *The Arabian Nights*, and Lamb's versions of Shakespeare."

Emmie brushed her cheek with the silky green tassel. She doubtless did not mean these idle gestures to be distracting, but they most assuredly were.

"You have Dingle memorized," she said.

"So, I hope, do you and many a tired nanny or parent."

"You did not write those stories for the nannies and parents."

Dunfallon's panic rose higher, to the acid-in-the-back-of-the-throat stage. A cold sweat would soon follow if he didn't...

Didn't what? This was *Emmie*, who loved books and children and cranky old men and wayward cats. Emmie was not Papa bound on another excoriation of his third son's myriad egregious faults.

"The first volume of Dingle's stories went into a second printing," Emmie said, almost as if Dunfallon's world was not coming asunder with old memories and new fears. "Between the two printings, there were, of course, a few corrections—printers are not perfect. There was also one change, made apparently by the author. Nobody knows why. He changed the word 'commence' to 'begin.' The sentence loses a little of its loftiness, but being both accessible to children and a tad lofty is a hallmark of Dingle's style."

Dunfallon wanted to beat himself over the head with her pillow.

"When you read to the children," she went on, "you used the word 'commence,' found only in the rare first edition. Your publisher did not anticipate how wildly popular the stories would become, and thus the initial printing was quite modest. The second printing was much larger, and that's the one all those nannies and parents have. The first editions are largely in the hands of collectors."

Dane's late father would have thundered at her to cease her impertinence, to spare him further exhibitions of female insolence. Dane was torn between a pressing need to leap out the French doors and a yearning to hug the library cat.

In the midst of this old dread of censure, a single thought penetrated: If he asked Emmie for her discretion, she would not betray his authorship. She was not a mean, blustering duke, but rather, a woman who applied reason and compassion in equal measure.

You can trust her, laddie. The warning came not in MacAlpin's gruff baritone, but in the voice of a brother long gone to his reward.

Dunfallon took the pillow from Emmie and set it aside. "I promised my brother Secondus one thing as he gasped his last. Weak lungs, my father said. My brother expired of damned consumption, which isn't supposed to afflict ducal heirs."

"What did you promise your brother?"

"That I would not be like our father. Secondus was my friend and ally, the person who insisted that MacAlpin accompany me to Oxford. Secondus took the blame for many of my blunderings, because even Papa would not beat a consumptive, nor would he accuse his heir of lying."

She patted Dunfallon's arm. "I am so sorry."

"One does not express pity for a duke, Miss Armstrong."

Her next touch was more of a caress than a pat. "Is that what your strutting papa would have said?"

"God, yes, and then he would have treated the world to a good twenty minutes of shouted bloviations grounded solely in his conceits and fearful fancies."

Emmie rose to go to the door, and Dunfallon's heart nearly stopped beating. *Don't leave. I can try to explain. Please...*

She let in the cat and returned to the sofa, this time sitting at Dunfallon's hip. "I gather your father did not approve of your stories?"

Dunfallon was tempted to reassert his denials, to lie, strut, and paw and generally make an ass of himself before the woman he loved. *That's how a proper duke would handle the situation.*

From the depths of his imagination, Dunfallon heard four small feline voices reproaching him: *Use your head. Think before you act. Keep trying. Don't give up. There's always a way home.*

Though he was not an intrepid kitten, and the family seat was a distant, drafty castle full of grim memories.

Where was *home? Who* was home?

"Dane?" Emmie took his hand and let her head fall to his shoulder. "Please tell me the rest of your story."

Dunfallon's heart began to beat like one of those war drums. "Not much to tell."

Aristotle leaped to the sofa and sat at Dunfallon's other hip, close enough that the cat's purring was both a physical sensation and a soft hum.

"Tell me anyway."

He was helpless to decline her invitation. "My father *hated* my stories, almost as much as he hated me. My oldest brother should have been the duke—a great strapping, bonnie laddie who loved to ride to hounds, shoot, and drink. Secundus was at least handsome and witty. But Papa was left with me, a shy, gangly, bookish disappointment—a disgrace. When he found out I'd been writing for children, he had me sent to Spain, to a unit that saw a great deal of action. He admonished me to make a man of myself or die trying."

Somewhere between landing in Lisbon and surviving Waterloo, Dunfallon had figured out that one could be *a man* and still pen a few children's stories. He'd never had the satisfaction of sharing that insight with his father.

"Dane, the old duke was the disgrace, not you. Your stories are about helpless kittens winning the day—through cooperation, cleverness, and bravery. Your father apparently regarded those tales as literary treason against his mutton-headed authority and the peerage generally. The kittens are decent little souls, and those who menace them are always abusing positions of authority."

She saw without effort what Dunfallon had taken years to put together. "I sorted out that much in Spain. I also became an exemplary officer, then did my bit at Vienna, anything to avoid going back to my father's house." He would not call that dreary castle *home*, not in this context.

"And now you lead the matchmakers a dance here in London, when you aren't lugging coal for me. Who else knows that you are a brilliant author?"

"I'm not brilliant." Papa had been very clear on that point, and for the most part, Dunfallon agreed with him. "I'm a plodder, conscientious, and more than a bit stodgy."

"Shy." She hugged his arm. "And a brilliant author."

That little, affectionate squeeze did something to Dunfallon's heart. A weight slid away, a grief. "I am Christopher Dingle." The words should have felt portentous, imbued with the gravity of a long-overdue truth, but instead, they felt... comfy. True, in an unremarkable way. The same way mulling spices smelled good and a purring cat was a delight.

In this office, with Emmie tucked against one side and Aristotle purring madly on the other, to admit authorship of some children's tales was *safe*.

"Who else knows?" Emmie asked.

"MacAlpin, my old tutor. He would never betray me. Lord Belle-fonte knows. He read the stories to his oldest daughter, whose juvenile critiques helped shape the final drafts."

"How is it you entrusted the Earl of Bellefonte with this knowledge? He can be a bit frivolous."

"Flirtatious, perhaps, but don't be fooled by his charm. Nicholas is shrewd and ruthless when he has to be."

"And he is your friend. I'm glad. We all need friends who understand us and stand by us even when we aren't making much sense."

Emmie had seen what all of society had ignored: The current Duke of Dunfallon was a lonely fellow, somewhat adrift, and not at all enamored of his title.

Whose privilege was it to stand by Emmie?

"Nicholas was sent off to school without warning," Dunfallon said, "as I was. My oldest brother had just died, and my surviving brother was prone to a winter cough that lasted ten months of the year. Bellefonte had been separated from his older half-brother, and the parting left him heartbroken. Bellefonte was outlandishly tall even then, a giant among the other boys, with a heart to match. He took me under his physical and figurative wing and was no respecter of my privacy. We remained friends through university and beyond. That he liked my stories and did not laugh at them meant worlds to me."

That Emmie liked Dunfallon's kitten stories, *and liked him*, meant even more. "The countess knows of my authorship as well," he went on. "Bellefonte let the secret slip in one of their many marital moments, but he assured me her ladyship can keep a confidence."

"I haven't shown my stories to anybody," Emmie said. "I've pored over Dingle's every word, drawn diagrams of his plots, studied his sentence structures, but what I wanted most to learn from him was how to reassure the vulnerable and the overlooked that they are equal to life's challenges. You could write those stories because you know what it is to be without allies or influence. One would never think that of a ducal spare, but the truth is on the pages."

Perhaps that's why Dunfallon was determined to preserve the safety of his pseudonym—because the sad reality of life in his father's house was in those stories.

"I like Dingle's stories," he said. "They represent my riposte to all of Papa's lectures and sermons. I could never say, 'Papa, you are a selfish embarrassment...' But I could say, 'There's another way to go through life besides blustering and threatening when abusing one's authority doesn't see one's every wish satisfied.' The old man made me watch while he burned my first editions on his library hearth. I'm sure I was the picture of youthful devastation, but all the while, I knew the stories were safe."

"Because you'd had them published?"

"Because even Papa could not burn down every library in the realm. I suspect he was unwell, in heart, soul, and mind. As his family dwindled and his years advanced, he became fanatic about standards, decorum, and consequence."

Syphilis, perhaps, or the corrosive effect of meanness, drink, and loneliness.

"The children will want their story soon," Emmie said, resting her head on his shoulder. "Will you read to them?"

"With pleasure, provided I don't again find you napping with Mr. Johnson when I finish."

They remained behind the closed door with Aristotle for another half hour. Emmie laughed at Dunfallon's explanation of his initial foray into West Bart's Lending, and Dunfallon agreed to make comments on the draft of her story.

He emerged from her office a changed, happier man. He was a fellow who had only one more question to pose if his joy was to be complete.

"Before we join battle with the Vandal horde, Emmie, please say you will be my wife. I would go down on bended knee here on the mezzanine, but that would make a spectacle of what should be a precious moment."

At the top of the steps, she paused and gazed out over the library.

"I would love to be Mrs. Christopher Dingle, and I thought Dane Dunn was a very worthy fellow too. Becoming a duchess, though... even your duchess would be quite a step."

She deserved to be wooed, of course. He should not have rushed his fences with a woman who had every reason to view polite society —and marriage proposals generally—with a jaundiced eye.

He took her hand. "I would expect my duchess to be almost as devoted to libraries as she is to her duke."

"You have the right of that, sir. I'll not turn my back on West Bart's Lending simply to mince about Mayfair at your side."

"If we marry, I can promise you mincing about Mayfair will fall very low on my list of priorities." He kissed her ink-stained fingers, ready to beg if necessary. "Please say you'll have me, Emmie."

"I can still look after West Bart's Lending?"

"We can set up an endowment that will keep West Bart's, its urchins, pensioners, cats, and pickpockets in cider and sandwiches until Mary Smith is named queen of the May. I will court you before all of London, flirt with Mrs. Oldbach herself, and—"

Emmie put her fingers to his lips. "You mean it? About the endowment and about not having to flit about every Venetian breakfast, grand ball, and musicale in Town?"

Dane was more than happy to give the social whirl a rest, and Emmie had good reasons to be wary of society.

"Within the limits of my station, I promise we will socialize only selectively."

Emmie held his hand against her cheek. "Thank you. With those assurances, I can happily consent to be your wife, though I expect to wake up from a nap and find I have neglected my overdue notices while dreaming this whole conversation."

"You are not asleep, Emmie Armstrong, and you are making my dreams come true. Thank you. Clichés come to mind, effusive, paltry clichés, so I will content myself with thanking you."

Her smile was mischievous and sweet. "Is the sofa still too short?"

"It's getting longer by the minute."

"Naughty, sir. We've been spotted."

Mary was at her post at the foot of the steps, glowering doom at any who thought to put off the reading of the daily story.

"When we've dispensed with the morning's tasks," Dunfallon said, "we can discuss particulars pertinent to the immediate future. Perhaps a repast in your office will suit?"

"A repast in my office will suit nicely. And I can tell you right now that for my morning gift—after a very short courtship—I must have a new story by the estimable Mr. Dingle. If you truly seek to impress me, a new volume of stories would be even better."

She swanned down the steps and began assembling the children by the hearth, while Dunfallon remained on the mezzanine and hoped like hell that his beloved had been joking.

"Dunfallon's father was awful," Emmie said. "A martinet with no sense for his children's feelings. What sort of man *numbers* his sons?"

Leah, Lady Bellefonte, sipped her tea and marveled. For the first time in living memory, Emmie Armstrong was babbling. She had been holding forth since ensconcing herself on the love seat opposite her ladyship's perch on the sofa. The fire on the hearth in the countess's private parlor softly crackled, and flurries danced past the window, while Emmie Armstrong chattered gaily on.

And about time too.

"His given name is Tertius," she said. "The older brother was Secondus. He was consumptive and expired while Dane was in the military. Secondus held out until Dane could get leave so they at least took a proper farewell of one another. Secondus was also Dane's ally. I suppose I should refer to Dane as Dunfallon, but the children still call him Mr. Dunn, when I so want them to be able to call him Mr. Dingle."

Emmie was wearing a pretty frock for a change, in holiday red and green, and her eyes had taken on the sparkle Lady Bellefonte usually saw only when Emmie was critiquing Mr. Coleridge's poetical maunderings.

"Emmie?"

"Hmm?"

"Has His Grace declared his intentions?"

"Yes."

Nicholas had predicted as much. He'd said that if and when Dunfallon succumbed to love, he'd fall hard and not for a predictable diamond.

"Have you informed your brother?"

Emmie's sparkle dimmed, and she considered her tea. "Ambrose is in Town. I know not why. He sent a note, and my fingers nearly froze holding it, the tone was so chilly. 'I plan to spend the holidays on Humboldt Street. Please inform Aunt. Threadham.'"

"Now that is odd," Lady Bellefonte said. "He might have written to your aunt rather than to you, and by rights, a dutiful nephew should pay a holiday call on his auntie."

Emmie made a face at a cup of excellent China black. "You think he was warning me of such a visit? Or does he expect me to go down on my figurative knees, begging for his brotherly forgiveness when he's the party in the wrong?"

Her ladyship considered what she knew of brothers—she had grown up with two, Nicholas had four, and the lot of them were difficult, dear men.

"I suspect Lord Threadham wasn't clear in his mind about his own motives. He probably told himself you had a right to know his movements, that you and he might meet at some holiday function, and you are his sister after all. He would not have examined his reasoning more closely until after the letter had been posted, when it was safe to do so."

Lady Bellefonte knew Ambrose, Viscount Threadham, only in passing. That no gossip concerning the viscount had reached her ladyship spoke well of him, but perhaps both discretion and debauchery numbered among his talents.

"Ambrose was such a happy boy," Emmie said. "That he has become a grim, judgmental prig baffles and disappoints me."

"Dunfallon might understand the transformation. He's not exactly a dashing blade himself."

Emmie cut herself a slice of the gingerbread loaf that had as yet escaped predation by Nicholas or the children.

"Why do you think Ambrose wrote to me?"

"Because he misses you, and the holidays are a time to be with loved ones?"

"This gingerbread is wonderful," Emmie said, a little too brightly. "Lighter than the usual varieties."

"The recipe was developed by Nicholas's brother Max. He's something of a food chemist, and he has a blend of mulling spices that goes so perfectly with his gingerbread that the Regent ought to pay to serve it at court. Max claims pepper is the secret ingredient in both."

"If he admits it, is it a secret?"

"A family secret, then. I'll send some gingerbread to West Bart's with you. Have you and Dunfallon set a date?"

If they were wise, they'd make a start for Scotland after the first of the year and marry north of the border without any fuss—or with as little fuss as ducal nuptials could involve.

The parlor door opened, and as predictably as bees flew to blooming honeysuckle, Nicholas, Earl of Bellefonte, sauntered into the room, pointedly ignoring the offerings on the tea tray.

And still, after years of marriage, parenting, and muddling on together, Leah felt her heart leap as she beheld her golden god of a darling husband.

"Lovey mine, I did not know Miss Armstrong had graced us with a call. Miss Armstrong, you look positively radiant. Pray tell, what has put such becoming roses in your cheeks? Could it be you've had a sample of Max's gingerbread?"

"Paws *off* the gingerbread, your lordship," Lady Bellefonte snapped. "You will spoil your supper."

"A man of my generous proportions needs at least four snacks between luncheon and supper." He batted his lashes at Emmie. "Support me in my famished desperation, Miss Armstrong, or I shall faint dead away."

Emmie offered him the plate holding her half-finished slice of gingerbread. "I could not have a fainting earl on my conscience, particularly when allowing you to topple to the carpet would shake the rafters and frighten the children."

Nicholas took a bite and put the slice back on the plate. "A woman of keen understanding. I am told by a little ducal birdie that felicitations are in order."

Even for Nick, that was forward, but then, he was protective of his friends. Also of his family, his pets, his employees, and his enormous mare—Buttercup, by name.

"I have given Dunfallon permission to pay me his addresses," Emmie said, positively glowing to impart that news. "The rest of the situation requires further discussion."

Nick helped himself to the rest of Emmie's gingerbread, for which Lady Bellefonte would remonstrate with him in private and at length, which would probably result in his lordship resorting to some kissing. Not the most desperate tactic in his marital arsenal, but lamentably effective when a wife was trying to be stern.

"If Dunfallon should for any reason vex you in the course of this courtship," Nick said, looking for once serious as he took a seat beside his wife, "you will apply to me, and I will sort him out."

"If there's sorting to be done, my lord, that office falls to me as His Grace's intended. I've encouraged him to resume writing his children's stories, for example."

Emmie was quietly exploding with joy, from the look of her smile. Her ladyship had read the Christopher Dingle stories and been charmed by them. The tales worked well for children, and the prose was entertaining to adults as well. The wit was subtle and uproarious, and more than a bit irreverent.

Nicholas was eyeing the rest of the gingerbread loaf, which he could consume in its entirety as one of his fourteen afternoon snacks.

"Dunfallon has agreed to resume penning children's tales?" he asked.

"As my morning gift, I've requested a new kitten adventure, and I'm sure a second volume will be very well received. Christopher Dingle has a following, and we've been waiting years for more of his work."

"Have you met Dunfallon's sister?" Nicholas asked, edging his knee closer to the tea tray. "Impressive woman. Has three daughters, and in a very few years, they will be gracing the ballrooms."

Nick had just changed the subject, though he was among the most devoted of Christopher Dingle's followers. He'd read those stories to Leonie, the oldest daughter of the house, when she'd been in leading strings.

"Lady Crestwood will be at my open house," Lady Bellefonte said. "The one you will attend, along with your prospective spouse. I believe her ladyship is coming in part to watch her brother dodge all the mistletoe Nicholas is hanging in unavoidable locations."

"Please say you'll come." Nick took a sip of Lady Bellefonte's tea. "I want to see the look on Dunfallon's face when my brothers celebrate the season with you beneath that mistletoe."

"They won't find me lurking near the kissing boughs, my lord. I'll be assisting her ladyship to guard the gingerbread from hungry elves." Emmie rose. "I have tarried too long away from my duties, and I can see myself out. I'm busier than anticipated this holiday season, and there aren't enough hours in the day."

Lady Bellefonte stood and tugged her husband to his feet as well. "We'll both see you out, Emmie, and you—when next we are private —will regale me with an explanation for why a duke ended up sweeping the hearth at West Bart's Lending. I will hold the matter in confidence, but I am dying of curiosity."

"An interesting tale, I'm sure," his lordship said, all innocence. "Shall I escort you back to the library, Miss Armstrong? Send a footman with you?"

"You shall not," Emmie replied. "I'm traveling exactly two

genteel streets over, and one of the benefits of becoming socially obscure is that I can eschew some of Society's sillier rules. For now."

She was still beaming and blushing as she bustled out the door.

"So in love," Nick said. "Almost as in love as we are."

"You are enamored of the gingerbread on my tea tray and think to sweeten me up with flirtation. I neglected to serve myself a portion. For that reason only, you may accompany me back to the parlor."

"I am your most humble servant, though if you asked me to lug coal and sweep the hearths, I might be a bit... nonplussed."

"What was Dunfallon doing at a lending library, Nicholas? His castle probably has a library bigger than West and East Bart's combined."

Nick paused outside the parlor. "He was hiding, lovey. He dodged into West Bart's to avoid an encounter with Miss Peasegill. I waited half an hour for him to emerge, and yet, he tarried among the books. I understand why he'd enjoy a literary refuge, but I fear our Emerald is in for a rude shock."

Lady Bellefonte opened the parlor door. "He'd never play Emmie false, Nicholas. Duke or not, Dunfallon is a gentleman."

"He'd never play her false—not in that sense, especially not after this masquerading as a curate business—but he's also not about to resume writing children's stories. I've tried every way I know to get him to take up his pen again, but he's not having it. When a Scottish duke makes up his mind, only his granny or his conscience can make him change it, and Dunfallon has no living grannies."

Lady Bellefonte took her place on the sofa and gestured for her husband to close the parlor door. Nick complied, then came down beside her and curled an arm around her shoulders.

"Dunfallon dedicated his storybook to my Leonie," he said, referring her ladyship's step-daughter, who'd come into the world well before the marriage. "'To a very young lady of grace and charm.' He'd not met her, but she was his first critic, after me. You need a larger slice than that, lovey."

"This is your slice." She passed him his treat on a plate. "Why won't Dunfallon resume writing? His authorship has stayed secret for years, and it could surely remain so. Emmie seems to think more stories are both inevitable and to be prized above all other gifts. She's happy to marry the author, and willing to tolerate the ducal trappings that come with him."

"Emmie is bound for disappointment. Dunfallon says Spain changed him, but I think the loss of his brothers changed him more, and inheriting the title finished the job. He's entirely the lofty peer now, not a fanciful youth bent on literary rebellions. Why is your piece larger than mine?"

"Because, as God and all his herald angels know, I must keep up my strength."

"What about my strength?"

"Eat your gingerbread, Nicholas, and tell me why Spain or Waterloo or losing siblings would disincline Dunfallon to write more stories. He has the knack of crafting a tale that entertains and instructs without ever preaching."

Nick took a nibble of his gingerbread. He was a dainty eater, for all his size. "Dunfallon's father burned his stories, and that had to hurt like hell. To burn books your own son has written, lovely little stories about fluffy kittens and their intrepid feline adventures... I did not always understand my father, but I knew without doubt that he loved me in his way."

Lady Bellefonte poured herself another cup of tea. "My father hated me, and books were one of my few consolations. I hope His Grace does start writing again. That he resume the use of his talent seems to mean a great deal to Emmie."

Nicholas set aside his plate of half-eaten gingerbread. "I don't think it's that Dunfallon refuses to write more stories. I think it's that he *cannot*."

"That is a problem, given Emmie's expectations. Getting them to the altar will take more than mistletoe and kisses, Nicholas."

"I fear you are right, as usual, lovey mine. But speaking of kisses..."

"I saw you lock the door, sir. My holiday wish for Emmie and Dunfallon is that they are as prone to locking doors years after speaking their nuptial vows as we are."

"Don't neglect your gingerbread, lovey. You are soon to need *all* of your considerable strength."

Lady Bellefonte finished every crumb of her gingerbread.

CHAPTER SIX

"The house just wants some... warmth," Emmie said, frowning at a portrait of the fourth Duke of Dunfallon holding pride of place over the library mantel. "And a little less plaid, perhaps. You have plenty of books, and..."

Her voice trailed off as she studied the fourth duke, whom Dunfallon had always considered the merriest of a sober lot. The old fellow actually smiled. He held the reins of a muscular hunter with one hand. With the other, he stroked the head of an adoring brindle hound. The portrait had caught a happy moment in what surely must have been a happy life.

He'd been well-liked, a perennial favorite for Scotland's parliamentary delegation, and his nine children had had nothing but pleasant memories of him, if their diaries were to be believed.

"He has your nose," Emmie said, skimming glances between Dunfallon and his ancestor. "You have the same humor in your eyes. I suspect he read to his children, and his letters to his wife were tender and sweet."

"Papa burned those letters too. Claimed they were a lot of sentimental tripe unbecoming of a duke's dignity." Though they had been tender and sweet—also bawdy in places—and Secondus had copied the best of them before Papa could destroy them.

Dunfallon busied himself poking at the fire. In a room this size, even three hearths would need more than a day to chase off the chill, but Emmie had asked only yesterday to see the official Dunfallon town residence.

He would rather have had the staff tidying and dusting for a week, but the staff, such as it was, amounted to an elderly couple and their grumpy middle-aged son. All the dusting in the world would not get rid of too much plaid and too few comfortable places to sit.

"How many volumes do you have here?" Emmie said, slowly turning a circle.

"Too many that haven't been read in a century. I hope you are equal to the task of sorting the lot. I look in on the place from time to time, but it's not... I prefer more modest quarters."

"And the Albany doubtless likes the cachet of having you on the premises." Emmie took the poker from him, set it aside, and wrapped him in a hug. "When you are writing stories again, you will need two studies. One for when you are the duke and one for when you are the author."

She did this—dropped little references to his renewed efforts with a pen, and each one made Dunfallon feel more like a false suitor. She also bestowed lavish affection upon him—hugs, caresses, kisses to his cheek—and that made him joyous and a little wary.

He gave her a squeeze and stepped back. "Would you like to see the ducal suite?" They'd already toured the cellars, kitchen, pantries, and maids' quarters, along with endless parlors. Mr. and Mrs. Peyton were off visiting a cousin and they'd taken their grumpy son with them, so this reconnaissance mission was blessedly private.

"I'd like to see everything. The music room, the sewing room, the apartment you had in your youth. The whole lot."

"Then see it, you shall." He led her by the hand from the library, which was more of a book museum than a place to read and repose, and took down a lamp from a sconce. On a winter afternoon, the house was frigid and gloomy. Young Peyton—a mere lad of fifty-some —had lit a few candles, which made the corridor feel even darker.

"You don't have good memories of this place," Emmie said.

"London was a challenge. Papa brought us down from Scotland to show us off and to subject us to tea dances, though dancing for Secondus became unsupportable. We were to do the pretty, charm everybody, and uphold the family honor without exception."

"You were making a perpetual come out," Emmie said as they mounted the stairs. "My aunt uses that phrase to refer to the ladies who are dragged by the heels from the schoolroom at barely seventeen and still among the hopefuls five years later."

"Were you counted in that number?"

"My parents' deaths meant I was spared until the antediluvian age of nineteen, but the five years among the ferns and wallflowers applies. Then word got around that I had decent settlements—thank you, dear Auntie—and the bachelor midges began to swarm."

"Speaking of settlements, I should meet with your brother or send my solicitors to meet with his."

"I'd rather you met with Aunt."

They traversed another shadowed corridor and stopped before a carved oak door.

"I am calling upon your aunt tomorrow," Dunfallon said. "Will you be there?"

Emmie traced the horn of a rearing unicorn on the door panel. "I should be at West Bart's."

She moved her fingertips over the smooth curve of the creature's neck, the sweep of his back, the muscular curve of his rump, and Dunfallon was abruptly aware—very aware—that he was alone with his intended and about to step into the private suite of rooms where they would, heaven bless the notion, spend many a night together.

And possibly some afternoons, the occasional morning, and the odd predinner nap.

"Emmie, how much time do you spend at West Bart's Lending?"

She ceased caressing the rampant beast. "A fair bit."

He moved closer. "Emmie?"

"I'm there most days, at some point. I open and close most of the time. The library is not open on the Sabbath, of course, but the rest of the week, people need to read. Let's have a look at the master suite, shall we?" She lifted the latch and sailed ahead of him into a surprisingly warm space.

The fires were more effective here, or Mrs. Peyton's supervision of her menfolk more apparent. The hearth was blazing, and the screens had been moved to flank the windows, blocking the worst sources of drafts.

Emmie chafed her hands before the flames and scowled at the painting of Dunfallon Castle in all its craggy splendor above the mantel.

"Why so few pictures of family, Dane?"

"Papa allowed no pictures of family outside the gallery at Dunfallon Castle, but I had the fourth duke dusted off to keep an eye on the library. He's the forebearer I am most proud of. Wouldn't hear of clearances, while my own father..."

She held out a hand to him, and he took it. "Your father cleared his tenants from the land?"

"We own a pair of islands, and yes, he cleared the one. Engaged in the proverbial midwinter evictions, complete with sobbing women, howling babies, and shivering children. The steward was able to see that every family's possessions were transported to the mainland, and he settled any who wanted to remain in Scotland as best he could—a total of eleven families. The other six were given passage to Nova Scotia and as many coins as I could spare. At sixteen, I hadn't all that many coins."

The warmth of the room faded, replaced by memories of the bitter salt-sea air, and Papa sitting snug in his coach, watching a bedraggled parade of former tenants troop off the dock and into a bewildering and difficult future.

"All for his bloody sheep," Dunfallon added quietly.

Another memory joined the bleak assemblage in his mind. "The old women, one by one, spit upon Papa's fine coach. They were no longer his tenants and not on his land, so he could do nothing by way of retribution. Instead, he fired the steward that day, before those seventeen families, citing unreliable loyalty as the unpardonable sin."

"What did you do?"

"I stormed off to university and wrote stories about kittens. I came into a competence at seventeen and set up a decent pension for our former steward. His son is the current steward. When MacAlpin wasn't drilling me on my Roman philosophers, I tasked him with locating our departed tenants. Nine of the families who remained in Scotland have since returned to the island. Sheep, as it turned out, are a poor investment."

Emmie settled into a wing chair. "I thought Scotland and Wales were awash in sheep."

"In England and Wales, the climate allows for some variety in the breeds, but for my family's holdings, only the hardiest stock can stand up to the winters. Those sheep produce coarse, cheap wool, and because every laird and landowner is now raising sheep—the crofters having all been chased off the land they farmed profitably for centuries—the market is glutted. The military—now at peace—was the largest single purchaser of finer wool, so the higher-grade products are also glutted. Then too, any country can find a breed of sheep adapted to its climate, so wool exports have also declined."

Emmie made a lovely picture seated beside the fire. Dunfallon took the second chair without asking her permission. They were to be husband and wife, after all.

Also duke and duchess.

"Are those nine families happy?" she asked.

"They are struggling, but I am determined that they will eventually thrive. Sheep are a blight on the land, and in another few years, the damage would have been irreversible. We're making progress, but reclaiming the island is slow going."

Emmie unfastened the frogs of her cloak. "I wanted to see this house because we will live here at least part of the time. I thought I would come away from our tour with happy imaginings about re-stocking the library and donating older titles to West Bart's. I gather you'd like more than the library taken in hand."

She was clearly keen on managing the library, at least. That left only fourteen other rooms abovestairs immured in plaid.

"I was hoping," Dane said, "that you might, that is... new wall-paper in the music room, fresh curtains in the family parlor. The touches that can banish ghosts and turn a museum into a home."

Emmie wrinkled her nose. "This is important to you?"

"I hadn't put it that way, but yes. The house reeks of my father's grand consequence, and yet, I haven't the resolve or the time to tackle the changes needed."

"New appointments as well?" She still sounded less than enthu-siastic.

"Carpets too, if you're up to that. I had thought to hire a deco-rator but I don't want my home to look decorated, I want it to look as West Bart's does—inviting, dignified, comfortable, secure." He fell silent rather than lapse into pleading.

"Very well," Emmie said, smiling slightly. "I will besiege the house, but don't be surprised if every room ends up with at least one shelf of good books."

"You may buy out every stall in Bloomsbury, and put bookshelves on every landing, and in the servants' hall. I was also hoping you might like to see the bedroom."

Now, where had *that* come from?

"A cheering thought, the bedroom. As you explain to me about sheep and evictions and burned love letters, I am gradually realizing that I will be a duchess. Sorting through the library here will be the least of the tasks expected of me, won't it?"

Dunfallon rose and offered Emmie his hand. "We will go on as we please, my dear. You can expect sweet, tender correspondence from me, I assure you. I regard Papa's greatest redeeming feature to be his use as a bad example. I may not have a clear idea of how I will execute the duties of my station, but I know how I will *not* go on."

Emmie kept a grip on his hand after she'd risen. "You will write more wonderful stories, for one thing."

That again. "I will not evict loyal tenants. I will not insist on being part of the parliamentary delegation to ensure that my interests take precedence over those of my equally deserving neighbors. I will not expect our children, should we be blessed with offspring, to puppet about Mayfair in tartan get-up while they spread lavish false-hoods about the wonders of the family coffers or our Scottish holdings."

He tugged her into his embrace, and she bundled close with wonderful enthusiasm. "This will be a happy household, Dunfallon. If it is within my power to make it so, we will have a happy house-hold. You will need peace and quiet for your writing, but if the chil-dren come along—and I pray they do—we will also have laughter, and raids on the gingerbread, and music, and love."

What courage she had, to envision so sanguine a future for them.

"And what of your own stories, hmm?" he asked, speaking with his lips against her temple. "Will you need two parlors, and will you write under a dashing pseudonym?"

Emmie eased away. "Let's have a look at the bedroom, shall we? I'm dying to see how the bed compares to the sofa in my office." She opened the door to the next room and disappeared from sight.

Dunfallon was left wondering what she could possibly mean—comparing the ducal bed and the office sofa—and hoping she meant what he thought she meant.

Being a duchess in theory was one thing. Every girl of means and standing was raised to envision herself with a circlet of jewels sparkling atop her head. The fairy-tale duchess wore gossamer cloth-ing, spoke only in the sweetest tones, and uttered only wise, kind, or clever words.

She did not fall asleep among the biographies. She did not come to her exalted station at such an advanced age that half her child-bearing years were behind her. She did not spend most of every weekday at West Bart's Lending, the closest thing she'd had to a home in recent years.

These thoughts followed Emmie into the bedroom, as did a few hollow platitudes.

Every bride had misgivings.

Every ducal bride doubtless brought a duchy's worth of doubts with her to the altar and never mentioned one of them.

Long courtships were for couples who lacked the means to establish their own households.

And yet, when she beheld the ducal bed, a commotion ensued in her belly. She would spend her nights for a significant portion of her remaining years in this luxurious enormity.

"It's huge." As large as many a housekeeper's parlor, the bed curtains the blue and white of the Scottish saltire. The counterpane was more blue and white with touches of gold and rose. "One expects hot-air balloons to float about beneath the canopy."

Dunfallon had come into the room and closed the door. He used a taper to light two candelabra on the mantel and a third on the bedside table.

"I had this room made over in blue, white, and rose, which were my mother's favorite colors. The late duke was for waving plaid about on every occasion. I've nothing against plaid, but as a decorating theme, it becomes busy in small doses."

"Hence the library."

"And the servants' hall, the first formal parlor, the second formal parlor, the family parlor... I promised myself I would never wear a damned kilt once I became the duke."

Emmie moved a blue silk-covered pillow near the head of the bed so the arrangement was symmetric. "Now that is a shame. I'm as susceptible to the charm of a kilted laddie as the next woman."

Dunfallon tossed the taper onto the crackling fire in the hearth. "You are as impressionable as Aberdeen granite, Emerald

Armstrong." He prowled closer. "For you, I'd put on the whole kit, provided you assisted me to get out of it."

Touring the house had been a bad idea. With each room visited, Emmie had felt her spirit sinking and her confidence as well.

The porcelain *room*—not a porcelain cabinet.

The silver *room*—not a silver chest.

The *third* formal parlor, reserved for receiving bankers, solicitors, and stewards representing other peers.

But the bedroom reminded her of a singular and comforting fact: She was marrying Tertius Dane MacManus MacTavish Dundee— she'd made a little tune to help her recall all those names—and he was a very dear and desirable man.

Emmie leaned near enough to whisper. "I will assist you to remove the ensemble you're wearing right this moment, if you're amenable, Your Grace."

"Dane," he said, drawing her into a hug. "When private, or anytime you please, my name is Dane. Are you intent on ravishing me, Miss Armstrong?"

"Is that hope I hear in your voice?"

"Is that worry in yours? I did not bring you here to enable a seduction, Emmie. We'll have to make a home of this place, and I rely on you to guide that process."

"We will also have to make a marriage as well in this place, among others, and engaged couples are expected to anticipate their vows." Emmie hadn't planned to seduce Dane on this inspection tour, but how much more important was it that they inspect *each other* rather than a lot of parlors and pantries?

He sat on the enormous cloud-bed, where he looked entirely at ease. "Join me, and we will talk about this marriage of ours."

Emmie was seized by a desperate reluctance to talk. She would analyze her motives for propositioning her intended later, probably a dash of bridal nerves, braided with a pragmatic need to get the first encounter behind them, and a touch of fear that, unless she took this step now, her courage might falter.

And if she dithered, then Dane might decide that a bluestocking duchess wasn't such a fine idea after all.

As Emmie settled beside him on the bed, her feet a good ten inches from the floor, she admitted that her duke was... formidable. Lord Hercules had not been formidable. He'd been arrogant and underhanded, and Emmie hadn't understood the difference.

Dane was not arrogant. He was kind and patient, and lovely, and —did this even signify to him?—a successfully published author.

"Does one negotiate the ravishment of one's prospective husband?" Emmie asked, hands folded in her lap.

"One discusses a significant step to be taken with one's prospective wife, because it's not a step that can be untaken, Emmie. How awful was the fumbling Lord Hercules?"

"I haven't any way to assess that. I did not enjoy his attentions, and Aunt says that means he mucked it up beyond all recall. I do enjoy your attentions—so far."

Dunfallon looped an arm around her shoulders. "Promise me something."

"I'm listening."

"Promise me that if you are uncomfortable for any reason—the light is in your eyes, you don't like where my hands are, you don't care for the position, I'm going too slowly or too quickly—don't let matters get to the beyond-all-recall stage before you demand an intermission, Emmie."

She was bundled against his side, a wonderful place to be, and yet, she had questions too. "How long do you expect this to take?"

He brushed a kiss to her temple. "Until early spring, if I had my way, but alas, half the afternoon will have to do."

The commotion in Emmie's belly became a full-blown riot. "Half the afternoon?"

"At least."

"I suppose we'd best get started."

Dane laughed and rose from the bed.

Dunfallon had spoken the truth. His intention had been to show Emmie the house, nothing more. That she had taken it into her head to consummate their courtship left him...

Pleased, of course. He cared for her deeply and desired her madly, and she was right: Even in polite society, couples typically engaged in intimacies on the way to the altar. Emmie knew that all too well.

And yet, something about the quality of her determination made him uneasy. She did not appear overcome with lust for his person, and she had not planned this assignation—he would bet his Shakespeare First Folio on that.

Some notion had taken hold of her, a now-or-never sort of desperation, and Dunfallon honestly could not decide where the honorable course lay.

If he rejected her overtures, she'd be hurt. The strutting-male part of him also loudly bellowed that he'd be a fool to deny himself shared pleasure with his intended when she was sitting on the very bed.

If he consummated their courtship, and Emmie did not care for the experience, where would that leave her? The answer hit him like the flat of a claymore to the chest: She'd be free to *change her mind*. To go back to her books and prodigies and leave Dane to the dubious joys of duking.

"Let's start with your hooks, shall we?"

Emmie's gaze turned wary. "My hooks?"

"If we are to all the pleasures prove in that bed, then shedding our clothes comes into it. The room is toasty, I'll warm the sheets, and then we will set the mattress aflame."

Emmie rose and gave him her back. "I wasn't sure. Hercules favored perching me on tables or bending me over the nearest chair."

Lord Hercules was about to lose his coach and four and his favorite riding horse over a polite hand of cards. Polite, but not friendly. If Hercules was foolish enough to accept an invitation to spar at Jackson's, his losses might include a few teeth as well.

"The bed for us," Dunfallon said, stroking his thumbs over Emmie's bare nape. "Lots of pillows, a pleasant nap between romps, soothing caresses, and passionate kisses." He pressed a lingering example of same to her nape. "All the time in the world."

"You'll use your toothpowder?"

Ye mischievous fairies, Lord Hercules deserved to lose a testicle. "Of course, and you are welcome to borrow my toothbrush as well. This suite is kept in readiness for me no matter how reluctant I've been to dwell here."

Emmie's dress was simple, the buttons fewer than Dunfallon would have found on a more fashionable creation. He loosened her corset strings while he was making himself useful and treated himself to lazy kisses along her shoulder.

"You're sure, Emmie?"

"Oh, yes. Very sure." She sounded determined rather than enthusiastic.

"Why don't you nip behind the privacy screen, and I'll get out of my boots?"

She turned, hugged him, and rustled off to the corner screened by a japanned panel. Again, her air was not that of a woman anticipating a pleasurable interlude, but rather, that of a nervous bride.

Perhaps, Dunfallon thought as he divested himself of all but his breeches, Lord Hercules should lose the deed to his house too. But no, probably not. Lady Hercules was already serving penance enough.

Dunfallon ran the warmer over the sheets, heard water splashing against porcelain, and reveled in a sense of humming desire. Good fortune had given him a bride intent on sorting matters out before she found herself married to a bumbler, and this was simply more proof that Emmie would be a spectacular duchess as well as a wonderful wife.

She deserved to try his paces, and she deserved—more than

deserved—to change her mind if she found him wanting.

Which, centuries of bred-in-the-bone Highland pride thundered, *he would not be.*

"Your turn." Emmie had emerged from the privacy screen wearing her chemise and a banyan of green silk that did marvelous things for her eyes. Her hair was a dark braid over one shoulder, and her feet were bare. She studiously avoided any glances at the vast bed or at Dunfallon's naked chest.

Tenderness cut through his desire, or rather, blended with it. "That dressing gown looks much better on you than it ever did on me. Give me two minutes."

He spent closer to five, making liberal use of the toothpowder, washing *everywhere* for good measure, and dragging a brush through his hair.

When he emerged from the privacy screen, Emmie was standing by the bed, looking pensive and precious.

He loved her. Loved her courage and pragmatism. Loved her disdain for polite society's games. Loved her affectionate nature and her devotion to her causes. He held out his arms, and she bundled into his embrace.

"I'm nervous, Dane. I'm trying to pretend to a sophistication I cannot claim. You are right that Hercules was... distasteful. He was brusque and hurried and less than particular about his hygiene."

Dunfallon was coming to love the way they fit together and to treasure the bodily trust Emmie showed him. He positively hated Lord Hercules.

"I'd cheerfully kill him for you, my dearest, but murder charges would interfere with our honey month. I suppose ruining him will have to do."

"You can do that?" She sounded hopeful, bless her.

"In the space of seventy-two hours, I will wreck him, foot, horse, and cannon, if you like."

She sighed, and Dunfallon felt some of the anxiety flow out of her. "Lord Hercules's ruin is a cheering thought—I consoled myself with dreams of his downfall for months—then I began to write fiction instead. Dashing cads never end well in my tales. I'd rather you spend your energies writing more kitten stories, Dane."

He stroked her back and wondered how much literature had been born of an author's sense of discontent and defeat.

"Dashing cads should never prevail," he said, "and dashing damsels should always win the day—and the duke." He kissed her, hoping discussions of Lord Hercules and blasted kittens could be set aside once and for all.

And thank the celestial powers, Emmie kissed him back. Dunfallon was developing a sorting system for her kisses. The peck on the cheek signaled he'd said something she approved of. The gentler buss indicated he'd tugged at her heartstrings. The smacker conveyed lustier joy…

Emmie wielded words well, but she was an orator with kisses.

In the ducal bedroom, she added blatant passion to her repertoire, taking a taste of him and then daring him to reciprocate. Though desire rode Dunfallon hard, he tried to go slowly and considerately, to be all that Ham-fisted Hercules had not been.

"I'm panting," Emmie said, linking her hands at Dunfallon's nape. "I'm panting like the heroines in all the Gothic novels. I do believe my bosom is actually heaving."

She studied the indicated part of her anatomy, as did Dunfallon —for about two mesmerizing seconds.

"You are so wonderful," he said, scooping her into his arms. "I want the whole of you heaving and panting and sighing. I want you shouting your pleasure to the rafters and then demanding the same again only better." He settled her on the bed, peeled out of his breeches, and came down over her.

"I want that too," she said, "providing you are heaving and panting as well."

He kissed her nose. "I am already panting. Kiss me some more, Emmie."

She kissed, she caressed, she sniffed, and stroked, and explored, and Dunfallon's grasp of reason began to unravel.

"This is why you said we'll be here half the afternoon, isn't it?" Emmie asked, straddling him. "Because there's so much more than hurried couplings behind the parlor door."

"Hurried couplings behind the parlor door can be delightful," Dunfallon said, tracing her breasts through the soft linen of her chemise. "An unexpected bit of heaven. With you, I want everything. The stolen moments, the sleepy joys, the towering passion. I want quiet nights by the fire and rousing political arguments over breakfast. I want... I want *you*, Emmie. All of you, and I want to give you all of me."

He wanted her in the next five minutes and for the next fifty years—at least. She curled down to his chest and snuggled close.

"The things you say, Dane. Now my heart is heaving."

So was his, and among the wishes and thoughts bobbing around on his emotional sea was a regret. Nobody had ever loved Papa like this, clearly, or the old fool would not have gone so far astray from what really mattered. For all his wealth and consequence, the previous duke had died unmourned and alone, and worse, he had probably died lonely without even realizing it.

"I love you," Dunfallon said, gathering Emmie closer. "I love you madly, Emerald Armstrong."

"And I love you, Dane MacTavish Dundee and all those other names that have flown straight out of my head. Someday I will slip and call you Mr. Dingle in a muddled moment."

"Just please not Tertius," he said, though her mention of Mr. Dingle sent a wisp of misgiving through him. "Emmie, I think you should know I'm unlikely to ever again write children's stories."

"Nonsense." She kissed his chest. "We'll make time for that, Dane. I realize that you're a very busy man, peer of the realm, manhood's finest flower, et cetera and so forth. But you've put off taking up your pen for too long. A hundred other peers can make speeches in Parliament. Only you can write more kitten stories."

"No, I cannot." He needed for her to understand this. "Like you,

I wrote out of discontent with matters beyond my control. That is behind me now, and rather than writing silly little stories, I have other means of exerting my influence."

Emmie angled up, using her elbow on his chest for leverage. "Silly... little... stories? Are you quoting your father?"

"Not intentionally. Just because he was a martinet doesn't mean he was always wrong." And in that pronouncement, Dunfallon had indeed sounded ominously like dratted Papa.

Emmie dismounted and sat beside Dunfallon, the covers swaddling her to her armpits. "But you are a *writer*. A brilliant, gifted, clever, published writer. You cannot walk away from that."

Dunfallon sat up as well rather than lounge around on his back when Emmie was apparently off on some female flight of illogic.

"I already have walked away." That statement had come across as disdainful, so Dunfallon tried to explain. "I was *marched* away from my literary ambitions years ago, Emmie. Lectured at length on the folly of those aspirations while my personal copies of the book were burned before my eyes. My associations with published authordom are not cheering, and I do not intend to renew my literary efforts."

"How can you sound like a duke even when you aren't wearing a stitch?" she muttered, worrying a nail.

How could she carp on Dunfallon's youthful folly when she was all but naked in their bed?

"Emmie, I *am* a duke. As you've said, some things cannot be helped. I have the ear of the Regent, I dine on occasion with Wellington, I have connections in many a foreign court, thanks to my tour of duty in Vienna. These privileges make it incumbent upon me to spend my time on affairs that matter—bills, parliamentary committees, estate problems. Intrepid kittens are no longer on my schedule."

Tell me you understand.

Tell me you are disappointed but bow to my unassailable reasoning.

Tell me you love me.

Emmie flipped back the covers and hopped off the bed.

CHAPTER SEVEN

Tell him you understand, Emmie's conscience bellowed. *Tell him he's not wrong, though you are disappointed to agree with his conclusions. Tell him again that you love him.*

"I must think about this," she said, making straight for the privacy screen. "I must... I simply assumed that you would write more of those wonderful stories. But then, I assumed Lord Hercules cared for me. I assumed my settlements were a secondary consideration for him. I assumed—however briefly—that you were a particularly fashionable curate, and I further assumed I could adjust to becoming a duchess."

Dunfallon folded his arms over the top of the privacy screen, all lazy masculine grace and bare, broad shoulders.

"Emmie, please don't turn a minor misunderstanding into some great drama. You appreciate my stories, and I'm glad you do, but there's more to me now than little feline fables. Of necessity, there must be."

Emmie regarded her reflection, a rosy, rumpled version of herself who had been having a *delightful* time in the sky-blue bed with her intended.

Meet him halfway, you henwit. Don't storm off in high dudgeon.

"You are attempting patient reason with me, Dunfallon." She was attempting patient reason with herself, too, and failing to achieve the desired result.

"Forgive me if I appeal to logic, Emmie, but I grasp how much I ask of you when I invite you to be my wife. Even if we refuse most invitations, we will still be subjected to interminable court functions, formal dinners, endless processions of guests during shooting season, most of whom we cannot in any capacity regard as friends. Gossip about infidelities neither of us has committed, fawning from syco-phants who can't even bother to be witty."

This recitation turned his expression bleak and suggested to Emmie that, in some ways, Dunfallon was still the lonely, bewildered youth who'd been sent off to learn the manly art of patriotic slaughter in Spain.

"Doubts on your part are only to be expected," he said, straight-ening, "but please don't drag my adolescent literary rebellion into the affray. To be very honest, it's not that I refuse to write more stories, it's that I cannot."

"Of course you can."

He wandered away, probably to put on a shirt and breeches, and that... that disappointed Emmie. They were having a proper row—one she'd started—and clothing was a sort of armor worn in the marital lists. She used some chilly wash water, then wiggled her corset on over her chemise and brought the strings to the front for the usual maiden-lady compromise between fashion and pragmatism.

"Let me do that," Dunfallon said, prowling around the screen, fully attired save for his coat. "When you are my duchess, I will perform this courtesy frequently, and while we are airing opinions, you need to know that I am an enthusiastic appreciator of the natural female shape."

He laced her up with just the right touch of snugness and then held her dress over her head. Because of his superior height, he could work the garment down in tidy stages. Emmie was soon fully clothed, though her hair needed attention.

"Please have a seat at the vanity," he said. "I can manage a chignon, and not because I've enjoyed a string of exotic mistresses. My older sister liked for me to brush out her hair when I was quite small."

Emmie perched on the vanity stool. "As a bachelor duke, exotic mistresses were your due."

"Do I take from your tone that a married duke isn't to indulge in such frolics?"

"You absolutely do."

"Good," he replied, undoing her braid, "because I have no intention of being a fashionable husband in that regard. I proposed to you because I esteem you, Emmie. I esteem your integrity and your character. I'm sorry the afternoon hasn't gone as planned. I'm glad we can be honest with each other."

He *esteemed* her. Not long ago, he'd said he loved her, and the difference in the words wasn't half so troubling as the difference in the tone with which he'd spoken them.

"In the spirit of honesty, Your Grace, you need to know that I am disappointed in your decision to stop writing for the children." To turn his back on the part of him that had first captured Emmie's heart, and that she'd been so sure would make them close companions as well as a devoted couple.

He wielded the brush with competence and care. No lingering caresses, no little pauses for kisses or whispered endearments.

And that is my fault.

"In the course of a long and loving marriage, my dearest, I'm sure we will weather occasional disappointments, but we will remain allies and friends." He separated her hair into three skeins and began a braid that curled over her right shoulder.

"Your parents were not friends or allies?"

Dunfallon paused in his plaiting. "I hardly recall. Mama had presented Papa with an heir and two spares, though she'd had the bad form to start off with my older sister. The duchess had earned a certain measure of independence. When I was eight, she died of a lung fever, and I have few memories of her before that. Her death did not change life at the castle all that much."

He resumed braiding, and Emmie was assailed by the urge to cry. Nobody had read stories to the youngest Dunfallon son, that was certain.

"You think your kitten tales don't matter," Emmie said, "but they do."

"They are pleasant little bagatelles useful for sending children docilely to sleep when a tired parent reaches the end of the day." He plucked the hair ribbon off the vanity and tied a secure knot. "I do not flatter myself that I accomplished more than that. Are we still engaged, Emmie?"

He began fashioning a bun at her nape, as briskly as if he were her usual coiffeur and she preparing for yet another evening entertainment.

"Why wouldn't we be?"

"Because you are disappointed in me."

While Dunfallon silently pinned her hair into a bun, Emmie considered that proposition. "It's worse than that. I am bewildered by you." And to some extent by herself, because he was right. She was making drama out of proportion to the moment, but she was also genuinely stunned that he'd belittle his own creations.

He finished and stood behind her with his hands on her shoulders. "Can you explain your bewilderment?"

To pose a question rather than make a demand had doubtless cost him some pride. Emmie realized her pride was also involved, if not the driving force behind this whole altercation.

Pride had a place in marriage, but arrogance did not, and she owed Dunfallon honesty—his word.

"Books saved my life, Your Grace. I had no desire at all to be launched into Society, but Aunt insisted that marrying was my first responsibility when my brother and I emerged from mourning. She explained that if I was mooning about the ancestral pile, the most desirable parties would pass over Ambrose because his sister already held the reins at the family seat. Getting leg-shackled was to be my salvation and my duty."

Dunfallon took a seat on the chest at the foot of the bed, and Emmie turned on the stool to face him.

"And you failed at that duty for five years?" he said.

"Failed miserably. I was the butt of jokes, the subject of wagers. I was the despair of my aunt and handed around from one modiste and milliner to another. All of them attempted outlandish experiments in an effort to cast me as an original. They turned me into a freak. One of them insisted that I be laced so tightly I fainted at Lady Dandridge's Venetian breakfast, and the talk only grew worse from there."

"I'm sorry."

"I do not want your pity. I want your understanding—your comprehension."

Something cool and wary came into his gaze. "Go on."

"In all these years," Emmie said, "the years of mourning, the years of social tribulation, the years since my only other suitor tossed me over, I've had the consolation and inspiration of books. Not only fiction, Dunfallon. I've read Mary Wollstonecraft, despite the scurrilous drivel her late husband heaped on her memory. I've read Sir William Blackstone's commentaries on many aspects of the law. I've read poetry and travelogues and fables and novels."

"You are a bluestocking. I like this about you. I enjoy good literature too."

Despair joined the bewilderment wrapped around Emmie's heart. "I owe *my life* to books, Dunfallon, and I mean those words in their least flattering sense. When Lord Hercules threw me over and then put it about that the fault had been mine, I ran out of fortitude. I stopped eating. I stopped going out. I would not receive the visitors who came to tour the ruins of my life. I lay in bed by the day and the week, and I longed to die."

"You? And your brother *allowed* this?"

"I lived with my aunt, and Ambrose and I had grown apart. There was no *allowing*, Dunfallon. Even a duke cannot force a woman to eat, to care about a life that proved over and over that she was a failure at everything."

He looked genuinely puzzled, and as if he was perhaps resisting the urge to argue. "You were in a bad way."

"And you are being kind. I was a wreck, but Aunt insisted I leave my rooms at least often enough for the maids to clean. I sought refuge in her library, and Aunt is well-read. That's where I found Wollstonecraft, who paints a very different picture of polite society's treatment of women than I'd been raised to understand. I found Mrs. Burney, who in her fashion said the same things Mrs. Wollstonecraft had said. I found that rascal Lord Rochester, and despite all, his vulgar, clever poetry made me laugh. I found Mr. Dingle's stories and his unrelenting faith that there is always a way home, if only we are resourceful and true to ourselves and to our loved ones."

Emmie stopped speaking rather than descend into ranting. The bleak eternity after her broken engagement had piled in on top of mourning, loneliness, homesickness, and that terrible row with Ambrose, and the only beacon of joy in the whole gloomy heap had been books.

And most of those, according to Dunfallon, had been *silly little stories*. He did not understand, and *of all people*, he should.

"Don't cry, Emmie, please don't..." Dunfallon passed her a handkerchief redolent of that majestic-forest scent Emmie associated with him. "Please don't... Your tears break my heart."

"Those *little feline fables*," she said in a low, determined voice, "gave me a way home when I had no home, when all of me, not only my heart, was broken. You belittle and malign those stories at your peril, Dunfallon—you break *my* heart—and you turn your back on the ability to write more of them when I know how very, very important such stories are."

He rose and drew her to her feet and then into his arms. "You are important to me," he said. "I am so sorry that life brought you that low."

Emmie allowed herself to rest against him, because this recitation, this argument, had conjured too vivid a recollection of that old seductive darkness and despair. Safety and sanity had been rebuilt one book at a time, one outing to the quiet order of the library at a time.

Then had come the magical day when Emmie had attempted to write a story of her own.

"Life brings many of us low, Dunfallon. Illness, misfortune, broken hearts, a ducal ass for a father, and we can bear it if we're not alone and if we can find a way home. I did, you did. That matters."

He'd asked her a question: Were they still engaged? Emmie wanted to say yes, to say that this painful discussion had brought them closer, and they were more engaged than ever. But if intrepid kittens were no longer on his schedule, that left only the busy duke to become her husband.

The busy duke, along with carpets, wallpaper, appointments, curtains, and—heaven help her—formal occasions of state.

Emmie remained silent in Dunfallon's embrace, weary to her soul. The man who'd read stories to small children, who had *written* those stories, and who had patiently hung greenery over the library door, had been a passing ghost. A figment of Emmie's imagination and Dunfallon's holiday sentiments. The duke himself did not love books—he *enjoyed good literature.*

She feared very much that she and His Grace, as lovely and dear as he was, would not suit.

"So how did you leave it wi' yer lassie?" MacAlpin asked, passing Dunfallon a wee dram.

"Awkwardly. I kissed her cheek, and she suffered my attention before bidding me good day." The memory stung, but not nearly as hard as the memory of Emmie recounting her worst, lowest moments. Years of grief, Society's cruelty, and loneliness had reduced a lioness to lurking in her lair with only her miseries—and some books—for company.

"What the hell is wrong with her brother, MacAlpin? Where was his handsome young lordship when his sister needed a strong arm to lean upon?"

MacAlpin lowered his considerable bulk into the opposite wing chair. This study had been crated up, down to the last quill pen and ink pot, and carted from Perthshire to Oxford and then to London. The chairs were familiar, as was the portrait of the mighty stag on his misty Highland crag.

So, too, was the sense that Dunfallon had come to this place to sort out a life that baffled him, though his last visit to MacAlpin's study had been prior to his departure for Spain. In recent years, he and MacAlpin met for dinner at MacAlpin's literary club or strolled amiably in the park on sunny mornings. They even took tea in Mrs. Mac's parlor.

At some point, they had stopped conferring over Dunfallon whiskies in MacAlpin's masculine sanctuary.

"And just how useful were you to your sister?" MacAlpin asked. "Her ladyship had a hard road, and she also lost her mama too soon."

"*Slàinte*." Dunfallon took a diplomatic sip of very smooth whisky. Her ladyship was eight years his senior, a law unto herself, and had been determined to quit the castle on the arm of the first remotely eligible suitor.

Which she had done, much to her youngest brother's heartbroken dismay.

"I was a boy," Dunfallon muttered. "Lord Threadham is a peer of the realm."

"Whose sister you intend to marry, without bothering to discuss the matter with him."

MacAlpin had many fine qualities, from a hearty singing voice to a fine sense of humor. He was patience personified around fidgety boys, and he could quote Shakespeare by the scene. At some point during Dunfallon's university education, MacAlpin, accompanying him as his personal tutor, had also acquired the credentials of a prosy old bore.

Since that time, his hair had turned snow-white, his beard had become luxuriant, and his eyes—if anything—more blue.

"You have attained curmudgeonhood, MacAlpin."

"Oh, aye. Mrs. MacAlpin beat me past the post in that regard, but she does set me a fine example. What will you do about your duchess, lad?"

"She's not my duchess yet." And some traitorous, logical part of Dunfallon wondered if that was for the best. A peer of the realm, a duke, fifty-ninth in line for the throne—or maybe sixty-eighth or seventy-third—did not sit about on his backside spinning fanciful tales for children. "I know she's begun to harbor doubts of the you-do-me-great-honor variety."

"Miss Armstrong was cast aside once before, you know." MacAlpin lifted his glass. "*Slàinte mhath.*"

"The gossips put the boot on the other foot," Dunfallon said, "though you have the right of it. Lord Hercules treated her cruelly, and dealt a final blow to her spirits after years of buffeting. He treats a woman—a tender-hearted, valiant woman, a lady worth more than rubies—as if she were the party found wanting."

"You're listening to gossips now, laddie?"

"They will insist on gossiping where I can hear them. I paid this call so I might listen to you. As much as I esteem my intended, I cannot allow Emmie to begin our marriage ordering me about."

MacAlpin nosed his glass and peered at the exposed ceiling beams. "Of course not, Lord Tertius."

"I haven't been Lord Tertius for ages."

Which was, of course, the point. Lord Tertius had had a ducal martinet for a father, few friends beyond his horse and MacAlpin's cats, and little ability to change his circumstances.

"I don't intend to order Emmie about either, if that makes a difference."

"Prudent of you. Mrs. Mac is always vastly entertained when I get to putting on airs. My strutting and snorting has her in a fine humor for days, though I can't say sleeping on yonder couch does much for my lumbago."

Usually, when MacAlpin was at his most vexatious, he was also at his most wise. Dunfallon had taken years to figure that out.

MacAlpin was being very vexatious.

"The stories I wrote can be excused as a youthful flight, the passing fancy of one not yet in line to inherit."

"You were always in line to inherit. Kevin was reckless and Secondus sickly. The old duke couldn't control his heir and couldn't cure his spare, so he whaled away on you all the harder. His version of preparing you for the title, I suppose. Fatherly devotion, however misguided. He would not listen to me, of course. No reasoning with a desperate duke."

Oh, that was subtle. "*Dùin do bheul*, MacAlpin."

"I'll no' be shuttin' my mouth until I've had my say, Your Dunder-headedness."

"I am all ears, hoping to nourish my flagging spirits with the ambrosia of your wisdom, also with some decent whisky."

"Then finish your whisky and heed me. Your stories are fine little tales."

Dunfallon waved a hand, though from MacAlpin that was high praise.

"They are also damned clever, because they said all the things your father could not hear. You were ready to enlist—to bloody enlist with the common soldiers, to take ship, to steal away with the traveling people —anything to escape your father's control. You know what it is to be much buffeted, laddie. You wrote your stories for all the folk out there feeling much buffeted, and you wrote them because you hurt like hell."

"I hurt worse in Spain." Too late, Dunfallon realized that he had not argued MacAlpin's assertion that the stories were more than passing amusements from a rebellious youth.

"No, you did not. The suffering in Spain was universal. The bitter cold, the violence, the blistering heat. Mr. Dingle's suffering was personal. Different business altogether." MacAlpin rose by slow heaves to fetch the decanter. "Goddamned winter is hell on an old man's bones."

Dunfallon had ever enjoyed his tutor's colorful language, though he'd also taken for granted that MacAlpin would always be *there*, always have a welcome for him, and a kind, if gruff, word. Watching the old man navigate around his sanctum brought a stab of sadness.

MacAlpin would not live forever, and then how would Lord Tertius, His Grace of Dunfallon, or Mr. Damned Dingle find his way home?

"You think I should resume writing, but, Mac, what would I write? I haven't had a decent story idea for years. Nothing I could come up with now would be any good."

"True. Everybody would laugh at you, assuming they learned of your pathetic little hobby."

Papa had called Dunfallon's writing a pathetic little hobby. "I could kick you."

"I can be fast when I have to be, and you, apparently, can still be quite slow. More whisky?"

"No, thank you, though I appreciate the hospitality. If I do marry Emmie, will you stand up with me?"

"Mrs. MacAlpin would be horrified if I were to so far forget my humble station. Get that giant earl fella to stand up with you. He's a decent sort."

"He will dwarf me at the altar, while you, in your Highland finery, will make a very fine picture."

"We'll see what Missus thinks on the matter, but from what you've said, the nuptials are in doubt. I rather admire a young lady who can see past the duke to the man, and to the boy the man used to be. Shows discernment. Too many young people today lack discernment."

"Please, MacAlpin, not the young-people-today tirade."

Dunfallon's host waggled the decanter in an admonitory fashion. "Be off with ye, lad. Stop by the stable to look in on wee Caspar before ye go. He's my favorite kind of boy—bright, stubborn, and determined. Missus adores him, and she has discernment by the barge-load. Witness, she married me."

Emmie adored Caspar, too, but did Emmie adore her intended? Dunfallon hoped she did, because he still very much adored her, which just made the whole situation hopelessly complicated.

"I'm for the stable, and you will give my love to Mrs. MacAlpin, please."

"Take on that fraught task yourself, my boy. She's in her parlor, knitting socks or spinning the fate of dukes. If you're thinking of scurrying off to the castle after the young lady dumps you, at least look in on us before your blow retreat."

"Dumps me?"

"Like a load of wrinkled ducal linen." MacAlpin raised his glass, winked, and downed the whole.

I am being dismissed. The experience had become novel, but Dunfallon bowed and took his leave like the good boy he'd once been. He made his obeisance before Mrs. MacAlpin, who insisted on sending him on his way with a packet of shortbread.

The day was bitterly cold and gray, though Dunfallon was in no hurry to return to the correspondence, ledgers, reports, and bills awaiting him in his bachelor quarters. The ever-so-important matters on which he squandered the bulk of his days.

Looking in on the boy would be a far better use of his time, and to blazes with the account books.

～

Dunfallon let himself through MacAlpin's back gate, crossed the alley, and entered the little stable that housed Mrs. MacAlpin's cart pony and Mac's old riding horse. They shared a roomy stall, the pony clearly the head of the household.

A few hens roosted in the rafters. A pair of nanny goats curled on a pile of straw in the second stall and chewed their cuds contently. The air was scented with hay, livestock, and leather, and while far from cozy, the stable had a snug feel.

Something about a stable in winter would always appeal to Dunfallon. He'd sought refuge in his father's stables, and at school, he'd often...

A twitch of movement caught his eye. Something white and furry slipped out from between the pony's hooves and leaped through the bars of the hayrack. A feline wound itself around Dunfallon's boots, purring madly.

"You're a friendly old thing."

She peered up at him out of jade-green eyes and slowly blinked. Not a young cat, a bit plump and saggy. A dowager queen. Dunfallon knelt to offer the requisite scratch about the ears, and the cat launched herself at his chest.

A shivery feeling passed over him as she grazed her cheek against his chin. "Jewel?" How many green-eyed white cats could MacAlpin own? "Are you my old Jewel?"

She licked his chin and tried to nuzzle her way inside his greatcoat. The shivery feeling turned to joy out of all proportion to the moment. Jewel had been a snuggler as a kitten and as a young lady. She'd outgrown such undignified behavior when the tomcats had caught her eye.

"She's allowed the freedom of the city in winter," a young voice said. "The rest of the year, she's a house cat. MacAlpin says she's had enough kits to last her a lifetime. Her name's Jewel, like in the stories."

Caspar came down the ladder as nimbly as a squirrel. He was

cleaner than Dunfallon had ever seen him, and he'd lost the worst of the gauntness in his cheeks.

"I like it out here," he went on. "The beasts are good company, and Mrs. MacAlpin says Mister Mac is getting on and shouldn't try to look after the chores all by hisself."

Caspar's speech had changed, acquiring a faint burr and much more careful diction. MacAlpin was nothing if not a miracle worker. But then, Mrs. Mac's shortbread also had wondrous qualities where small boys were concerned.

"We miss you at the library," Dunfallon said, taking a seat on a bench while the cat persisted in her efforts to investigate his greatcoat.

"I miss West Bart's too," Caspar replied. "Missus says we can visit on Thursday, though Mister Mac has nearly as many books as West Bart's does. Did Miss Emmie send you?"

"Yes, in a sense."

"That cat sure does like you."

"And I like her. She was a friend when friends were few, and she's apparently not forgotten her old chum."

"Our mates matter," Caspar said, brushing his fingers along the cat's tail. "Mr. Dingle says that."

Dunfallon undid the top buttons of his coat, and Jewel secreted herself next to his chest. Her proportions had changed, her purr had not.

"Mac says I'm old enough to read anything I please for myself." Caspar took the place beside Dunfallon on the bench, scuffing his boots—new boots, from the look of them—on the dirt floor. "Mrs. Mac says reading to me helps keep her eyes sharp. They are nice people, but..."

"But you don't trust them," Dunfallon said. "I was about your age when I met MacAlpin. He was big, loud, and used words I'd never heard before, as if he was some kind of linguistic fencing master. I knew not if he was a demon or an angel, so I decided I would watch him closely and make up my mind when I had a better sense of his motives."

The recollection of those early days under MacAlpin's tutelage was both sweet and sad. Such a lonely boy, though any other child in the realm would probably have envied him.

"I should go," Dunfallon said to nobody in particular.

"Mr. Dingle says we oughtn't to try to solve a problem until we know all we can learn about it. Like when the bridge froze. The kittens didn't know if the river would ice up overnight, and they didn't know if cat snatchers lurked beneath the bridge... I woulda punched any cat snatchers where it counts, I can tell you that."

Cat snatchers figured prominently in Dingle's tales. Nasty, speechifying old men who stank of pipe smoke and frequently threatened to teach small kittens respect for their betters. The cat snatchers were invariably foiled, only to turn up more determined and odoriferous in the next story.

Jewel situated herself so she could peek out beneath Dunfallon's chin.

"If you give MacAlpin a chance to earn your trust, Caspar, you will not regret it. I consider him a friend."

Caspar glanced over at the goats, the skepticism of the ancients in his young eyes. "You ain't just sayin' that?"

"MacAlpin all but saved my life. He certainly saved my soul. Do you suppose wee Ralph might join you here, or Mary?"

"Mates stick together," Caspar said. "Mr. Dingle—"

Dunfallon rose. "Mr. Dingle is not the universal authority on all questions of substance, Caspar."

Caspar scowled. "He's a pretty smart feller, you ask me. O'Keefe the Thief tried to recruit me and Ralphie for his gang. We said no, because O'Keefe *ain't* loyal to his mates. He's rich, he has the watchmen in his pocket, and he's got manners, but boys go missing from his gang, and nobody will say where they went. He don't stick with his mates."

Dunfallon sank slowly back to the bench. "You are eight years old."

Caspar kicked at the dirt. "I might be ten. Petty says boys from the stews come small for their age. I'm a good fighter, though."

Dunfallon's head was filled with a thousand tasks he ought to be seeing to, a dozen other places he could be, and yet, he could not seem to leave the stable.

"You are eight years old," he said again, more softly.

"Mary is eight too," Caspar replied. "O'Keefe tried to give her money, but she wasn't having any of that. Bevins says we need to take special care to walk her home, but we was already seeing to it. We also look after Miss Armstrong. Petty and Bevins help with that." Caspar took a particularly hard kick at the dirt. "O'Keefe has a few girls in his gang. They disappear too. I wish the cat snatchers would grab O'Keefe and toss *him* on a boat."

"But you stick with your mates so you are safe from O'Keefe. What else have you learned from Mr. Dingle, Caspar? Jewel and I are curious."

The boy prosed on, about cat snatchers and kittens, West Bart's, and goats. Sticking with your mates, listening to your ma, washing your paws before a meal, keeping track of the streets so you didn't get lost, and always finding the way home. He chattered as happy boys were meant to chatter, while Dunfallon, who was not a happy boy, listened.

"Would you like some shortbread?" he asked when Caspar paused between diatribes.

"Is it Mrs. Mac's?"

"Yes. Freely given to me to ensure my continuing good behavior." Dunfallon produced the bag and passed over a piece.

"Do all curates talk like you?"

"I thought we had established that I am not a curate."

"So what are you?"

Dunfallon took a piece of shortbread as well. "I thought I was a duke."

"A bleedin' duke? Cor. No wonder you talk so toplofty. And Mr. Mac taught you how to talk, dint he? Does Miss Emmie know you'm a duke?"

"She does. So does Mr. MacAlpin. He was my tutor, long years ago."

Caspar munched his treat. "Is it fine being Yer Grace? Miss Emmie's brother is a lord, but she don't care for him much."

No, it was not fine—yet—but it could be. "A peer can be a lonely fellow," Dunfallon said. "Everybody pretends to be your friend, and it's hard to tell who your mates really are."

"Do dukes allus go around with cats stuffed in their coats?"

Would this child never run out of questions? Dunfallon hoped not. "In the normal course, a cat is not part of ducal sartorial splendor, but I suspect successful authors of children's tales are permitted the occasional feline fashion accessory."

Lucky fellows, those authors. Jewel was a warm, rumbling weight over Dunfallon's heart, and the shortbread was as wonderful as ever.

Though who were his mates? Did he have any mates? Who did he *want* for his mates? Lord Bellefonte was a good friend, but as for *mates*...?

The image of Emmie dozing against Dr. Johnson's life story came to mind.

Bevins and Petty, a two-man court of inquiry.

Wee Mary, demanding her stories and deserving every one of them. Ralph, a young fellow in want of confidence who nonetheless knew who his mates were.

"I am a duke, Caspar, but I am also Christopher Dingle. I used that name to publish my book so nobody would know I'd written the stories."

"Izzat like you have a gang name?"

"Something like it."

"God's bodkin, you be a duke *and* you be our own Mr. Dingle. You should tell Miss Emmie you wrote those stories. She'll fall pure in love with you, and it won't matter you're a duke. She don't like lords, but she'd make an exception for you."

"Have another piece of shortbread," Dunfallon said, shoving the whole parcel at Caspar and getting to his feet. "In fact, keep it, or share it with the goats."

"I'm not giving Mrs. Mac's shortbread to no goats. You still have a cat in your coat, sir."

"Where she apparently thinks she belongs. Caspar, if you were to write a story, one worthy of Mr. Dingle and worthy of our friends at West Bart's Lending, what adventure would you send the kittens on?"

Caspar popped another piece of shortbread into his mouth and studied the goats, who chewed their cud as if they, too, were enjoying some shortbread. The pony and Mac's old horse peered at Caspar through the slats of their stall as if also awaiting his opinion.

"I dunno about adventures, but I like the map game," Caspar said. "The map game can help the kittens find their way home, and you can dedicate the story to West Bart's Lending."

Dunfallon considered the suggestion and caught a tantalizing whiff of literary possibilities. He tousled Caspar's hair—how often had MacAlpin tousled Lord Tertius's hair?—and took his leave.

He was not in a hurry, for once. He had a tale to spin, and the story had to be not simply good, it had to be worthy of Dunfallon's mates.

CHAPTER EIGHT

"Ambrose." Emmie set down Mr. Johnson's Scottish travelogue with a *thump*. "My lord, rather. Welcome to West Bart's Lending." She bobbed a shallow curtsey, which earned her a stiff bow in response.

"Happy Christmas," she added grudgingly. Happy Christmas Eve, more accurately, and to be absolutely punctilious, not all that happy, after all.

The older-sister part of Emmie assessed Ambrose's health, mood, and attire, while another part of her resented him with unseemly intensity for intruding on her sanctuary now of all times. She had parted from her intended three days ago and had not heard from Dunfallon since. Nor had she sent him any cheery little note signaling a return to former good relations.

Her reticence was based on instinct rather than reason. Yes, a duke could be too busy running his duchy to write children's stories, but before he'd been a duke, Dunfallon had been Christopher Dingle. Emmie knew what she owed the duke as a prospective spouse —respect, affection, loyalty. She was less clear about what she owed Mr. Dingle, or what a duke would owe her.

Ambrose did not look particularly pleased to grace West Bart's

Lending with his lordly presence, though he was the pattern card of masculine elegance.

And a small, unignorable part of Emmie rejoiced simply to see her only sibling looking so fine.

"Who's he?" Mary asked, fists on her skinny hips in a manner that presaged forcible ejection of unwanted intruders.

"This is my brother," Emmie said, slipping a hand through Ambrose's arm. "Miss Mary Smith, may I make known to you Ambrose, Viscount Threadham, late of Kent. His lordship is in Town for the holidays. My lord, Miss Mary Smith."

Mary popped a curtsey that would not have been out of place in the boxing ring. Chin barely tipped, hands still planted on her hips. "Now you bow," she said. "Miss Emmie introduced you to me first, because I'm the lady and you be the gent. That's the rule. Now you bow."

Bevins and Petty had roused themselves from their early-midafternoon naps, and Ralph had paused after his seventh pass down the only banister not festooned with ribbons.

Ambrose, to Emmie's shock, offered Mary a proper bow. "Threadham, at your service. Delighted to make your acquaintance, Miss Smith."

"You can call me Mary, but I'll beat yer arse if you get fresh. Caspar showed me where to kick a fellow what gets fresh."

Ambrose's dark eyebrows rose to celestial heights. "You may be assured of my best behavior."

Some of Mary's pugnacity faded. "Will you read us a story? Mr. Dunn reads to us, and he's better at that than even Miss Emmie, but he doesn't come every day. Miss Emmie is very good at readin' stories. I can read too—some."

Drat the child for mentioning Dunfallon, whom Emmie had half hoped to see lugging the day's usual buckets of coal.

"Mary, we've had our story for today. Perhaps you'd remind Ralph not to slide down the banister for me?"

"Ralph! Stop polishing the banister with your butt. Miss Emmie says."

Aristotle, in the midst of his early-midafternoon contemplation session, opened his eyes and glowered at Mary.

"I weren't polishin' the banister," Ralph yelled back.

"Cease squabblin'," Petty barked. "Decorum in the li-bree so a fella can catch a few winks!"

A few months ago, even a few weeks ago, Emmie might have been embarrassed by these displays of informality, but recent days had shifted her perspective. West Bart's Lending was her refuge, and also her castle, more than strong enough to endure raised voices and unruly children.

Ambrose appeared to study the portraits ringing the mezzanine or perhaps the mistletoe that hung beneath them.

"Are you preparing for a journey to Scotland?" he asked.

"Scotland?" Home to the Dukes of Dunfallon since antiquity had acquired its first mist?

Ambrose nodded at Mr. Johnson's travelogue.

"No, of course not. I was just... reshelving the prodigals. Patrons browse, and the books end up wandering, or being wandered. What brings you here, Ambrose?"

"You do, or rather, Aunt's suggestion that I would find you here does. Is there someplace we might talk, Emmie?"

She was in no mood for a lecture from her baby brother about her proper place being in Kent—for *another* lecture. She was also in no mood to be further harangued about the impropriety of her attachment to the library, and she was in no mood *whatsoever* to explain her situation with Dunfallon to his lordship.

"Emmie? Are you well?"

"In the very pink." That had sounded mulish, and Ambrose, whatever his failings, had been a noticing sort of little brother.

"You look as if the dog chewed your copy of *Cecilia* again."

Well, in a manner of speaking... "I enjoy roaring good health. I can offer you tea in my office."

"Thank you."

She'd expected a demurral, if not a protest, but in the past two years, Ambrose had apparently learned some true self-possession to go with his lordly pretensions—and his excellent taste in tailoring.

"The lady goes up the steps first," Mary called, "so you can catch her if she falls on her bum."

"Hush, child," Petty rejoined, though he was smiling.

"That girl has a fixation," Ambrose muttered.

"On manners," Emmie said. "A fine subject for a young lady's focus."

Ambrose let her have the last word, which only increased Emmie's sense of unease. As a boy, he'd battled fiercely—if for the most part fairly—for the final say on any topic.

He's growing up. Emmie considered that complicated thought and revised her conclusion. *He has grown up.* While she'd been dusting biographies and buttering bread, Ambrose had become Lord Threadham in truth.

She could doubtless respect his lordship, but she missed the mischievous, affectionate little brother whom she'd actually liked. Not only was he lost forever, he'd grown a good six inches taller than she, though he wasn't quite as tall as Dunfallon.

Why are the holidays always so hard, and when will I hear from my intended? "In here," she said, pushing open the door to her office. The room bore the aroma of greenery, and that, too, made her think of Dunfallon.

Whom she also missed, drat him.

"Books," Ambrose said, turning a slow circle. "Why am I not surprised?"

"Because West Bart's is a lending library?"

"If I say spinsterhood does not agree with you, you will figuratively kick me in a location Miss Smith would approve of, but, Emmie, I note the books because this is *your* office. Were your office in a shipping warehouse, a convent, or a gaming hell, you would fill the space with books."

Emmie took the kettle from its stand and set it on the parlor stove. "Please have a seat, and I apologize for my shabby manners. You have ambushed me, Ambrose. I thought we might run into each other in the park or at some musicale. I did not expect you to brave West Bart's Lending."

He settled on the old sofa, arm resting along the back, legs crossed at the knee. That Ambrose was tall and well turned out came as a shock, but that he had become *elegant*... How had that happened without her being aware of it?

Without her playing any role in his transformation?

Though she knew how. "I was so angry with you," Emmie said quietly. "So *disappointed* in you." The word brought to mind Dunfallon's assurance that spouses occasionally disappointed each other. But then, Dunfallon was never far from Emmie's thoughts. She had the nagging sense that she'd wronged him by insisting on more stories and an equally nagging sense that for him to refuse to write them was also wrong.

"You are as direct as ever," Ambrose said. "I've missed that. You never let me get away with being the indulged heir and only son."

"Somebody had to prevent you from becoming an ogre."

He smiled slightly, a ghost of his old boyish grin and even more charming. "Or a troll. You had very little patience with trolls. How are you, Emmie?"

The kettle whistled, so she gained a small respite preparing the tray and fetching milk from the window box. When Ambrose ought to have prattled on about the weather, the autumn house parties, or Aunt's choral group, he remained silent.

"I am better," Emmie said, setting the tray on the low table and taking a seat on the sofa. "I needed time, privacy, and some good books after my debacle with Lord Hercules. Aunt saw to it that I had all three, and now I am back on my mettle. Now tell me, *how are you?*"

"You relieve my mind. I am contrite."

"Did you drop Papa's prized Turkish lodestone down the wishing well again?"

"Old business, and you cannot fault my reasoning. If tuppence brought luck, then tossing in an item valued in antiquity should have brought an avalanche of good fortune. Besides, I apologized, and I retrieved Papa's treasure."

"After I told you to go fishing with an iron lure."

"I retrieved the lodestone, and the next harvest was quite good."

They shared a sibling smirk, and Emmie was abruptly pleased to see her brother. The situation with Dunfallon might be irreparable, but cordial relations with Ambrose would be no small holiday boon.

"You were not at Lady Bellefonte's holiday open house," Ambrose said, his expression becoming once again serious. "I had hoped to find you there."

"I sent regrets." Emmie checked the strength of the tea. She rearranged the linen table napkins stacked on the side of the tray. She set out two cups on saucers. "I don't suppose you ran into His Grace of Dunfallon at Lady Bellefonte's?"

"I did not. He was kept away by the press of business, apparently, but I did make the acquaintance of a Miss Peasegill. Interesting woman. She was the only one not making frequent passes beneath a kissing bough. We argued about the mistletoe tradition, and... Well, she put me in mind of you. I did not come here to talk about her or Scottish dukes or boyish pranks."

Emmie poured out two cups of steaming tea and passed one to Ambrose. "What are we to discuss?"

He took a sip of his tea, then set down the cup and saucer, and rose. "I owe you an apology."

Emmie had longed to hear those words, had written one letter after another—all unsent—explaining why Ambrose should offer them to her. His long-awaited apology was of curiously little comfort.

"Apology accepted. How long will you be in Town?"

He went to the window, which looked down on a humble alley

made slightly less disreputable by the light snow dusting everything in white.

"Don't be like that, Emmie. You are the most stubborn woman I know. Don't accept an apology while holding on to your grudge. I was wrong. I behaved very badly, but..."

"But Hercules was so convincing," Emmie said, "and he said enough true things about me—I *am* contrary, I *am* particular, my head *is* full of bookish notions—that you believed his falsehoods as well."

Ambrose sent her a disgruntled glance over his shoulder. "And I did not believe *you* when you stated the situation plainly. Hercules painted himself as the wronged party, the gallant wooer treated cruelly. He even suggested I might try to change your mind."

"A convincing touch, I'm sure, and you apparently declined to take on that challenge."

Ambrose returned to the sofa. "There is no changing your mind, Emmie. Gibraltar is a trifling lump of wet putty compared to your determination once you've dug in your heels."

"While you are the soul of amiable reason at all times?"

He took another sip of tea. "Valid point, but I am here now, and I apologize for my disloyalty. I served you an ill turn when you most needed a sibling's support, and I am deeply sorry for that. I should have listened to you, should have believed that you were being honest with me."

"What changed your mind? You and Hercules were thick as thieves at one point."

"Your tea will get cold."

"The better to dash it in your face when you attempt to prevaricate, Brose."

"Never make empty threats," Ambrose murmured. "You taught me that. Well, you use the word 'thief,' and as it happens, the term applies to dear Hercules. I'd heard rumors at the club, but clubs abound with rumors. Hercules married well, and other bachelors and younger sons found that vexing."

"What sort of rumors?"

"That he cheats at cards." Ambrose's tone expressed profound distaste. "That one doesn't trust him with the valuables at the odd house party. That his wife will hire only older, unattractive maids who prefer to work in pairs when his lordship is in residence. One whisper followed another, and still I thought it all so much idle talk, until he stole from me."

"He stole from us both, Ambrose." Emmie put the words gently, though she was entitled to remind her brother of the facts.

"I cannot call him out, Emmie, but I've considered issuing the challenge anyway."

"Fortunately, you remembered that I would thrash you within an inch of your title for such foolishness. Tell me how he stole from you."

"I invited him down to Kent between house parties, and when he left, I could not find your first edition of Christopher Dingle's *Stories for Young Children*. I wanted to send some of your library to you, if you were determined to bide with Aunt. I found, instead, a second edition. The housekeeper had seen his lordship paging through your more valuable copy. Upon inspection, Hercules had also helped himself to two other first editions and a few curios."

"Mrs. Burney's *Evelina* and Mrs. Radcliffe's *The Female Advocate*. I'd bragged to him about owning both, as well as the Dingle. *Evelina* is signed by the authoress."

"I was aware of that. I got myself invited to the house party Hercules was attending after his stay with me in Kent. I wandered into his lordship's rooms—purely by mistake, of course—and rifled his luggage, also by mistake. I traded the stolen books for the cheaper editions Hercules had left in Kent. I brought your first editions with me to Town and will convey them to you for safekeeping."

Good heavens. Ambrose had become... calculating. Dashing, even.

"Hercules must be desperate if he's stealing from a friend," Emmie said, feeling an unwanted twinge of pity for such a creature, and for Ambrose, who'd been taken in by Hercules's nonsense. "I truly, truly had a narrow escape."

"Hercules and I are not speaking—ever again—and he was not my friend. I should have listened to you, Emmie. I can only blame youthful stupidity and an excess of masculine pride."

"You were a dunderhead, Ambrose. I am not in the habit of serving falsehoods to those I love most dearly." She offered this mild scold because Ambrose seemed to expect it.

Even if Emmie had been inclined to gloat, some inchoate insight dissuaded her from indulging in that pleasure. She had been taken in by Lord Hercules, too, of course, and to as great a degree as her brother had, if not greater.

"Am I forgiven?" Ambrose asked, rising.

Emmie got to her feet, too, because the sounds of some commotion were coming from beyond the door. Mary and Ralph getting into yet another holiday scrap, or maybe the extra order of gingerbread Emmie had put in at the chop shop had arrived.

"You are forgiven," she said, "but I fear I must excuse myself. I don't suppose you can be persuaded to butter some gingerbread?"

"Am I permitted to sample the gingerbread once I've buttered it?"

"Yes," Emmie said, grabbing her brother in a hug. "You were good to come here, Brose. You are right that I am stubborn, though I prefer to think of myself as determined. Hercules made a fool of me, so don't feel too badly that he did the same to you."

Ambrose hugged her back, a good, solid squeeze. "I heard rumors at Bellefonte's do that Hercules is removing to the Continent. Some peer or other has lit a fire under Hercules's creditors and bought up some of his markers. Nobody will say who has performed this public service. Lady Hercules will not accompany her spouse. She's with child and unequal to a winter crossing."

"Good for her." And Emmie was fairly certain she knew who had lit that fire under Hercules's lenders. "I've missed you, Brose." To say that felt very good indeed.

"Missed you too," he said, stepping back as somebody let forth a whoop. "Ye gods and little fishes, what is going on in your library, Emmie?"

"A holiday riot, no doubt. Yuletide has put the younger patrons in high spirits, and we're to have an extra serving of gingerbread in honor of the season." She bustled out the door before those high spirits could turn destructive, just in time to catch Ralph and Mary each making a flying pass down the banister.

"Who the hell is that?" Ambrose muttered, joining Emmie at the top of the steps.

"That is..."

The Duke of Dunfallon, in a green cloak reminiscent of Father Christmas, was ordering a half-dozen footmen about as they set out parcels and boxes and placed a three-foot-high decorated fir tree on the central reading table. "That is an invading army intent on decking the halls. Though I haven't a clue who the white cat is, but she looks very sweet perched on His Grace's shoulder."

The footmen brought in a punchbowl of steaming cider, the spicy scent filling the whole library. Parcels wrapped in red and green cloth were arranged by the tree, and as Aristotle came to attention on the mantel, a veritable feast was laid out between the biographies and the travelogues.

"Emmie," Ambrose said quietly, "are you crying?"

"Of course not." She blinked madly and waved to Dunfallon. "I am not crying, and that is not the Duke of Dunfallon. That is Christopher Dingle himself, and I really must go wish him Happy Christmas."

Emmie stood at the top of the steps attired in the red and green Dunfallon had thought so fetching, a handsome fellow beside her. The real Mr. Dunn, perhaps, and Dunfallon detested him on sight. The man was too exquisitely attired to be a curate and standing entirely too close to the next Duchess of Dunfallon.

"Shall we bring in the rest of the parcels, Your Grace?" the head footman asked.

"You shall, and the corner pub has meat pies and rum punch for the lot of you, including John Coachman and the grooms."

The footman bowed and scurried off, calling to his liveried brethren.

Emmie regarded Dunfallon solemnly, then said something to the handsome blighter and came down from the mezzanine. As she approached Dunfallon, he could see that her lovely green eyes were shiny.

"Did that overdressed popinjay make you cry?" Dunfallon asked, setting Jewel down a safe distance from the Christmas roast. "Something has upset you, Emmie. Tell me what it is, and I'll—"

She launched herself at him and wrapped him in a hug. "You banished the troll. Thank you."

She bore the same brisk, beguiling lemon verbena scent as always, no hint of holiday spirits about her person.

"Emmie, West Bart's Lending would never allow a troll to pass through its doors. Do you refer to a fairy tale?" He held her gently, knowing only that she was upset, and he must restore her good spirits.

"I do, Your Grace. I refer to a fairy tale with a happy ending. We need to talk."

"My love, we must do much more than merely—"

"Will you read us a story?" Mary's strident question cut through the hubbub of chattering children, nattering elders, and Mrs. Oldbach—where had *she* come from?—arguing with two of her library committee members over the placement of the punchbowl.

MacAlpin and his lady arrived at that moment, Caspar swaggering before them like the library's self-appointed majordomo.

"Mary," Emmie said, easing from Dunfallon's arms, "we've had our story for the day. You must stop pestering every passing gentleman to read us a story."

"I pester ladies too," Mary said, chin dipping. "Mr. Dunn said I was the best page turner he ever had. That is a pretty white cat."

The white cat was having a sniff around the hearth while Aristotle watched from above.

"You could read for yerself," Ralph bellowed, "if you'd ever study your letters. I can write me name, and Caspar is almost as good a reader as Miss Emmie. But you be too stubborn and contrary to learn your letters, Mary Smith."

Mary's chin began to quiver, and Dunfallon learned the true meaning of panic. He snatched the girl up and perched her on his hip.

"I have, as it happens, brought a story along with me today. It's a holiday present for our Miss Armstrong from Mr. Christopher Dingle. I also brought the very Jewel herself who inspired Mr. Dingle's stories."

"Mr. Dingle wrote a new story?" Emmie asked. "For me?"

Oh, calamities and catastrophes, she looked ready to cry again. Dunfallon set Mary down within snitching range of a plate of buttered gingerbread.

"Wash your paws, children," he said, doing his best to imitate Emmie's sternest tones. "Then we will feast, and then we will—"

"Am I too late for gingerbread?" The Earl of Bellefonte sauntered in from the foyer, a small girl clinging to his back and a little boy holding his hand. "I heard a rumor stories and gingerbread were to be had for one and all at West Bart's Lending. I can smell the gingerbread, so don't try to hide it from me."

His countess came after him, a little girl dragging her by the hand, a young blond woman at her elbow.

"Next," said the countess, "his lordship will tell you he has been a very good boy. Don't believe him. Miss Armstrong, Your Grace, good day. Children, those are the loveliest cloved oranges I have ever seen."

Petty and Bevins stopped arguing long enough to push to their feet at her ladyship's arrival, and Aristotle squinted at her sagaciously from the mantel.

The popinjay chose then to stroll down from the mezzanine, and Dunfallon was tempted to tell the lot of them that the library was closed for the next thirty minutes in order that he have time to mend his fences with Emmie. Also to read his story to her in private to learn what she thought of his rough draft.

Though thirty minutes wouldn't be nearly long enough for the sort of fence mending he had in mind.

"We should eat before the food gets cold," her ladyship said. "Lord Threadham, a pleasure to see you. Nicholas, do not set a bad example for the children, or I shall be wroth with you."

"Wouldn't think of it, lovey."

Threadham? Dunfallon leaned close to Emmie. "Your brother is here?"

She nodded. "He apologized. We are in charity with one another, and I am dying to hear your new story, but we must also find some time to *talk*, Your Grace."

Dunfallon certainly wanted to talk with Emmie—talk too. "I am dying to know what you think of Mr. Dingle's latest tale. Caspar helped, but I'm out of practice, and penning years of business correspondence doesn't exactly hone one's talent for feline fables."

"Are we planning to do justice to all this lovely food?" Lord Bellefonte asked. "Or shall we stand around goggling at one another and whispering beneath the mistletoe?"

Emmie swept over to the earl and smacked the giant paw holding a slice of gingerbread. "Don't talk with your mouth full, my lord, and he who sets a bad example must say the blessing."

Bellefonte smiled. "Lovey, I think Miss Emmie likes me. She speaks to me in the same adoring tones I used to hear from you, once upon a time."

"Is he drunk?" Threadham muttered.

"He's in love," Dunfallon replied. "Let's find seats, shall we?"

The meal was merry and loud. Bevins and Petty flirted outrageously with Mrs. Oldbach and her committee members, and Aristotle and Jewel patrolled beneath the table. Bellefonte's brood started a game of hide-and-seek with Caspar, Ralph, Mary, and the other children, and a great quantity of food disappeared.

When the footmen came tottering back from their meal at the pub, Emmie gathered the children around the hearth, and Lord Threadham suggested they join in a song. He chose the ballad of Good King Wenceslas, which boasted at least seventeen verses, and Mrs. Oldbach and Petty knew them all.

As did the footmen, who were in very good voice.

Dunfallon enjoyed every verse, because each one gave him more moments to behold his beloved and to fashion the speech she was owed. She had been right—he suspected Emmie was usually right—and they *would* talk.

"Now we get a story," Mary announced. "Mr. Dunn said."

"He's not really Mr. Dunn," Caspar said. "That was just a nickname. He's really Mr. Dingle, but we have to keep that a secret."

MacAlpin stroked his beard, while Ralph looked confused.

"I have a lot of nicknames," Dunfallon said. "His Grace of Dunfallon is another, Earl of Angelsmere is another. Viscount Dingle is in the pile somewhere, and there are a few baronies as well."

"You're a nob?" Ralph asked.

Emmie would expect him to deal honestly with her patrons. "'Fraid so."

"So am I," Bellefonte said, "but I can't write stories like *he* can. I do have a lovely mare named Buttercup, though. The largest horse you will ever meet, and she can do tricks."

"I'm a viscount," Threadham added. "I hope you won't hold that against me. Miss Emmie is my sister, and she used to read to me."

"I'm just an old lady in the mood for a good story," Mrs. Oldbach said. "Might we commence?"

Mary squirmed beside Mrs. MacAlpin. "Don't you need a page turner?"

Oh, the hope in that question. "Very kind of you to offer, Mary, but this story is so new, it hasn't been printed as part of a proper book. I have only the words on foolscap, and I haven't yet done the sketches."

"When you have this story as a book, I will turn your pages. You have to start with 'once upon a time.'"

Mary enjoyed great confidence in her opinions, but she was sometimes in error. "I will start with the title and dedication. *Under a Mousing Moon* by Mr. Christopher Dingle, dedicated to Miss Emmie of West Bart's Lending, guardian of truth and worker of miracles."

The fidgeting and squirming subsided, and on the mantel, Jewel and Aristotle started up antiphonal purring.

"'Once upon a time,'" Dunfallon began, "'there were four mostly well-behaved kittens named Hammerhead, Mark, Luke, and Jewel...'"

The pages shook slightly in his hand, but by the time he'd reached the part about the kittens wandering the town in search of the merest morsel of food, and the children were calling out directions to the fictitious kittens, he'd hit his stride. Emmie's eyes were shining again—in a good way—and when the kittens found their way home, as they always did, the library reverberated with applause.

The gathering broke up in phases, with the footmen disappearing first, carrying boxes of leftovers. Mrs. Oldbach's contingent departed next, chattering like starlings about West Bart's Lending being the brightest gem in the committee's crown. The pensioners decamped with the ladies, providing escort and flirtation in equal measure.

Lord Bellefonte gathered up his family, though he did murmur something in Emmie's ear before taking his leave of her.

MacAlpin collected his wife, Caspar, Ralph, and Mary, along with the older boys who were so inclined, amid talk of a Christmas Eve map game tournament.

Last to go was Lord Threadham, who looked like a man with a few fraternal warnings on his mind.

"Don't disappoint her, Dunfallon," Threadham said as Emmie moved around the library, blowing out sconces. "She was ill-used once, and I could not call the blighter out because he was a commoner. You are titled, when you bother to recall your nicknames, so watch your step."

"I have already disappointed her," Dunfallon said. "We appear to have weathered my blundering. If you will take your splendid, lordly self off, I will make a proper proposal to my prospective duchess and pay my addresses to Mr. Dingle's intended."

Emmie paused to reshelve a book here and to tidy up a stack of magazines there. She was all of a piece with this stately old library, and yet, she shone like a jewel in her own right too.

Threadham extended a hand. "Welcome to the family, Mr. Dingle."

They shook. Threadham offered a farewell to his sister and promised to call upon her and their aunt Christmas morning.

Emmie waved and blew out the last sconce as Threadham took his leave. "Finally," she said, coming around the biographies to wrap an arm about Dunfallon's middle. "I would like to challenge you to a holiday sofa-measuring contest, sir, but first, I have a few things I need to say to you."

"Let's sit by the fire, shall we? Before you launch into the scolds I abundantly deserve, Emmie, allow me to explain."

She leaned against him, the sweetest holiday gift imaginable. "What utter rot. I was wrong, and you will allow me to make my apologies. Ladies first, Your Grace, or must we have Mary remind you of your manners?"

"I like it better when you call me Mr. Dingle and best when you call me Dane."

"I adore it when you tell me I'm your love. Let's talk."

She led him to the reading chairs before the hearth, while on the mantel, Jewel and Aristotle ever so delicately touched noses.

"Mary will learn her letters now," Emmie said, which seemed a safe enough thing to say while falling in love all over again with a duke who hauled coal, managed Christmas feasts, and wrote gorgeous little stories. "The children—I mean, the kittens—found their way home safely because they knew the map of London, and because they could read the street signs and building markers."

Clever of him, to weave that lesson into the adventure, but then, Mr. Dingle was a very clever fellow. "Mrs. MacAlpin," Emmie went on, "allowed as how she could use a little helper around the house, and I saw Mr. MacAlpin making a bird out of paper for Ralph. Ralph is clever with his hands, and he'll..."

Dunfallon smiled at her. "Yes, my love?"

"I can't think when you do that."

"Smile at you?"

"Call me your love in that purring tone. You are my love too."

His smile faded. "That is the greatest gift I have ever been given, Emmie. You were right, you know, about the stories—about me."

"No," Emmie said, rising and pacing before the hearth. "You will not apologize first, Dunfallon. I will apologize to you. *I did not listen to you.* You said not only that you would not write more stories, but that you *could* not. I *could not* face Society for a time—could not— and nobody but my aunt believed me. You are not some mechanical marvel who can produce stories merely because I adore what you write. You are a busy man, a peer, and I had no business trampling your truth."

One moment, Emmie was pacing with righteous determination. The next, she was perched in Dunfallon's lap, his fingers circling her wrist.

"Is Miss quite through with her diatribe?"

"No. You might have asked me to sit in your lap."

"You might have bestowed the privilege of your presence upon my person, and I hope in future you often will." He kissed her cheek, and when Emmie ought to have scolded him—where did Lady Belle- fonte get her fortitude?—she cuddled against his chest.

"My brother did not listen to me," she said. "I explained to him exactly what had happened with Lord Hercules at the time of that scoundrel's defection, and Ambrose could not credit my version of events. I could not *make* him listen, and I never want you to feel the misery that I did when my only sibling turned a deaf ear on my misfortune. I will tell you when you are wrong, Dunfallon, but I will also listen to you. Truly listen, not simply hoard up ammunition for my next volley in the argument. We can both be right, and we can both be wrong, all at the same time. You should write more stories—I was right about that—and I should have respected your demurral."

Dunfallon's fingers stroked Emmie's hair from her temple to her nape, a deliciously soothing touch. "You propose a sound bargain. I promise you both honesty and kindness, and that means listening to each other even when we are disappointed or dismayed, but it also means we don't lie to ourselves."

"You could never—"

"I did, or I failed to see what you were trying to tell me. Caspar sorted me out. Caspar and MacAlpin. I was becoming my father, absorbed with the honors and duties of my station, and those honors and duties are important. The stories, as you so easily grasped, are important too. It's not one or the other, I can do both, with proper inspiration and assistance. Do you know why Mary doesn't learn her letters?"

"Because she's a prodigy with numbers?"

"Because her mother cannot read. Mary has it in her stubborn little head that if she learns to read, she will make her mother feel stupid, and her mother—a streetwalker overly fond of gin, to hear Caspar tell it—is all she has. Mary also thinks that once she learns her letters, nobody will ever read her a story again."

"But Caspar reads fairly well, and he's..."

"He's off to greater ventures. Nobody is reading to him, or so Mary thinks. Caspar explained it to me."

Emmie wanted to catch up with the MacAlpins, take Mary by the hand, and explain to the child that nobody is too old to enjoy a story hour. Not too old, not too well-read, not too important.

She also wanted to close her eyes and snuggle closer to Dunfallon, so she did. "Dane?"

"Hmm?"

"When I am an old and crotchety duchess sitting on too many committees and fond of too many cats, will you still read to me?"

He kissed her cheek. "Of course, and you will read to me, and we will argue over our stories and over reform bills and gingerbread, but we will also listen to each other."

"You may have all the gingerbread you please. What else did Caspar say?"

Dunfallon's caresses weren't putting Emmie to sleep so much as they were easing away all the worries she'd stored up over the past few days and past few years. She was pleasantly aware of him in a physical sense, but more significantly, she felt restored to emotional closeness with him.

Honesty could do that. Honesty and love.

"Caspar said a great deal. He reminded me that stories have the power to fortify us against temptation, against bad decisions, against loneliness. He explained to me—not in so many words—that Mr. Dingle had done more to protect him against turning to a life of crime than all the sermons or charitable committees in London have done."

"Gingerbread and cider played a hand in keeping him safe thus far too, Dane."

"As did the physical refuge of West Bart's Lending and the friends he made here. I wrote those stories to fortify myself, Emmie. I had lost sight of what they might do for other people. I saw in myself only the duke my father intended me to become, and I had lost sight of Mr. Dingle entirely."

"Are you quite through with your apology, sir?"

He hugged her. "Yes. Happy Christmas, Emmie. Did you know that emeralds are worth more than rubies?"

"What are you going on about?"

"I am expounding on my heart's greatest treasure. Will you marry me?"

She kissed his cheek. "Happy Christmas, Dane. Yes, I will marry you. Have you more story ideas?"

"As it happens, I do, and I'm sure you do, too, but might we discuss them later?"

A lovely glow spread through her. "You are inclined to measure my office sofa with me?"

"Something like that."

"I thought you'd never ask."

She led him between the bookshelves and up the steps, past all the kissing boughs and portraits, past the plays and periodicals, to her cozy office, where His Grace of Dunfallon found that—contrary to his earlier supposition—Miss Emmie's office sofa was a perfect place to celebrate a holiday engagement.

And they lived happily—also noisily, lovingly, and honestly—ever after!

TO MY DEAR READERS

Oh, dontcha just love a holiday happily ever after? I wrote this story in part because I delight in seasonal romances, and also because I delight in books. My local library figured prominently in my middle-school years in particular, and started me on a path that ultimately led to a degree in music history and many lucrative and enjoyable hours at the piano.

If you want some interesting reading, try binging the lives of the composers. Yikes!

But if you're in the mood for more romance, my fifth Mischief in Mayfair title, ***Miss Dauntless,*** will be available in November from the **retail outlets**, and on October 4 from my **web store**. My Lady Violet Mystery series wraps up with ***Lady Violet Says I Do*** (**web store** on sale in December, **retail outlets** in January), and then it's on to more Mischief next spring. Do I have the best job in the world or what?

As you think about your TBR pile this holiday season, please spare a thought for your local library too. Most of them have donation options on their web sites, and they enrich our communities with so much more than "just" books. In my county, the public library is not only a wonderful place to borrow books, hear great stories, gather for activities, and further a job search, it's also the only dedicated daytime cold weather shelter, and one of few available cooling stations. Libraries truly do change (and save) lives!

And if all goes well, look for another holiday novella next year. Lord Ambrose and Miss Peasegill just might come to blows over the only first edition copy of *Stories for Young Children* for sale in all of London. Or they might look up and see that kissing bough right overhead... Wheee!

Grace Burrowes

Read on for an excerpt from **Miss Dauntless**, Mischief in Mayfair —Book Five!

EXCERPT—MISS DAUNTLESS

"That is an earl, Thomas," Matilda Merridew said quietly. She'd crouched down to admonish her son at eye level. "The Earl of Tremont is a peer of the realm, an important man, *a lord.*"

Also a bit stuffy, based on what little Matilda knew of him. His lordship was a young man, and attractive enough. He was dark-haired, lean, tall, and turned out in exquisitely understated good taste. His reputation among the former soldiers who'd served with him was one for rules, policies, and proper decorum.

If any force on earth was *not* inclined in those boring directions, it was Matilda's five-year-old son.

"I am an important boy," Tommie replied, grinning. "My mama loves me best in the whole world!"

He'd nearly yelled that proclamation, his voice carrying to every corner of the church hall. Vicar Delancey sent her a pained smile, Mrs. Oldbach flinched but otherwise ignored Tommie's outburst, and Mr. Prebish—current *dominus factotum* of the pastoral committee—glowered at Tommie, then at Matilda.

The earl, fortunately, remained in conversation with the vicar's son-in-law, one Major Alasdhair MacKay.

"I do love you best in the whole world," Matilda said, putting a hand on Tommie's bony little shoulder lest he hare off to make a cave out of the cloaks and coats hanging in the corridor. "I also want to be proud of you, and if I'm to take the minutes for this meeting, then you must stay out of trouble."

"I'm always in trouble," Tommie said, puffing out his chest. "Mrs. Oldbach says I'm a proper limb."

A limb of Satan, did Tommie but know it. "You are not always in trouble. You are simply lively." Exhausting was a more accurate term. "For the next hour, you will please look at your picture book, practice writing your name, and *be quiet*."

Tommie would try, he truly would. He'd turn a few pages of his picture book, he'd even pick up the pencil and wave it about or make a few scratches on the paper Matilda had fetched from Vicar's office, but Tommie had a constitutional aversion to extended periods of quiet while awake.

Mrs. Oldbach clapped her hands. *"Tempus fugit,* my friends. Lord Tremont is a busy man, and it's time we brought our meeting to order."

Mrs. O was a fixture at St. Mildred's. White-haired, imperious, and well to do. She exuded a perfect balance of Christian good cheer and elderly ruthlessness. Matilda kept Tommie as far from Mrs. O as possible.

"Please be good," Matilda said, kissing Tommie's crown and moving to the table in the center of the hall. She took up her post as scribe at the right hand of the chairman's seat and angled her perch to give her a clear view of Tommie's corner. He'd plopped himself on the floor and dutifully opened a picture book, but his gaze was leaping all over the hall.

Matilda had packed not one but all three of his picture books, the old stuffed horse that he now sought only at bedtime, two pencils—Tommie invariably broke his pencil points—and some string. The church cat could be counted on to entertain Tommie for two minutes at a time if that good beast was in residence.

Tommie cupped his hands to his mouth and bellowed. "I'll be good, Mama!"

More winces and scowls greeted that announcement. The earl glanced over at Tommie as if noticing the boy for the first time. Matilda mentally prepared for lordly disdain—children did not belong at business meetings, not even church business meetings.

Tommie waved wildly. "Good day, Mr. Earl! Do you want to see my picture book?"

Merciful angels, deliver me now. St. Mildred's was a prosperous congregation, though a far cry from St. George's in Hanover Square. Peers did not frequent St. Mildred's, and the earl was very much a visiting dignitary.

The whole room went quiet, with gazes ricocheting between the boy and the peer. Mr. Prebish looked positively eager to hear Tommie on the receiving end of a tongue lashing.

Another tongue lashing.

His lordship excused himself from his conversation with Major MacKay, and walked over to where Tommie sat on the floor.

Matilda did not care that Tremont was an earl, a wealthy man, a noted philanthropist, and a former officer. She marched over to Tommie's corner, prepared to inform his lordship that nobody scolded her only begotten son for merely being friendly.

Tremont extended a hand in Tommie's direction. "Tremont, at your service, Master...?"

Tommie scrambled to his feet and wrung the earl's hand. "I'm Tommie. Tommie Merridew. This is my mama."

Tremont extricated his lordly paw from Tommie's grasp and bowed to Matilda. "Madam, you have me at a disadvantage."

"Matilda Merridew, my lord." She bobbed a hasty curtsey.

"My amanuensis on this august occasion, I believe. Tommie, a pleasure to have made your acquaintance. I was told St. Mildred's is a congenial house of worship. Your Mama and I must tend to business for the nonce. You will keep that story book in good repair until I can make a proper inspection of it. Mrs. Merridew."

The earl gestured in the direction of the table. Tommie, for once, was silent, so Matilda preceded his lordship to the table and managed not to faint from shock when he held her chair.

The earl called the meeting to order, and a discussion began of hiring former soldiers to look after St. Mildred's grounds. His lordship's charitable endeavors included housing a dozen such worthies. Setting them up in some sort of business was his present aim.

The sexton had vociferous objections to anybody tending to the churchyard but himself, until Lord Tremont suggested that any lot of former soldiers did better when somebody was appointed to supervise their efforts. Moreover, gravedigging was a skill known to all veterans, alas, and one suited to younger men who benefitted from regular vigorous exertion.

Matilda bent over her notes, while keeping one eye on Tommie, who was imitating Tremont's hand gestures. The earl's hands were graceful, his manner dignified, but more than anything, his voice held Matilda's attention.

Tremont moved the discussion forward with polite dispatch. Whether he agreed with the committee member who held the floor or not, he thanked every participant for sharing their thoughts. He *listened*. He asked sensible questions, and again *listened* to the answers.

Nobody dared interrupt or talk over anybody else, nobody dared make a ribald aside. The meeting was the most civilized and productive exchange of ideas Matilda had observed. That Tommie was a witness to this gathering gave her all manner of maternal ammunition for good examples.

The orderliness of the proceedings aside, Lord Tremont had the makings of an orator. Before he spoke, he took a moment as if gathering his thoughts, and when he replied, his words were chosen for precision and economy. All that was lovely—the fellow made sense even as he flattered his listener—but what upended Matilda's usual indifference to any and all things male was the beauty of Tremont's voice.

He created a flowing stream of golden elocution in a well modulated baritone. His words resonated with courtesy, reason, benevolence, respect for his audience... all the gentlemanly virtues made audible.

If he ever set out to be charming instead of polite, he'd be dangerous. Matilda mentally shook herself for even speculating on such a topic, and pretended to add something to her notes.

Has beautiful voice.

She was erasing that nonsense when Tommie began to sing. Being Tommie, he did not sing a venerable old hymn or a sweet little nursery rhyme. He burst forth with Burns's "Green Grow the Rushes, O," an earthy tribute from a man to the charms of the ladies.

While Matilda scrambled about for a means of discreetly distracting her son, Tommie caroled on. *The sweetest hours that e'er I spend/Are spent among the lasses, O...*

Had the Earl of Tremont not been present, Mr. Prebish would have been leading a charge to silence Tommie's warblings and assign him a penance. Instead, the committee of the whole waited to see how a peer of the realm dealt with a Proper Limb.

But gie me a cannie hour at e'en/My arms about my dearie, O!/An' warl'y cares an' war'ly men

May a' gae tapsalteerie, O!

"Master Merridew." Lord Tremont's voice carried without having been raised, and yet Tommie paid him no heed.

For you sae douce, ye sneer at this/Ye're nought but senseless ASSES, O! The wisest man the warl' e'er saw/He dearly lov'd the lasses, O....

The vicar looked as if a post in Cathay had developed compelling appeal. Mrs. Oldbach's lips were pressed together very firmly, and Major MacKay was grinning.

Worse than that, much worse, was MacKay joining in for the next verse. *Auld Nature swears, the lovely dears/Her noblest work she classes, O!/Her 'prentice han' she try'd on man/An' then she made the lasses, O!*

"Master Merridew." Tremont sounded quite stern, and Tommie was not accustomed to proper address. The boy fell silent at long last.

"While we appreciate your impromptu serenade," the earl said, "we yet have work to do. Come here if you please."

To Matilda's astonishment, Tommie did not order the earl to instead come to him. Tommie viewed matters logically, which often made him sound impertinent. Superior height, for example, did not make adults superior in any other way, otherwise—according to Tommie's reasoning—the tallest man would be king, and the shortest a beggar, but there were tall beggars and short kings.

And yet, Tommie scampered over to stand by the earl's chair. "Mama taught me that song, but she has a much prettier voice than I do."

"Very gallant of you to compliment your mama," Tremont said, hoisting Tommie onto his lap. "Pay attention, young sir. This is a gavel."

He held up the chairman's gavel, but did not let Tommie grab it.

"It's a hammer, Mr. Earl."

"Not a hammer, a gavel. When the chairman applies his gavel thus to the tabletop, silence reigns. Give it a bang if you don't believe me."

Tommie walloped the table with the gavel and the whispering among the committee members stopped.

"There, you see, lad? Not a hammer, a gavel with all the special powers attendant thereto. As the vice-chairman of this meeting, you will bang that gavel when I tell you to, as many times as I tell you to. You will not permit anybody else, not even your dear mama, to touch the gavel during the progress of the meeting. Three whacks now, for practice."

Tommie thumped the old table three times.

"Very good. When you are not required to man the gavel, you may draw toads, if your mama would oblige you with some paper and a pencil. All gentlemen acquire basic artistic skills, and the sooner you start the sooner you will master the challenge. If you are already

proficient rendering toads, you may attempt a dragon or the very difficult unicorn. You will please recall the meeting to order."

Tommie twisted about to send Matilda a questioning glance.

"Two raps," she said. "One right after the other. And then you
say, "This meeting will now come to order."

Tommie vigorously executed the duties of his office. For the next
forty-five minutes, he seemed quite content occupy the earl's lap, and
draw all manner of mythical beasts while quietly humming Burns's
ode to the ladies.

Order your copy of ***Miss Dauntless***, and read on to enjoy Christi
Caldwell's holiday novella, **Diamond in the Rough**!

A DIAMOND IN THE ROUGH

By Christi Caldwell

DEDICATION

A Diamond in the Rough
By Christi Caldwell

To Librarians Everywhere:

Thank you for being the guardians
of a haven so very desperately
needed in this world!

OTHER TITLES BY CHRISTI CALDWELL

All the Duke's Sins
Along Came a Lady
Desperately Seeking a Duchess
All the Duke's Sin's Prequel Series
It Had to Be the Duke
One for My Baron
Scandalous Affairs
A Groom of Her Own
Taming of the Beast
My Fair Marchioness
It Happened One Winter
Heart of a Duke
In Need of a Duke—Prequel Novella
For Love of the Duke
More than a Duke
The Love of a Rogue
Loved by a Duke
To Love a Lord

Her Duke of Secrets
The Read Family Saga
A Winter Wish
Memoir: Non-Fiction
Uninterrupted Joy

COPYRIGHT

A Diamond in the Rough
Copyright © 2022 by Christi Caldwell
Kindle Edition

For more information about the author:
www.christicaldwellauthor.com
christicaldwellauthor@gmail.com
Twitter: @ChristiCaldwell
Or on Facebook at: Christi Caldwell Author

CHAPTER 1

Mayfair
London, England
Winter 1815

In a world where women were largely powerless, one might expect the daughter of a duke and goddaughter of the King and Queen of England had *some* power. At the very least, power over her own life.

The world, however, would be wrong. As the Duke of Devonshire's daughter, Lady Diamond Glain Carmichael knew that very well. From the subjects taught by her governesses. The pastimes she must learn and adopt as hers. The food she ate. Even the books she read. Certain topics and studies and authors were deemed appropriate.

Most were not.

Glain had learned early on and long ago the expectations had for her. The Duke of Devonshire and the long line of stern, soulless governesses he'd employed had drummed into Glain, precisely what fate and future awaited her as a duke's daughter, and also the way he, along with Polite Society expected her to behave.

Unfortunately, her younger sister, Opal, had proven a far less apt study.

Seated upon the striped Hepplewhite sofa that overlooked the quiet London streets below, Glain added another diamond stitch to her whitework embroidery. The winter season brought with it a welcome peace. This time of year, when the *ton* retreated to their country estates, always brought a reprieve from the inanity of it all.

Or, at least it *usually* did.

"You are being ridiculous," Opal whispered, stomping her foot in a noiseless way upon the rose-pastel carpet.

That attempt at silence proved Opal may have gathered more than Glain had credited.

It didn't change anything.

"No," Glain said calmly, threading the tip of her needle through the monochrome background in her frame. She paused to assess her needlework, angling the fine muslin. "I *am* being rational. That is entirely different and eminently better."

"I shan't ever become you, Glain. Never, ever." With every reiteration of that word, her sister stamped her foot for emphasis. "*Ever!*"

Alas, her sister would. At thirteen, however, she'd just not realized it.

Unlike Glain whose earliest remembrances were age seven when her father had entered the nursery and discovered her writing her own fairytale stories upon the empty pages her kindly governess had provided.

The duke had stormed the room, grabbed the sheets, and into the hearth they'd gone.

The governess whom she'd loved, a woman who'd encouraged Glain, even at that young age, to think bigger, to dream of more, had been sacked, only to be replaced by a new sterner, colder, pinch-mouthed woman, who'd been unafraid to wield a switch to Glain's knuckles when she'd deemed Glain's work inappropriate.

Eventually her sister who loved both art and books with the same intensity Glain once had, would realize the limitations placed upon them both. Opal had simply managed to escape the certainty of her future until now.

She'd discover what Glain had, and what all women ultimately did—their voices weren't their own. Neither were their interests and passions. In the end, first their fathers, and then their husbands dictated who a woman must be.

To resist was futile.

A small hand waggled before Glain's face, and Glain went briefly cross-eyed as she concentrated on those paint-stained fingers.

"Hullo? You're not even listening to me. Have you heard *any* of what I said?"

"On the contrary." Glain angled her frame and resumed her sewing. "I've heard *everything*. It's why I'm now ignoring—"

Opal yanked the wood frame from her sister's fingers, hid it behind her own back, and glared. "I don't know why you always insisted on being called Glain. *Diamond* suits you far better. They're cold and icy. You are incapable of feeling anything."

It was because of their mother. Her mother had been the one who'd chosen the name Glain...the duke had insisted his daughter be a 'Diamond' in every way. As such, Opal's charge struck in a place deep within her heart, the pain making a liar of her sister.

"I *am* capable of making safe decisions," she said calmly, keeping her features perfectly even.

"Safe," Opal's face pulled. "Bah, how dull and how very boring."

"Dull and boring essentially mean the same."

"It is a circulating library," Opal entreated. "A circulating library. Why can't I go?"

"Because there is no board of directors who oversee the type of books offered. The library is largely sponsored by the Duke of Strathearn." A duke whose reputation preceded him.

"Well, if a duke is a sponsor, that should be good enough for father."

One would *think*.

"It would be, if the establishment was more selective in who it allows memberships to."

Her sister stared confusedly back. "And who is that?"

"Anyone and everyone, regardless of station or...reputation." Prostitutes. Notorious mistresses. Self-made men.

Opal wrinkled her nose. "That's snobbish."

"I don't disagree, but my opinion doesn't matter." In a tyrannical world, no woman's did.

Fury poured from her sister's eyes. "I *hate* him."

There was an area they could come to a consensus on.

"Opal," Glain tried again. "You have books here. Ones—"

"Ones hand-picked by father, and boring and dull."

"Which both still mean the same thing."

Opal clasped her hands against her small chest, and her eyes took on a faraway, romantic glimmer. "But not all books are the same. *These* books, Glain, they are...magical." She whispered that latter word with an awed reverence one might bestow upon a newly discovered land or rare gemstone.

"Magic doesn't exist, Opal," Glain spoke gently, but as firmly as she could. She cast a watchful look at the doorway. "And certainly not in the gothic stories you read," she whispered.

Opal dropped her arms to her side and glared. "They are magnificent, and clever and you would judge them."

"*Father* will. And when he does, gone they go. Spare yourself that hurt. You are better off not indulging in them."

"Reading is *not* an indulgence."

Her sister scrambled onto the sofa, going up on her knees beside Glain. She gripped her with desperate little hands. "Look at me and tell me there's nothing that's ever brought you joy the way my books do. Because I don't believe it."

Glain held her sister's eyes. "Opal, I was six when I," *learned*, "Accepted how my life would proceed. You would do well to remember that pastimes like reading or painting, or whatever it is... they aren't worth," *Losing loved ones over.* "Angering the duke."

Opal sank back on her haunches. "It is no wonder you find yourself Princesse de Glace," she said. Had those words been shouted, with her sister glowering and stomping, it would have been easier than this...quiet acceptance.

Ice Princess.

Yes, the world—her own sister—believed her the flawless, unfeeling Glain, a woman so flawless, so perfect, even after two Seasons she'd not found a man worthy. What they'd failed to realize was how lonely Glain's life truly was. That not even Opal her beloved sister realized as much, would never not hurt.

Glain, however, had discovered something altogether more agonizing—having people ripped from her life. Her late mother who'd been banished by their father for daring to encourage Glain's inquisitiveness. The governess who'd been dismissed for daring to encourage Glain's inquisitiveness.

"Did you hear me?" Opal demanded. "I said you *are* the Ice Princess. Don't you even care I'm calling you names?"

"There are certainly worse things than being referred to as a princess, Opal."

Glain's was a bald-faced lie. That title cast upon her, whether spoken in the King's English or French form, stung.

Sadness filled Opal's light-blue eyes. "You are unbearable, *Diamond*, and I will never, ever, become you." Somehow the somberness with which the younger girl spoke sent an even greater spiral of hurt through her.

"Never, ever, ever."

Opal cocked her head.

"You forgot one of your 'evers'."

Opal's eyes bulged, and then with a piercing shriek she tossed her arms up.

Glain should have expected her tenacious sister was not done. She kept her features even. "I know I'll not do anything scandalous, and I'd advise you to learn that important lesson, and quickly, Opal."

"Why?" her sister asked with an unexpected and sudden calm.

In a reversal of roles, Glain tipped her head in an accidental mimicry of her sister's early befuddlement. "I don't...?"

"Why are you so determined to be the flawless lady?"

It was a question never before put to her. Glain found her voice once more. "Because it is the way *we* are expected to conduct ourselves."

Fire blazed within her sister's eyes. "Well, it is a *stupid* way."

And within Opal's expressive gaze, Glain saw herself of long, long ago. Back when she'd believed she'd always be as effervescent as her. But then, Glain had been a small child when she'd transformed herself into someone she despised.

Opal, on the other hand? She'd retained hold of her merrymaking ways far longer. Odd Glain should find herself both resenting and envying the younger girl.

Giving up her seat, Glain joined her sister.

"As ladies, we *must* conduct ourselves in a manner that is above reproach, Opal." She rested a hand on her sister's shoulder. "You'd be wise to learn that now. Otherwise, you'll learn what fate awaits those who don't conform to Father's expectations."

"It is only a book," her sister entreated.

This forlorn side of Opal, one who was so desperate for her books, threatened to wear Glain down.

"You know he'll not countenance it, Opal."

The books in question were gothic stories, ones of grizzly death and murder.

"Bah. He's a curmudgeon. Either way, he barely knows we're alive."

That was only true in part. "Barely or not, he knows, and when he finds out—"

"*If*," Opal shot back.

"*When*. The duke discovers all. And when he does, he will burn your books and fire your governess, Mrs. Fernsby for daring to encourage your reading such works."

And she'd not have that for her sister.

Opal's cheeks went a pale shade of white.

Good.

At last, Glain had managed to penetrate her sister's pertinacity and seemingly unflagging determination to visit the circulating library.

Mrs. Fernsby genuinely cared about Opal and nurtured the girl's soul. The sole reason Glain and Opal's tyrannical father hadn't removed the woman from her post was because Glain had taken care to shield the governess and her charge from the duke's scrutiny. She couldn't protect Opal forever, and eventually His Grace would snatch that slight happiness enjoyed by his youngest daughter.

Opal found her voice. "If he burns my books, Glain, then at least I'll have had the joy of reading them and will carry the memories of what I read for all of time."

With that, her sister did something Glain never recalled the younger girl doing—she turned ever so quietly and made a slow, silent march from the parlor. She closed the door not with a bang, but a small, nearly indecipherable click.

As specks of ice lightly pinged against the frosted windows, Glain stared after Opal a long moment, wavering between calling her back or running after her.

In the end, she shook her head and picked up her embroidery.

Nothing she said would make her sister happy. Nothing Glain shared would undo the unwanted truths about their circumstances— both as ladies, and more specifically as the Duke of Devonshire's daughters.

As she worked, however, guilt and regret all swirled in her breast. Guilt that she'd been the bearer of bad truths for her younger, still hopeful, sister. Regret that their father—that the world, on the whole —was not a better, more tolerant place for women. And frustration... there was that, too.

Restless, her embroidery in hand, Glain pushed to her feet and headed over to the floor-to-ceiling length windows covered with a light frost.

She pressed one of her palms against the chilled glass, warming it enough so that she wiped away the residual of ice there. She pressed her forehead against the slight view she'd provided herself of the quiet Mayfair streets below.

Glain knew when her sister looked at her, what she saw and believed. And not only because Opal didn't spare anything when it came to telling Glain precisely what she thought of her.

Her sister hadn't discovered the truths yet. But she would.

In a world where men were free to be whom they wished to be, traveling the Continent or world if they so wished, or studying the subjects they wanted—or as this case would have it—even reading the books they wanted, women of their station found themselves relegated to the role of ornamental objects, voiceless. *Powerless.*

"You want to go play?"

Glain gasped, and whipped around, finding the owner of that small, child's voice.

Her ten-year-old brother, Flint, stared hopefully at her.

At Glain's silence, he joined her, walking with measured steps better suited to a grown man.

Whereas the duke largely ignored his daughters, his son received all his attentions and energies. And for all the ways in which Glain lamented the unfairness that came in being born a female in a man's world, she also found herself pitying Flint for the pressure and attention the duke gave him—*suffocated* him with.

"Do you?" her brother pressed. "Want to play? You're looking out the window the way I do when I'm in the middle of my lessons." He gestured to the lead panes behind her. "I wanted to play with Opal."

Glain lightly ruffled the top of his blond curls. "And any sister will do?"

"Yes," he said with all the honesty only a child was capable of. He swatted her hand.

"No," she said. "I," *can't,* "don't want to play. I was just..." *thinking of how life was and regretting so much of it* "...watching the snow fall." She settled for that easier, simpler answer. "Are you and Opal quarreling?"

Her brother shook his head and similar to the way Glain had moments ago, he cleared himself a spot upon the frosted glass and pressed his nose against the pane. "I can't find her."

"Opal is upset," she explained.

"Why?"

Guilt reared its head once more. "She wanted to go somewhere, and I thought it better we not."

"The circulating library?"

She bit the inside of her cheek. Even her brother knew that. Which meant it was only a matter of time before the duke did.

Flint puffed out his small chest. "When I'm duke, I won't care what books my sisters read. I'll let them buy whatever ones they want, and they shall read them whenever and wherever they wish. Why, if you want to read one of those gory books Opal loves in the middle of Sunday sermons, I shan't say a thing. Why...why... I'll see them installed in the pews in place of the boring missals there."

So much love for him filled her breast. Glain settled her hands upon Flint's shoulders and gave him a light squeeze. "You are a wonderful brother and will make the best duke," she said softly. "But until that day, His Grace expects us to conduct ourselves in a manner befitting a nobleman's children."

Not unlike Opal of a short while ago, fire lit his eyes. "That's another thing. When I'm duke, I'm not going to require anyone call me His Grace or duke. Not the way *he* does. I'm going to order everyone to call me Flint."

A small smile twitched at the corners of her lips. "What if you don't order *anyone* about, and instead, *allow* them to call you by your given name?"

He scrunched up his heavily freckled nose, a product of his love for the summer sun that left him with those long-lasting remnants through the subsequent seasons. "Very well. I shall *invite* them to call me Flint. The staff and my friends and everyone. But if they call me

His Grace, I shan't like it." Suddenly the boy's eyes brightened, and his entire face lit up. "Ooh! It is snowing," he exclaimed, scrambling closer to the window so he could stare out, and shifting the topic as only a child could.

While Flint stared wide-eyed out the window, Glain made no attempt to hide a sad smile.

Alas, her brother would inevitably change. He'd develop a similar expectation of how he'd be treated, and how others referred to him. It was only a matter of time. Right now, the duke ceded nearly all control of Flint's schooling and life to the tutors whom he'd personally interviewed. But that wouldn't be forever. One day soon, he'd take Flint under his wing completely, so that he might shape him in his image.

Her brother yanked on her hand. "Why do you look sad of a sudden?" he asked worriedly, sounding very much like the boy who'd gotten into the inkwells in their father's office, painted the walls with that same ink, only to find Glain and the tutor he'd escaped from upon him. "You can't be sad. Look!" He lifted his small, slender arms in a way that framed the tiny flakes falling rapidly outside. "It's *snow.*"

"I'm not sad," she promised, lying. "I was merely thinking."

"Thinking about sad things."

Even at ten years of age, he proved entirely too astute, and far more in tune with her or her sister's feelings than the man who'd sired them.

Leaning down, she placed a kiss on her youngest sibling's smooth cheek.

Flint instantly blushed a bright bred. "Go on now," he muttered.

Frantic footfalls echoed from out in the corridor.

Just like that, all the color leeched from his freckled face.

Warning bells went off. "Flint, what have you done?" she demanded on a whisper as the steps drew nearer.

"I...may not have finished my lessons completely," he muttered grudgingly, scuffing the tip of his buckled shoe along the floor.

She briefly closed her eyes, and instantly springing into action, she gripped her brother by the shoulders and steered him down behind the sofa just as a light knock fell on the door.

"Enter," she called out in the crisp, aloof tones she'd become well-noted for amongst both Polite Society and the duke's household.

The panel instantly opened, and a small, wiry fellow with wire-rimmed spectacles and a prematurely balding pate stepped inside.

His small mouth was pinched like he'd been born sucking upon a lemon and hadn't stopped in the thirty and however many so years he'd been on this earth. "I am looking for his lordship," Mr. Crowley said in a no-nonsense tone, one that had become more obsequious and curter the longer his tenure with the duke. "He has escaped his lessons."

"I am afraid he is not here," she said coolly.

The tutor flattened his lips. "This will not do, at all. The boy has responsibilities, and yet his flights of fancy and his flights in general interfere with his edification. I've no choice other than to report his latest escapade to the duke." Spinning on his shiny black, buckled shoes, Mr. Crowley turned to go.

Glain glanced down to where her brother knelt at her feet still. Frantic worry creased Flint's high, noble brow and glittered in his panicked eyes. She whipped her gaze up to the entryway.

"I would advise against that," she said in tones steeped in frost and disdain as only she had managed to perfect these years.

The tutor turned back with a frown. "My lady?" He spoke with all the disdainful arrogance afforded him as the duke's personal hire for his heir.

Well, Glain could do disdainful arrogance with the best of them. "Do you truly believe His Grace will take well to an incompetent tutor who cannot properly watch after the future duke?"

Mr. Crowley blanched.

Glain pressed her point. "I assure you, he won't," she said warningly. "You will be the one held responsible for his show of rebellion, and it will be you, in return, who finds yourself suddenly unemployed."

The spindly-looking fellow yanked at his elaborately folded white cravat. "Perhaps...his lordship can enjoy just a small reprieve," he said, his voice squeaking. "After all, he proved extraordinarily focused and on-task prior to his es—uh..."

She narrowed her eyes into thin slits. "Break?" she supplied.

"Y-Yes. Th-that. His permitted break. In fact, if I'm being completely honest, I was the one who s-suggested we have a break. Why, he's likely even now headed back to the schoolrooms."

At her feet, Flint giggled, and Glain cleared her throat loudly, covering what would be a damning giveaway. "Good day, Mr. Crowley." With her words, expression, and attitude, she imbued all the ice, befitting the moniker Opal had hurled Glain's way.

The tutor dropped a deep bow and then, backing out of the room, he drew the door shut behind him. Frantic footfalls, these ones departing, filled the quiet of the room, ultimately fading all together.

"Brava!" her brother cheered entirely too loudly and clapped his hands as he did.

"Shh!" She stole a frantic look at the doorway, more than half-expecting that she and Flint had stepped into one of many traps set by the duke to test his children.

"You did it." He hopped to his feet. "You kept me safe from mean Mr. Crowley."

He gazed upon her with far more adoration than she deserved.

"I cannot do that forever," she said. "Soon, you'll need to begin conducting yourself in a way the duke will approve of." And then he'd be forever changed.

Flint's blue eyes flashed. "He can go han—"

She clamped a hand over his mouth, muffling the remainder of that curse upon the duke. "Have a care. He can," *and would*, "make your life a misery."

Her brother shrugged. "Donff care," he said around her palm.

And she believed it. She believed him. Glain closed her eyes once more. Not unlike Opal, Flint still possessed a backbone that hadn't been broken, but it would be. "You will care," she warned. Because ultimately, the duke determined what a person cared about, and used that to bend their will, and shape people into moldable objects he approved of.

Flint shook his head. "No, I—"

The door exploded open, and he instantly dove to the floor.

Her heart racing, Glain looked to the front of the room.

Only it wasn't an enraged duke there to take Flint away and twist him into his image. Relief filled her breast.

"Sally," she greeted her maid.

Relief that lasted only as long as her maid's next words. "She's gone," the young woman whispered, her voice breathless and her cheeks flushed, like she'd run a great race.

She puzzled her brow. "Who—"

"Lady Opal," the maid rasped.

"She is not." A master at hiding, Opal often took to sneaking about and remaining hidden until she decided it was time to come out. "I'm certain she's just—"

"One of the stableboys saw her sneaking outside."

"Then she's in the stables," Glain said calmly, with an ease she didn't feel.

"Already had one of the footmen look there." Sally twisted the fabric of her immaculate white apron. "She's gone."

"Gone," Glain repeated dumbly. Where would the girl go? And didn't she know the wrath she risked if the duke suddenly recalled he had another daughter? One at that who was still unyielding and an even greater handful than Glain had ever been.

"I don't know, my lady," Sally whispered. "We have to inform His Grace."

Oh god. No. This would be the thing that crushed Opal. The duke would never tolerate—

"Don't!" Flint exclaimed. "She is fine."

Glain and the maid switched their attention to the boy.

He instantly dropped his gaze to the ivory floral Aubusson carpet.

Glain narrowed her eyes. "Flint," she said warningly.

He shuffled back and forth on that handwoven carpet, putting her in mind of a penguin she'd once observed long ago when her mother had been present and had taken her to the Royal Menagerie.

"She is fine," he repeated.

When he said nothing more, Glain looked to Sally.

The girl instantly took that signal, dipped a curtsy, and hastily ducked out of the room.

The moment she'd gone, Glain found herself alone with Flint. "Out with it."

"The c-circulating library. You wouldn't go with her, and I wanted to go, but she said I really needed to help provide a distraction."

She should have expected something was suspicious when he'd sought out her to play with instead of Opal. Glain pressed her palms over her face. "You are going to be the death of me." Letting her arms drop, she headed for the door.

"Where are we going?" he asked, following close at her heels.

"Where do you think I'm going, Flint?" *Not we.* "You have your lessons."

"Well, if you think I'm staying," he charged, "then I'm going to tell Father."

"Let's go." Glain grated out those two syllables. She didn't believe for a moment he would, and yet neither was it safer to leave him here alone in possession of that information about their middle sibling.

Her brother flashed a triumphant grin.

If it was the last thing she did, Glain was going to fetch her sister back before the duke discovered her gone and tamped out the younger girl's fire once and for all.

CHAPTER 2

He was the unlikeliest librarian.

That was what had been said, anyway, about Mr. Abaddon Grimoire.

Nor were the people who'd said as much been wrong, either.

Born of the roughest streets of East London to a common street whore and sold into a child gang belonging to the notorious William Wilson, Abaddon would never be what a person conjured when they imagined the keeper of a circulating room.

But then, as a young man of fourteen who'd been determined to escape oppression and live free of the influence of men who'd have him murder and steal for their pleasure, he'd also known they would find him if he didn't lose himself the last place those kings of the underworld would look—a circulating library.

As an illiterate boy who neither read nor owned a book, Abaddon's greatest skill had been gladiatorial in nature. He'd been used for fights the way cruel men might a dog or cock. He'd also been clever enough to realize the *last* place they'd ever look for him, would be among the aisles of musty volumes, filled with inked words none of them could make sense of.

That day Abaddon found shelter in the Chetham's Subscription Library, he'd believed the only value to be found there came from the cover it had provided. He'd spent days, hiding among the shelves.

Until the proprietor, an older fellow with white hair and big spectacles and even bigger cheeks, and without any family, took Abaddon in as his own. He'd taught him to read and write and understand all that went into overseeing the library. And when he'd died, he'd ensured care of it remained in Abaddon's hands.

But Abaddon had never forgotten what it was to hide.

A person never did fully shake free of the chains that bound them. For a man or woman born in the Dials, those chains were mighty and strong. Even if one was fortunate to escape—as Abaddon had done—the ugly remembrances lived on. The memories were forever there, reminding him of how miserable life had been...and how very easily it could go back to the worst ways.

Yes, Abaddon knew what it was to hide. And why he recognized it so easily in others.

As this particular case would have it, a small someone other, with her blonde curls tucked under a too-big-for-her-head cap.

The breeches and coarse wool jacket she wore were better suited to a stableboy but were of higher quality to mark her different from someone who'd just escaped the grasp of London's greatest gang leaders.

She wasn't a street thief, either.

Or at least, she'd not made an attempt to stuff any of the small leather volumes she'd been perusing into the leather sack flung over her small shoulder.

If she was a common street thief, she was bloody bad at her line of work.

A thief's first job was to blend in with their surroundings, attract no notice, and be discreet in every movement.

This girl, however, periodically stole long, obvious glances about as if she were searching for someone before returning her focus to the book in her hands.

Unlike Abaddon who'd also hidden behind a book long ago, holding it upside down because he'd not known the damned difference, this child held it the proper way, and close to her nose—as if she were reading, and then recalling she was hiding, before being drawn back to the words on those pages.

From where he stood at the end of her aisle, he folded his arms. "That's a good one," he remarked.

The small patron gasped, lost her grip on the book in her hands. It hit the floor with a quiet thump.

She eyed him nervously. "Sir?"

Abaddon nudged his chin at the small volume beside her feet. "That one."

She glanced down. "I've not read it yet. Have you?"

"Aye. Read most of them, I have." Strolling over, he dropped to a knee and rescued the book lying indignantly upon its spine. "And I'm not a sir. Just a regular mister. Mr. Grimoire." He held the book out, and she took it with eager fingers.

Interest sparked her eyes. "Even the horror ones, you've read?"

"Especially those."

"Then your name suits you." She giggled. "Mr. Grim."

"Grimoire."

"I like grim better. I wish *I* had a gothic-story-type name."

Not only did he possess a gothic-story-type name, but a dark, dangerous path to go along with it.

"What name do you have?" he asked.

She eyed him warily. "Opal."

It didn't escape his notice that she deliberately withheld her last name.

He felt the girl's gaze on him as he examined the small stack of books she'd sorted into three piles at her feet.

"What have we here?"

"Those are my keeper ones," she said of the largest pile. "And those are my maybes." She gestured to the slightly smaller stack of volumes alongside it.

Abaddon looked at the third and also the smallest pile. "The 'no' pile?"

She shook her head. "I don't have any 'no's'. I like all books, but some more than others. Just some are at the bottom of my reading list."

"And you have the space for all these books?"

She hesitated. "No?"

There was the slight uptilt of a question, one that hinted at the lie.

Opal No-Last-Name brightened. "But a person can always find space for books." She considered her selections for a long while. "I can purchase these from you," she offered.

Reaching inside her jacket, she withdrew a small lace reticule, made of silver satin and adorned in pearls, it was as fine an item as he'd ever himself stolen during his thieving days.

She wagged that extravagant bag at him. "See, I have the money." Opal gave her bag a little shake, setting the coins a'jingle.

Her precise tones, that money, and the quality of that article bespoke a child who came from wealth.

He gently pushed the bag back towards her. "If I sold you these books then other readers won't have the joy of exploring them."

Opal troubled at her lower lip. "I...I hadn't thought of that. I forgot for a moment I was in a lending library." she said, her elfin-like features crestfallen, as she reconsidered the large stacks at their feet. "I was lost amongst all the books."

"Well, given you can't read them all at the same moment, seems you don't have to worry about not taking them all up today."

"Yes, but what if someone else comes in here," she asked, frantically, jabbing at the largest of the piles. "What if they want the same books I want, and *they* don't return them and then I never get to read them, Mr. Grim?"

"Ah, so that is the reason for that larger pile."

She nodded. "My you-might-lose-them-and-will-I-ever-be-the-same-if-I-cannot-find-a-copy-again pile?" Her pixie-like features grew solemn, and she slowly shook her head. "And I honestly cannot say that I will be, be able to find them again, Mr. Grim."

"We can't have that."

"No, we can't." She added her consensus to his.

Dropping his hands to his knees, Abaddon leaned forward so he could meet the little girl's big, blue eyes. "Sometimes, we just have to trust that people are capable of good."

At the front of the shop, the tinny bell jingled, announcing Abaddon's latest patrons. The bell had been the first recommendation he'd made when Mr. Baughan took him in, as a way of noting people coming and going.

Abaddon spared a brief glance over his shoulder, before returning his attention to the small girl.

He knew everyone who stepped foot inside this circulating library, along with details about them, where they sat, the manner of books they read, how often they came. "You don't have a membership," he remarked.

"No," Opal fished around the reticule. "But I can. Only..." She stared forlornly at the coins in her hand. "Are you certain you will not sell me the books because..." She paused. "I don't know if I'll be allowed to come back," she finished on a forlorn whisper.

As Opal dropped her sad-eyed stare to the leather volumes on the floor, Abaddon felt tension whip through him.

So, there was someone who had the girl under their thumb. Having been oppressed himself, he easily recognized the look of someone suffering that same fate.

Abaddon continued to observe her. All the while, the latest patrons who'd entered moved through the library: a pair of footfalls, one light, the other lighter. A mother and a child. His time spent in East London had provided him all number of necessary skills to survive, one being the identification of a person's footsteps—how close they were, how heavy they were, and which ones were to be avoided.

When it became apparent Opal didn't intend to volunteer

anything more on the people barring her from visiting and reading, he posed the question. "Who is preventing you from—?"

"Opal," a woman cried. Stiffening Abaddon looked up to the picturesque beauty striding over.

Nay, gliding. A tall, willowy woman didn't stride—she floated, her graceful movement leant a shimmer to the silver satin cloak.

Gazing at the ethereal vision before him, Abaddon at last understood the ancient Greeks' portrayal of those goddesses as women of height. With the lady's golden curls intricately twisted about her head like a coronet and tucked in place by diamond studded pins, she may as well have been Helen of Troy herself, come to life.

Brushing past him, she gripped the younger girl by her shoulders. "Opal," she repeated, more than half-breathless. With relief? Fear? Both?

A young boy joined the pair of ladies.

Then, as if realizing the girl was in fact, fine, his latest patron stiffened, her enormous hazel eyes, flecked with specks of greens and golds and browns, hardened. "Whatever were you thinking?"

She might be a golden Aphrodite in the flesh, but as she spoke to the girl, the lady was a cold as the marble statues erected of that deity.

"You *know* you were explicitly forbidden from coming here."

Abaddon tensed.

There it was, then. Verification of just who had been barring the young girl from visiting the circulating room.

And there could be no doubting the woman before him was anything but a lady. Far too young to be a mother and far too high in the brow to be a governess, she'd some connection to the girl she continued to harangue.

He slid his assessing stare over her slim face, the bold, sharp slashes of her cheekbones. The only hint of softness to the lady was a set of lush, full, red lips. Lips that would make even an honorable man think of sinning.

And he was no honorable man.

Suddenly, the boy, largely forgotten until now at the lady's shoulder shoved an elbow into her back.

The young woman grunted. "Flint, what—" She followed the boy's not-at-all discreet gesturing to Abaddon.

Her attention flew his way, and she inched her gaze slowly, ever more slowly up his person. The lady quickly released Opal's shoulders and straightened.

She lowered sinfully long golden lashes, hooding her eyes.

During his life, he'd been reminded at every turn of his standing in the world. But he'd never given a shite what people thought and didn't let some toff or lady shame him. Certainly not the ones who entered his business.

He stared back boldly, unapologetically.

Color flooded the high planes of her cheeks as if she were offended he, a mere mortal, should dare that affront. She flattened her mouth, turning those lovely lips down at the corners. "Who are you and what are you doing with my sister, sir?"

Ah, the sister, then.

CHAPTER 3

Glain's voice was steady.

Under ordinary circumstances that was no abnormal feat.

She'd perfected the art of cool, clipped, refined speech. One she'd mastered as a girl then refined as a young woman who'd been declared a Diamond by the queen and suddenly found herself sought after by marriage-minded men.

This, however, was certainly not an ordinary circumstance.

Just as this was not a prim, polished, proper gentleman, the kind she'd become all too adept at repelling.

None of those men had dared stare so baldly, so unapologetically.

And certainly, none of them had looked like *him*.

At least four or so inches taller than her almost six feet, he was a broad, powerful man, heavily muscled, as if he'd been cut from a swath of stone and then stuffed into mildly respectable black wool garments.

Her gaze crept up to his face. He possessed an iron jaw and a slightly bent, hawkish nose. Hooked as it was, it hinted at a man who'd had the appendage broken—mayhap several times.

Her brother pushed an elbow into her side. "It's rude to stare," he scolded in an outrageously loud whisper that sent the stranger's lips tipping up and heat exploding to her cheeks.

"Hush," she mouthed.

Alas, there was to be no mercy this day, for Flint did what he was being groomed by his tutors to do—he dug in, determined to have his words acknowledged. "What? You are, and it's rude."

"They always do this," Opal explained matter-of-factly to their audience of one.

"Ah," the man murmured, lifting his head in acknowledgement. The queue at the nape of his muscular neck slid over his shoulder.

Glain found her footing with him. "I asked you a question," she said. Taking a step closer, she gripped her sister lightly by the wrist and pulled her away.

Or attempted to. Opal dug in.

"What are you doing with my sister?" Glain demanded.

"Two," he said, suddenly, unexpectedly, and she tipped her head in confusion.

He lifted two fingers. "You asked two questions: Who am I and what am I doing with your sister?"

At that less than subtle shade of mockery, Glain drew back. The heat in her cheeks blazed several degrees warmer.

"You have to forgive her," Opal said. "She's not used to people challenging her."

The man flicked a stare up and down her person. "That I can believe." The look he gave Glain was one that indicated he found her wanting.

Fury and annoyance tightened in her belly at being called out, and yet at the same time, dismissed.

"I'll not ask—"

"This is Mr. Grimoire," Opal interrupted, and it didn't escape Glain's notice that her sister did so because *Mr.* Grimoire had no intention of supplying an answer to either of her questions. "He operates the circulating library."

Glain recoiled for entirely different reasons. "You are the librarian?" she asked incredulously.

This six foot-four-inch specimen of heavy muscle and chiseled features? With a lion's mane of Teutonic gold hair, overly long and drawn haphazardly into a que at his nape, he'd more the look of one of those long-ago gladiators she'd read of than a keeper of books.

"Expect somethin' else, darling?"

His speech contained of roughness to it, slightly over-emphasized enough to make her think he exaggerated those tones.

To scare her? To shock her? Well, he did. But not because of his tone. Because of his blunt speech and the way his gaze seared her all the way to her soul.

No one looked at her the way he did, direct, and without apology. In fact, no one met her eyes with theirs. People went out of their way to dip their stares deferentially when she passed.

She'd long hated it, yearning for someone to just *see* her. Only to have this man look squarely at her and find herself unnerved to the point of wishing him to move his focus to anything and anyone except her.

"Cats got your tongue, darling?" he drawled.

Her brother and sister giggled and Glain glared. Only Opal attempted to hide that hint of mirth behind her fingers.

Mr. Grimoire glanced at her siblings and winked.

There was something so gentle and warm in that flutter of his lashes. Something inside grated that he should respond so to her sister, while treating Glain like she was the dung upon his badly scuffed boot.

"We are going," she said tersely, grabbing each of her siblings by a hand. "Now."

"Hey," Opal cried out in protest, grinding them to a stop once more. "I'm not finished here."

Glain cast a warning look her sister's way. "You most certainly are," she gritted out.

"You've got a problem with my circulating library?" That low growl better suited a primal beast than a man.

But then, mayhap that was what the unlikeliest of circulating library owners in fact, was.

"She does," Opal answered for her.

"Opal," she bit out.

"She does not like books," Flint piped in, and at the look Glain shot his way, he lifted his shoulders in a half-shrug. "What? You *don't*."

She felt Mr. Grimoire's stare upon her once more. "I like books just fine," she said between her teeth, not sure why she felt the sudden need to defend herself to a man who looked at her so.

"Oh?" he drawled. "Which ones?"

God, he was insolent and audacious and infuriating.

"Respectable ones," she shot back, glancing pointedly at the stacks of books at the floor between them.

"Boring ones," Opal added.

Their brother spoke in tones pitched high to mimic a lady. "Ones about manners and peers and how to conduct oneself."

"And do not forget." Opal wagged a finger at Flint. "All the skills a lady must master in order to catch herself a husband." With that, brother and sister stepped into one another's arms and proceeded to perform the scandalous steps of a waltz down the narrow aisle, knocking into the piles, and bumping into the shelves as they danced.

Glain closed her eyes and prayed for patience. Drat if she didn't possess two outrageously disloyal siblings.

She caught Mr. Abaddon's grin.

He looked to her siblings. "I'd be remiss if I didn't mention circulating library etiquette."

Opal and Flint immediately stopped waltzing. Why, they listened to this big stranger better than they'd ever listened to her.

"May I have a moment?" he asked the young pair, and the two hurried off.

The moment they'd gone, Glain gritted her teeth. "I don't need you to go ordering my sister and brother about."

"What?" he asked lazily. "You want that honor all for yourself?"

Glain gasped, a hand flying reflexively to her breast. "How...dare you!" she stammered— stammered when she *never* did so. "How—?"

"Dare I?" he supplied in cool, mocking tones.

She jabbed a finger at him, several times. "You...you..."

He inclined his head. "Mr. Grimoire is the name you are looking for."

"Are crass and rude and boorish and mocking and perturbing and...and..."

He lifted a tawny eyebrow. "And?"

"Rude!" she repeated, because it really bore repeating.

"*I'm* the boorish one."—That slight emphasis sent heat from her neck up to her face, and by god, if this man wasn't going to paint her red forever. —"This from the lady who entered my library, ordered my patron about, and—"

Dropping her hands to her hips, Glain swept closer. "She is my sister."

He didn't miss a beat. "Your sister who is also my patron."

"She is no such thing!" she shouted, her voice pitching to the rafters. "She is a young lady. A proper, respectable young lady."

Her brother and sister ducked around the corner, both staring at Glain with wide, disbelieving eyes.

As they should.

Because Glain didn't shout...she didn't even raise her voice. She kept it careful and measured and modulated. What was it about this man that drove her to this show of temper?

Glain forced a serene smile she did not feel, and waved a hand, urging them on.

Thankfully, this time, they did as she bade, though knowing the imps as she did, they also no doubt hid behind the column and listened in on her exchange with the infuriating shop owner.

When she looked back at Mr. Grimoire, she drew in a slow,

calming breath. "My sister is not patronizing your circulating library," not taking her gaze from his unswerving one even as the piercing intensity of his hazel eyes left her quavering inside, "and she will not be taking these books out."

From somewhere over Mr. Grimoire's shoulder, she caught her sister's quiet cry and Flint's shushing sounds.

Regret: it cleaved away at her breast, but Glain forced aside that weakening. "This is for the best," she said. For him? For Opal? Or herself? Mayhap it was really all three she sought to convince. Giving her skirts a snap, she made to step around him.

"The best for whom?" he jeered, stopping her in her tracks with that echo of her very thoughts.

"All involved, Mr. Grimoire," she said icily.

He chuckled, that low, rumble, devoid of real humor, and a perfect expression of mockery.

Do not ask. You don't care. It doesn't matter.

"What?" she asked impatiently, stunned even as that question tumbled unchecked from her always careful lips.

"It's just I find it amusing, is all." He leaned forward and then swept out a hand, nearly brushing her with his gloveless, ink-stained fingertips.

"I don't see anything amusing about this. You are challenging your patrons."

"You aren't my patron," he said coolly. "My patrons read real books. Not some lessons on how to catch yourself the most powerful husband, and how to mold yourself into a colorless, vapid, unfeeling princess."

Glain recoiled.

She didn't know him beyond a handful of moments, and he knew her not at all, and yet...how very strange that his words—those specific ones, at that—should hurt so, that they should leave her hot with shame and regret and also fill her with the sudden, over-whelming urge to cry.

Colorless. Vapid. Unfeeling.

"What do you care what the girl reads? Because then she'll be different from you?"

All his words struck Glain in the chest, somewhere very near her heart, and overcome, she turned swiftly, and presented him with her back.

Opal *was* different, and in all the best ways. She'd retained the ability to smile freely, and think even more freely, and did so without any inclination of how precarious her existence was, at how quickly it could all just go...away.

Bloody fucking hell.

She was going to cry.

And he didn't deal well with tears.

Hell, he didn't deal with them at all.

In fairness, he hadn't had to deal with them.

The people he'd grown up amongst hadn't shed those drops, those marks of weakness, when a person living on the streets of London couldn't afford to be anything but hard.

He'd only spoken the truth. That's what had brought her—them —to this moment.

Strangely the thought didn't make him feel any better.

He swiped a hand over his face. "Stop."

She came to a sudden, jarring halt but remained with her back to him. Her narrow shoulders were proudly erect, her spine as straight as if a rod had been inserted within it.

"I was only speaking the truth," he said tightly.

"Is that your idea of an apology, Mr. Grimoire?"

"I don't apologize for telling the truth."

If possible, her back came up even more. "Good day, Mr. Grimoire," she said stiffly.

Despite himself, a slight smile twitched at his lips. That ice princess with her perfect manners.

"Darling—"

She whipped around. "I'm not your darling, and it's rude to call a woman with whom you are not familiar—*or* for that matter, to call any woman 'darling'."

"I don't have your name."

For a moment he thought she intended not to give it.

"Lady Diamond—" She grimaced. "*Glain* Carmichael."

Glain.

Welsh-sounding and slightly lyrical for the way it lingered and then rolled from the tongue, it was far softer and slipped from her lips more smoothly than that first she'd shared.

"You called me vapid, Mr. Grimoire. And I'm not. Do you know what I am?"

He opened his mouth to tell her, but she beat him to it.

"I'm reliable. Calculable. I'm not someone given to flights of fancy."

"Why?" he asked.

She drew back. Her golden eyebrows snapped together into a single, baffled line that accentuated the fascinating birthmark between her brows. "I don't know what you are—?"

"Why are you so determined to crush the girl?"

This time he may as well have struck her for the way she blanched and hunched into herself. And damned if he didn't feel like the worst of the bullies he himself had encountered in the streets of London.

Abaddon tried again. This time he gentled his tone.

"You really think flights of fancy are such a bad thing?"

The lady's jaw worked, and for a moment, he thought she wouldn't answer, that she'd back down. He should have known better and expected more from a bold princess.

"They are if one is determined to protect oneself from being hurt."

She spoke of *suffering?* He scoffed. "What do *you* know about pain?"

The lady narrowed her eyes. "You mean, because I'm a lady?" Gathering her skirts, she swept over. "Because what could a lady born of the peerage possibly know about that real emotion, or *anything*?" Hers was a rhetorical question, and damned if he didn't feel small under her condescending stare and sharp words. "And tell me, Mr. Grimoire. Do you think you somehow know more about everything? Pain and how and why a woman should or does conduct herself all because you are born outside the peerage? That your world experience gives you an understanding about how everyone lives?"

A muscle ticked irritatingly at the corner of his eye. "You don't know nothin' about me," he growled slipping into his roughed speech. The insolent princess.

"No, I don't," she said, instantly, too readily. "I know you have a slightly rough accent you worked at concealing and that you dress well enough, but not as fine as a nobleman." She hurled those truths at him. "I didn't presume to know *anything* about you because of it. *You* on the other hand felt more than comfortable sizing me up because of *my* birthright. Making assumptions that fit whatever narrow opinion you may have of people from my station. Now, I bid you good day, Mr. Grimoire." She collected her skirts for a third time, spun on her heel, and made to take her leave.

Abaddon stared after her proud, retreating figure.

The lady wasn't wrong. He had formed his own assumptions based on her icy veneer and intent to drag her sister off. After all, what other opinion could he have been expected to reach?

And yet, it also left him wondering at the words she'd spoken. And about the lady herself.

"It's not because of your birthright, you know."

She stopped again.

This time, he marched over, sliding himself in her path, lest she leave. For he knew, if she did, she'd be gone forever.

"I don't have a problem with ladies," he said. "Not all of them."

She pursed her lips. "Just me, then. I am honored."

He'd ruffled her feathers.

Abaddon flashed a half-smile, the one he'd used to disarm people through the years.

Lady Glain, however, proved unflappable—singularly unaffected, her features a smooth, frosty, detached mask.

"In fact, I respect the ones who come in my library. They aren't the judgmental sort." *Like her.* "They know what they like to read and aren't afraid to borrow it, regardless of opinion."

Pain flickered in her eyes. "Yes, well, not all ladies have that same luxury," she said softly, and he sharpened his gaze upon her expressive face.

It wasn't the first she'd spoken of pain or a harsher existence than the one he imagined she knew.

"You do know something of it, don't you?" he murmured.

Her expression instantly shuttered. "I don't know what you are talking about," she said stiffly.

"I think you do. I think you're pretending you don't so you don't have to reveal anything more than you already have."

Her eyes grew wary, but she said nothing.

"Well, that's fine, princess. I won't press you for your secrets. I won't ask you to share anything you don't want to share with me."

What accounted for his sudden yearning to know those details about this woman, ice on the exterior but with revealing eyes that glimmered with hurt.

"A-And why should I want to share anything with you?" She tipped up her chin. "I don't know you. Nor do I intend to ever again step foot inside your library."

Aye, he expected she believed that. But he also knew he didn't intend to allow her to disappear as she wished. "It's not all bad here," he murmured. "In fact, you might discover your sister isn't wrong about this place and the books you can find here."

The lady flattened her mouth into a firm line. "I highly doubt that, Mr. Grimoire."

She was a prickly one. That should be a great killer of desire for the hoity-toity woman. And yet her disdain and indifference had an altogether different effect on him. The lady posed a challenge.

Abaddon caressed a finger along the side of her tense lips, and that lush, slightly pouty flesh trembled slightly.

In desire? Horror? Perhaps a blend of both?

"Wh-what are you d-doing?" she whispered, not pulling away.

He'd bedded enough women of her station to know he could make even the loftiest lady cry out with passion when the wanted a bit of the rough. He also knew they equally were repelled by his station and thrilled at the prospect of slumming with him.

"Like satin you are," he murmured. His hunger for her made him careless with the speech he'd long ago practiced and perfected with the man who'd adopted him. The lady's plump pillow-like lips went soft and a whispery exhalation slipped past them.

He leaned nearer. "I've got a proposition for you, Glain."

The lady froze. And then as if she'd been dunked in the icy Thames, she gasped loudly and jumped back a step. "How *dare* you?" she whispered furiously, slapping a hand to her breast, drawing his gaze briefly to the fabric pulled more tightly against her shapely form.

Abaddon flashed a lazy smile. "Not *that* kind of proposition."

She stilled and a pretty pink blush filled her cheeks. "Oh."

Did he imagine the disappointment there? He rather thought he didn't. In fact, he'd wager his circulating library on it.

"W-Well, that is good," she said. "But neither should you touch me or use my name."

"Are those equal affronts in your world?"

"They are. A man does not just go about calling a woman by her given name or touching her. It bespeaks a level of intimacy that is scandalous and would see a lady ruined."

"And that would be the last thing you'd want?" he jeered, not sure why her disdain should chafe. He was well accustomed to it, but something about *this* woman, and that sentiment coming from her, rankled. "Being ruined by a tough from the streets."

"I'm not looking to be ruined by anyone, Mr. Grimoire," she said coolly, with entirely too much ease for him to ever doubt her sincerity.

And yet...

"I expect if I had a fancy title attached to mine name, it'd be a different story, then." He flashed another cold smile.

"There you'd be wrong. *Again*."

Again. The audacity of this one.

Abaddon folded his arms at his chest. "You expect me to believe a lady who reads books on catching husbands wouldn't be all warmth and smiles were it a duke or marquess taking such liberties?"

"I don't read those books."

"You said—"

"I said I read books befitting a lady, Mr. Grimoire," she said impatiently. " My siblings were the one who assumed those books were about marriage."

He caught his chin between his thumb and forefinger and made a show of studying her, doing so deliberately to pique her curiosity. "Hmm."

"Hmm, *what*?" She wrinkled a surprisingly lightly freckled nose, an appendage that had been dusted from its time in the sun, hinting she had a far freer spirit than he'd previously credited her with.

"It seems you and I have gotten off on the wrong foot. Both of us have made assumptions about one another."

"I haven't made any assumptions about you, Mr. Grimoire. *That* honor belongs entirely to *you*."

"You've got a problem with my library, do you not?"

"I'm sure it's fine enough—"

"But not fine enough for your sister."

"Not safe enough for my sister," she corrected.

"Because I'm here."

"Because—" The lady stopped herself abruptly.

His ears perked up, and he waited for her to finish that thought and give him the reason she was so adamantly opposed to her sister shopping here. Once more, however, she remained tight-lipped.

"I'll strike a deal with you, princess."

A brighter color bloomed red on her cheeks. "My name is not 'princess.'"

"Fine. Glain, then," he said.

She gasped. "I most certainly was not suggesting—"

"You spend a week here. One week," he went on, continuing over whatever unwanted lesson on propriety she intended to dole out. "An hour each day. You read my books. Different ones than whatever nonsense you've been occupying yourself with over the years. And if at the end of the week, you don't find yourself head over toes for the new books you read—"

"*When* I don't."

"And you still don't want your sister here, I won't interfere."

The lady didn't reject his proposal outright. He'd more than half expected she would.

He touched a hand to his heart. "You have my word, Glain."

She chewed at her lower lip, studying him warily. "You expect me to trust your word, and yet, I do not know you at all," she spoke haltingly, as though engaged in a battle with herself.

From the corner of his eye, he spied Lady Glain's siblings as they ducked their heads from around a tall bookshelf.

With their eyes, elder sister and younger sister engaged in a silent exchange. The younger girl fairly pleaded with her gaze.

"Please," Opal silently mouthed from across the way.

Lady Glain closed her eyes tightly, and when she opened them, she sighed. "Very well, Mr. Grimoire. You have one week. An hour each day, and not more than that. And at the end of our time together, I expect you will honor your promise and cease interfering in my relationship with my sister."

From that nearby aisle, a happy squeal went up followed immediately by the boy shushing her to silence, muffling that tell-tale happiness with what Abaddon suspected was his hand.

His mouth twitched even as Glain firmed her lips. No wonder they existed in a perpetual pout. Not that he minded. They were perfectly plump and lush and put a man in mind of forbidden, wicked imaginings.

"Now, if you'll excuse me, Mr. Grimoire."

He touched the brim of his brow. "Glain," he said, and this time, as she swept off, he made no attempt to stop her.

Suddenly, Abaddon smiled, very eager for tomorrow, and the challenge before him.

CHAPTER 4

Sometime between yesterday's meeting with Mr. Grimoire and this very moment, Glain had lost her mind. There was no other way of explaining it.

Pure madness was all that *could* account for the agreement she'd made with the fiercely handsome librarian, at a circulating library so scandalous for the people it catered to, and the shocking selection offered.

Standing across the street from the modest establishment, Glain peered at the cheerful front window, adorned with a ring of garland and a bright crimson bow at the center. When was the last the halls of her family's household had been decked so for the holiday season?

Her eyes slid shut, as a buried memory from many winters past slipped in: Glain and her mother, hanging garland, and as they did, singing *Christ Was Born on Christmas Day* so very loudly they'd not heard the duke. Until they had. Until his shouts had drown out their revelry.

"Decorating? As if you are bloody servants! And we do not cele-brate as the plebians do? Is that—?"

"Ahem."

Glain came whirring quickly back to the present.

Kenneth, her family's driver, stared at her with a concerned gaze. "Do you... require anything, my lady?"

She gave her head a slight shake, clearing the cobwebs of unwanted memories. "No. Nothing, Kenneth. Thank you. I'll be along shortly."

With that, Glain gathered the hem of her cloak and dress, and continued the rest of the way to Mr. Grimoire's library. The sooner she got this over, the better she'd be.

Only, as she found herself on the stoop, staring at a wreath entirely too big for the door, she braced for the expected rush of horror or panic that came from being here. But it didn't come. Instead, there was a stirring of excitement inside.

It had been so long—longer than she could remember—since she'd done anything she wasn't supposed to. She'd been unfailingly prim and proper and conducted herself at all times above reproach. Until now.

Now, she'd set out on her own, without even the benefit of a maid all so Glain might read whatever unsanctioned books it was she pulled from Chetham's Subscription Library shelf, where anyone could come.

Or is it the prospect of seeing him? Is it really that you have never met a man so bold, so insolent, and so dangerously handsome?

Her breathing increased. The warmth of it stirred a little cloud of white in the winter air and she pressed a gloved palm to her chest in a bid to slow her suddenly pounding heart.

Stop. He is just a man, and these are just ridiculous, silly books he'd have you read, and there is absolutely nothing at all seductive about him or this forbidden visit. At all.

A pair of nearly obsidian eyes met hers through the circle made by the wreath, and she shrieked. Glain buried the remainder of that startlement in her gloved fingers.

As if to put the final nails upon the coffin of her flighty musings, the proprietor lifted his watch fob, and pointed to the timepiece.

"You're late," he mouthed perfectly. Slightly mocking, and more than slightly condescending, and also absolutely the perfect killer to whatever nonsense had previously been filling her head.

And here you were, waxing on romantic, forbidden thoughts.

Grateful for the cold that would no doubt conceal her blush, she clasped the handle, and let herself inside.

"I'll have you know, I'm not late, as we set no time." she said, pushing the hood of her cloak all the way down.

He lounged a lean hip against a nearby display table. Her heart did a double-time beat at just how provocative he was in that casual repose.

"There's a difference between arriving and sitting outside for the whole of the agreed upon time," he said. "Either way, given your aversion to this place, I'll attribute the delay to you working up the courage to be here." He straightened and held out a heavily callused, ink-stained palm.

Glain unfastened the frogs of her cloak. "I'll have you know," she said, placing her velvet-lined cloak in his waiting hands. "I am quite punctual, always...except when circumstances require a delayed entrance. This, however, was not one of those times."

"What are?"

Confused, she stared at him.

"What circumstances require you to disregard a person's time?"

"I'm not someone who disregards a person's time, Mr. Grimoire," she said, suddenly finding it important that he didn't think she was the manner of person who didn't value another's time. "There are expectations, however, when attending certain events that one arrives fashionably late."

He snorted. "Likely so some self-important people can be sure there are more eyes on them. Sounds a touch self-important. Doesn't it?"

Glain made a show of removing her gloves, refusing to let herself be bothered at how easily he judged her.

Let Mr. Grimoire have his unfavorable opinion of her. It was better this way. The last thing she either needed or wanted was to have some manner of friendship with him.

"Despite your opinion, my adherence to that way of thinking—" *She'd always quite despised it.* Suddenly, for reasons she didn't understand, it seemed very important this man who continued to judge her know that. "Is one insisted upon by my father, Mr. Grimoire."

Her father would not have it any other way. He had insisted she be on display for the crowded ballrooms so that she could attract the notice of all.

"I take it he's a powerful, self-important man."

She waited for him to tack on: who raised a self-important daughter. This time, however, that insult did not come. "He *is* a very powerful, self-important man." She hesitated, withholding that final detail that would at last cement this man's respect. As all people were summarily impressed and awed by that title. "He is a duke."

"Ahh," he said, stretching out that singular syllable in a way befitting the discovery that her father was in fact a step away from royalty.

She braced for the change.

This moment where he treated her differently because of that discovery.

Glain stared at him.

He stared pointedly back.

She bowed her head slightly.

He matched that movement. "What?" he asked, confusion wreathing his voice. "What is it?"

And then it hit her—he didn't care. He didn't reveal the slightest hint of awe or reverence. He didn't treat her at all differently, rather, he treated her precisely as he had since they'd crossed paths yesterday. "Nothing," she said, feeling a lightness inside. "I...it is just people behave a certain way towards me when they discover that detail."

"I'm not most people, darling..."

"No, you aren't, Mr. Grimoire," she murmured, hopeless to stop herself from trailing her gaze over those sharp, angular planes of his face, nicked and marred with small scars she'd failed to note before now. They only leant an air of raw realness to his otherwise perfectly beautiful face.

He flashed a half-grin. "I'm sorry, *Glain*," he corrected, and this time, she didn't correct him. This time, she also felt more than a trace of regret at his dropping that familiar endearment of 'darling'.

"You still intend to use my Christian name."

His smile widened. "Absolutely and every time."

"Very well," she said, tipping her chin up a fraction. "What is it?"

"What is *what*?"

"Given you intend to address me so informally, it is only fair I return that familiarity."

Tawny eyebrows shot up above his hazel eyes.

She couldn't tamp down a triumphant smile. He'd thought her too lofty to ever dare such a boldness. Good. It felt wondrous, unnerving a person—that was, for different reasons than the icy demeanor she'd adopted.

He grunted. "Abaddon."

That dark angel of the abyss.

"Abaddon, then," she murmured, tasting and testing the feel of it upon her lips.

It was a sinister name, perfectly suited to a man who called for her to challenge everything she knew.

"Let's get on with it," he said, pulling her from her musings.

"Yes." The sooner they did this, the faster the time went, and the sooner she'd be free to leave, return home, and forget him and this outrageous arrangement.

He stared at her.

"What is it, Mr.... Abaddon?" she asked impatiently.

"Start looking."

Glain did just that, glancing around. "What exactly is it, I'm looking for?"

Abaddon gave her an incredulous look. "You're jesting?"

"I assure you, I do not 'kid' or make jests," she said impatiently.

The unlikeliest of circulating library owners snorted. "Now, that I can believe."

She bristled. *He's just trying to get you riled up. You've perfected being unaffected. You've come to embody a cool ice princess with everyone. This man was...or should be no different.* "Why, don't you just tell me what the problem—"

"The problem is, you're in a library. You look. You read some of the pages. You determine what stories you like to read."

He wanted her to peruse the shelves, then. Very well. *This* she could do.

Glain inclined her head. "If you might point me to the copies on elocution and—"

"The hell I will."

Heat exploded on her cheeks. "Cursing as you do, and in front of a lady, you'd do well to not only have a section, but to read those books yourself."

Abaddon dropped a broad, powerful shoulder against the end of the shelf. "Oh, I have those books. Smallest section I've got, and actually the least read by my patrons."

Annoyance ran through her. "And yet you won't direct me to them?" She fought the urge to stamp her feet, and instead made herself take a deep, steadying, and more importantly, calming breath. *Always be in control. Always be coldly indifferent and polite to the point of impolite.* "Very well, sir. Is that to be my test for the day? You shall find yourself disappointed as I can find the section well enough on my own."

He slid into her path. "That's not your test."

Which implied there was a different one he was putting to her.

"Well?" she snapped, drawing back as soon as that curt one-word syllable exploded from her usually-always-controlled lips.

"You're going to peruse the shelves, looking at different books than those stuffy ones you usually read, darling."

Darling.

Despite herself, a thrill of warmth invaded her chest and seeped out to every other corner of her being. It shouldn't. His was just a flippant endearment, and yet, she was hopeless to control the way her belly danced inside.

As if to highlight just how unaffected he was by her, in return, Abaddon removed his fob and let the golden string dangle before her face.

Glain instantly went cross-eyed as she attempted to bring those close numbers into focus.

The gleaming gold cylinder twisted and turned before her face, too quickly for her to either make sense of the item carved upon the back or make out the numbers there, and she found herself intrigued about the object of clear value and how he'd come by it. It looked old, but well taken care of and she wondered what it meant to him.

And worse, why she should care. She didn't. She drew back. She was just curious about this odd, gruff, lightly coarse-speaking fellow who challenged her at every turn. That was it, and certainly nothing m—

"Time's a' wasting, darling," he said, pocketing that item once more, and the spell was broken.

Grateful for the reprieve and welcoming the opportunity of putting some much needed distance between the, Glain found her legs and turned dismissively in the opposite direction. She continued a quick march to the end of the aisle and without pausing looped around the next row of shelving so that she was away from Abaddon Grimoire.

Closing her eyes briefly, she pressed her head against the row of musty-smelling books. *He is just a man. A rude, condescending man. Whatever interest you have in him is solely and strictly that.*

Glain took several more moments to repeat that mantra before opening her eyes once more and giving her head a hard, clearing shake. "Let's get on with it," she muttered under her breath, and grabbed the closest volume.

CHAPTER 5

The lady fascinated him. And Abaddon wasn't fascinated by any ladies of the peerage.

There'd certainly been enough of them coming through the doors of his circulating library. Many had come here slumming, eager to land themselves a spot in the bed of the notorious East Londoner who operated this establishment.

Not a single one of them had been like Glain.

She exuded an air that warned a mere mortal from daring to look at or touch her, and damned if that wasn't a greater lure than the apple Satan had put before Adam.

The young lady was an interesting conundrum—flawless and perfectly in control one minute, and then the next, there'd be a break in composure as she grew visibly impatient, her motions quick as she muttered to herself, before quick as that lapse came, regaining complete control of her temperament, so that where Abaddon watched the lady, wondered if he'd merely imagined that reaction.

"Ridiculous," she whispered under her breath, and his lips twitched up at the corners.

No, he'd not imagined any of it. "What's the problem, darling?"

The lady shrieked as the book went flying up and out from her grip before sailing quickly to the floor.

Thwack.

Muttering to himself, Abaddon rushed to retrieve the forlorn copy, all the while glaring at her. "Have a care. Books are precious," he said, inspecting the leather volume for injury.

"Then you would be well-advised to not go spying on a lady and sneaking up on her when she is perusing titles."

She'd a point there. He'd sooner turn the keys of his business over to a stranger and return to his days as a thief in the streets than admit as much.

Wordlessly, he handed the book over to now-gloveless fingers.

She snatched the volume and drew it close to her chest.

Abaddon's stare however, lingered upon her fingers.

In his years in the streets and in this establishment, he'd learned to tell a lot about a person by their hands.

Hers were soft. Lily white.

That display of her privilege should disgust him.

Strangely, it had the opposite effect.

As if she'd been unnerved, the lady dampened her mouth. "Was there something else you wanted?"

He should let her get back on with her search. For some reason, not wanting to leave her just yet.

"What's so ridiculous?" he asked.

She puzzled her brow.

"You said—"

"I know what I said," she said, a familiar blush filling her cheeks. "I barely whispered it."

"Yea, well, I hear all." His words were not mocking nor teasing. Rather, he spoke God's truth. A person who lived on the streets either developed heightened senses or perished.

She gave a toss of her head. "If you must know,"—Strangely, he must. — "I was merely thinking about the fact that the only way to determine if a book is one wishes to read is by—"

"Reading it?" he interrupted, dryly.

Glain nodded. "Precisely. But in a case, such as this," she held her book up and motioned to the area around them. "When one is surrounded by hundreds—"

"Thousands," he corrected. He was proud of his collection and didn't want her downplaying its true size.

"Even better, thousands," she continued. "How is one to ever determine in a timely manner whether a book simply by looking at its title is in fact what a person wishes to read? It seems like a waste of valuable time."

Her and her peculiar view on time. "That's the point of it." He slid closer. "And that's also the beauty of a circulating library, Glain," he murmured, reaching a hand out so close to her heart-shaped face he felt the quick inhale and exhale of her breath, a soft, warm sough upon his skin.

Forcing himself to focus on the lesson at hand and not this keen awareness of the beauty before him, Abaddon fetched a random volume and drew it out. "You can collect any number of books, fill your arms with them and set a stack down on a table...and you can forget time, Glain," he murmured. Close as he was, he appreciated the bold slashes of her high cheekbones. Her dainty, slightly pointed chin that added an air of interestingness to a face. Her face was a perfect model of those ancient Greek sculptors to have immortalized in stone. "You can just lose yourself."

Hopeless to help himself, he dusted a finger along that prominent cheekbone, and her long, blonde lashes fluttered wildly. "You can just lose yourself in..." He forced his arm back to his side, and the lady's eyes flew wide. "Whatever books you've discovered. And you can also know that when you're done, there's thousands more waiting for you. You can return time and time again."

And he imagined the tableau he spoke of: her visiting this place, and sitting herself down in one of the cosy, well-used, chairs, and burying herself in whatever books she'd collected. He smiled wistfully. All the while she'd be muttering to herself and whispering quietly about her selection, and whatever it was she read on those pages.

"I thank you." Glain glanced down briefly at the book in her hands. "But some of us don't have that luxury, Mr. Grimoire."

She used his surname when she was cross.

"Ah, yes, forgive me. That's right," he said, not bothering to keep the slight mockery from his voice. "You're entirely too busy to idle away inside my morally decayed library."

Color exploded on her cheeks. "How dare you?"

"Quite easily. I gather, you're far too busy seeing to important matters like—let me take a guess? Stitching flowers on some needle-point." By the way her blush deepened, he was on the mark. "I bet you're flawless on a pianoforte."

Her lips went brittle. "And that is a bad thing?"

So, she was.

He smirked. "I'd wager you also sketch and paint a solid bowl of fruit or country landscape."

Her color deepened, and if possible, her lips went even harder.

"Yes, those endeavors are far more important for you as a proper lady, aren't they? Tasks that don't require you to think or challenge you. Where you read all the books hand-picked by your fine governess about topics that don't really matt—"

"How *dare* you?" she cried, her chest heaving, taking him aback with the force of the emotion bleeding from her eyes. "At every turn, you continue to judge me. And yet, you know nothing about me. I sketch and paint, but I hate it. I mastered Latin and French and use it only when I talk to myself in my head, because I don't have the luxury of traveling the world as you, and all men, do." She took an angry step closer. "And I don't visit circulating libraries and sit down reading books for hours upon hours about," she slashed a hand behind her, "books about happily-ever-afters, and love and romance or magic, and do you know why?" Glain didn't allow him a word edgewise. "Because there is no place for it. There is no magic in this world."

She was right. As someone who'd both witnessed and committed any number of sins, he could attest firsthand for those truths she spit out. He passed his gaze over her face, touching his stare upon each plane of her spasming features. "I never knew…"

"That a lady could feel oppressed and miserable?" she asked bitterly. "I assure you, we can. For as impossible as your existence likely was, in ways you still have freedom of yourself and your decisions, and in how you carry yourself that is afforded to no women." She thumped a fist against her breast. "We, on the other hand, are at the mercy of first our fathers, and then, if we're lucky, our *husbands*," she spat those words in the clearest indication of just what she thought of the wedded state.

Her every word shamed Abaddon as he rightly deserved, but she wasn't done, and he deserved that, too.

"You've identified me as a self-centered, self-absorbed heiress, no doubt? The killjoy of her livelier sister's happiness." Grabbing her skirts, she stalked the handful of steps between them, tilted her chin, and glared fiercely up.

God, she was breathtaking in her fury.

"I am protecting my sister, and my brother, in the only ways I'm able. So don't you dare presume to judge me when you know absolutely nothing of our circumstances." With that blistering set-down, she turned on a furious huff.

He caught her lightly, gently, by the wrist. "Please," he said quietly. "Don't go."

~

Glain should go.

He'd given her every reason to leave.

He'd been rude and condescending. Yet, as coldly mocking as he'd been, hurling all the assumptions he'd made about her, *at* her, how tender and warm his voice was the next instant.

His baritone, a shade too deep, and slightly gravelly, coarse with street-roughened tones, had gone soft in a way she'd not expected this man to ever be soft.

And yet, she remained equally entranced by his hold upon her, impossibly tender and soft from a man whose fingertips and palms proved so large and callused.

She stood there, stiffly, warring with herself. Reluctantly, Glain nodded.

He released her, and she went cold in the place where he'd touched her.

"We'll begin again, tomorrow," he said quietly.

And why did it feel as though they spoke of something entirely different? Why did her heart race and her breath hitch, and her mind think only of new beginnings with this man who loved books and operated his own establishment.

Incapable of anything more than a nod, Glain remained mute.

He, however, may as well have been wholly oblivious to her and her fascination with him and this moment.

Rather, Abaddon perused the shelving beside them, using a finger to skim the titles as he looked. Dropping to his haunches, he stopped his search on one.

He tugged out a volume, and then straightened. "Try this one."

Fighting the magnetic pull of his hazel stare, Glain made herself look at the book he'd given her. "I'm not interested in romantic t..." Her words trailed off. "*A Vindication of the Rights of Women.*" This is what he'd selected for her? She glanced up.

He nudged his chin. "I think you'll enjoy that, and...probably agree with her on much."

Returning her attention to the small bound copy, she fanned the pages, pausing as she went.

"*My own sex, I hope, will excuse me, if I treat them like rational creatures, instead of flattering their fascinating graces, and viewing them as if they were in a state of perpetual childhood, unable to stand alone...*"

Glain continued skimming the volume.

"Taught from their infancy that beauty is woman's scepter, the mind shapes itself to the body, and roaming round its gilt cage, only seeks to adorn its prison."

Glain's breath caught for a second time that morn, but for entirely different reasons than the feel of Abaddon's touch, or the heat of his eyes upon her. But no less entrancing or seductive.

Hopelessly captivated, Glain read and the world ceased to exist beyond anything but the inked black words upon the pages of this seductive text given her by Abaddon Grimoire.

She wanted to keep reading of these philosophies, forever. She—

Glain stopped on a page.

"I earnestly wish to point out in what true dignity and human happiness consists of. I wish to persuade women to endeavor to acquire strength, both of mind and body, and to convince them that the soft phrases, susceptibility of heart, delicacy of sentiment, and refinement of taste, are almost synonymous with epithets of weakness, and that those beings are only the objects of pity, and that kind of love which has been termed its sister, will soon become objects of contempt."

She snapped it shut and reflexively Glain took several much needed steps away from him. "I...I can't read this," she said, her voice weak and breathless to her own ears. She held the book out toward him, both a plea and demand that he take it.

"Sure, you can," he said in that rough murmur. "That's the beauty of a library and books, themselves. You can read anything you want, and you can feel any way you wish to feel reading them." He took a step closer, and then another, effectively erasing all distance that she'd previously built between them.

She could feel as she wished, and yet...

In her mind, she replayed those damning words, over and over again.

"... I wish to persuade women to endeavor to acquire strength, both of mind and body, and to convince them that the soft phrases, susceptibility of heart, delicacy of sentiment, and refinement of taste, are almost synonymous with epithets of weakness, and that those beings

are only the objects of pity, and that kind of love which has been termed its sister, will soon become objects of contempt..."

Her throat worked, and she squeezed her eyes shut, in a bid to fend off the great swell of emotion threatening to drag her under.

"It's rubbish," she said, her voice tight and brittle to her own ears, and she knew her words were a lie, but God help her, she wanted a fight with him. "You've given me rubbish to read."

He placed his lips close to her ear, and her breath caught for a different reason. "You know I haven't, darling," he whispered against that sensitive shell. Delicious little shivers raced down her neck and all the way down her spine, leaving her giddy with a giggle she sought to suppress. "You know you read those words, and saw the value in them, and you know you want more."

He was right. She wanted...more.

Something in the air shifted, growing somehow more charged, more electric.

She should fight the pull. She should move away from him, and this moment, and yet, she angled her head ever closer towards him.

He edged slowly towards her, in that same way.

Two dissimilar people, moving in a like way, drawn towards one another like those magnets her brother played with. An irresistible pull between them.

Even as Abaddon shifted, lowering his mouth to hers, Glain leaned up, and touched her lips to his.

With a guttural growl better suiting a primal beast, he kissed her. His harsh, beautiful lips were a brand upon hers, as though with each slant he sought to learn the feel and taste of her flesh, imprint upon her, and then memorialize this moment for all time.

Sighing, Glain crept her arms about his thickly muscled neck and turned herself over to this. Nay, to the powerful, completely masculine Abaddon Grimoire.

Somehow, this was safer than their previous heated exchange. This man, and this kiss, safer than that bluntly expressed, so very accurate criticism of all that Glain was—of all that she'd let herself, nay made herself, become.

And there, amidst the bookshelves of a circulating library a stranger might enter at any moment, she gave herself over to the passion of this, her first kiss.

Nay, this wasn't a kiss.

This was an embrace. An all-consuming, passion-filled embrace.

Abaddon folded her in his powerful arms, and she pressed against him so close, she felt every defined contour and muscle of sinewy strength.

She felt the growl rumble in his chest, but that low-approving sound never made it past his lips, and it was as though even in passion, he possessed a mastery of restraint.

Suddenly, he shifted his lips away from hers and she whimpered at the loss.

He touched a finger warningly against her swollen mouth, silently reminding her of where they were, and what they did, and how imminent discovery was.

That should have been enough.

Enough for her to come to her senses, slap him, and then race from this moment, this library , and this man.

Only, God help her. She did not. She could not.

Instead, as he leaned closer, tempting her with the promise of another kiss, she lifted into it and him.

"Shh," he breathed against her ear, and she managed nothing more than a jerky nod, acquiescing to his warning and the continuation of his embrace.

He placed a kiss against her lips, and unlike the kiss before, he didn't devour her. He didn't kiss of her and taste of her, like a man who wished to consume, but rather, he explored like the most patient explorer, delving into unchartered territories to which he now staked a powerful claim.

He continued his quest, lightly nipping at her slightly fuller lower lip, and then licking at the corners of her mouth.

She clamped her legs together in a bid to alleviate the sudden pressure that had built there.

Her efforts proved in vain.

A liquid heat pooled at her center, and reflexively she moved her hips against him. That slight thrusting brought her flush with the hard ridge of flesh prodding against her belly.

He chuckled, the sound a low, triumphant, all-pleased masculine rumble.

It didn't grate.

Rather, as he continued to trail his lips down the curve of her neck, lightly nipping and sucking of that flesh, it fueled a heady sense of power that came from his appreciation of her body.

She wasn't a woman men desired.

That was, not a woman anyone desired beyond the size of her dowry and her lofty connection to London's most powerful duke.

But even those lures had never been incentives enough for men to see past the barrier she'd built to keep herself safe and unmarried.

Nay, they all avoided her gaze and her altogether.

Unlike this man.

Abaddon.

He was not repelled by her. Nay, he devoured her, and she went even several shades hotter inside at the realization of the power she had over him. This strong, primal, masculine man wanted *her*.

Abaddon filled a strong, powerful hand with her right buttock, and pressed her even closer to him.

She whimpered and rubbed like the kitchen cat in heat she'd observed two years earlier, and he swallowed that telltale sound of her yearning with his kiss.

He stroked his tongue against hers— a bold, angry lash—and she matched each glide in a dance more forbidden than the waltz.

Glain didn't want this moment to end.

She wanted to feel his hands on her. She ached to know what came after the kiss. She wanted—

The tinny bell at the front of the library jingled.

Abaddon yanked his mouth from hers, and it was all she could do to keep from crying out. As she slumped against the shelves, finding support and purchase as her knees trembled, she should be horrified at the prospect of discovery. Instead, an overwhelming urge to weep at the interruption filled her.

His embrace—nay, their embrace—had been the single most beautiful, special, magical moment of her entire existence.

Abaddon—

Her gaze went to him. A completely cool, collected, and wholly unfazed Abaddon Grimoire, who consulted his timepiece.

"Time's up, darling." He dropped the chain back into his pocket. "You're free to go."

That was what he'd say.

She felt a blush burn up her cheeks.

What in heavens had she done? She was hardly a woman given to lapses in judgement, She'd never, in the whole of her life, lost control of her senses. And in this moment, with this man, she'd done precisely that.

It was a mistake she'd not make again.

With all the aplomb she could muster, Glain straightened on still unsteady legs. "I thank you for your assistance this morning, Mr. Grimoire," she said loudly for the benefit of whichever patron now wandered the circulating room.

He bowed his head. "My pleasure." His heated gaze bore into hers. "It was all my pleasure."

Her heart thumped wildly. Surely, she wasn't merely imagining the double meaning behind that statement?

Slowly, he shifted closer, and her body of its own volition swayed nearer to him. She didn't care about the other patron present. Or the imminent discovery. She should. The threat of ruin should itself be enough to send her fleeing.

Only, she was powerless against this steely man's pull over her.

Abaddon reached out, and with a fluttering in her chest, Glain lifted her mouth to his.

He held a book out.

A book?

The world came crashing, screeching, and sliding to a jarring halt.

He winked, and that wildly beating organ in her chest increased to a frantic double-time.

"If you'll excuse me, I've other patrons to help."

With that, he turned on his heel, stalked off, and left her there fighting to regain control of her wits.

From somewhere in the room, his voice carried over to her. Whatever words he now spoke to his latest patron were muffled, but matter of fact.

As if not even moments ago, he'd been making love to her mouth, and she'd been rubbing herself against the hard, contoured muscles of his powerful body.

Because it clearly hadn't meant anything to him. She'd do well to remember that for the next time she saw him.

Even so, the memory of that kiss remained with her as she quit the library and made the journey back to her family's Mayfair townhouse. As she sailed up the steps a short while later, a dreamy smile played on her lips when the doors were drawn open by the duke's always dutiful servants.

"Where in blazes have you been?"

That cold, icy greeting brought her whirring, crashing back to reality, as only that frosty welcome could.

Her heartbeat slowed to a sickeningly slow halt. "Your Grace," she greeted. The duke had insisted he was always to be 'the duke' or 'Your Grace'. Never: Father. Never: Papa.

In fairness, six feet tall, with a hawkish nose, a harsh mouth, and possessed of a close crop of icy white, meticulously clipped hair, he didn't have the look of any beloved, doting Papa. He exuded power and influence, and in this instance annoyance.

"I've been looking for you, Diamond."

Diamond.

God, how she despised that name. She always had. She'd just not known how very much until Abaddon had laid claim to her given name of Glain.

The duke never sought her out unless he was displeased or unless he required something. Never in her adult life, however, had she given him reason to be disappointed.

Glain gave her maid, a desperate look.

The young woman hastened over.

"I was out," Glain said, quickly entrusting that book Abaddon had chosen for her, to the loyal servant's care. "I—"

The duke's gaze snagged on the title.

Go. Flee. Run. Before he notes—

Only—

The duke frowned, extending a hand that commanded as effective as any words.

Glain's maid hesitated, and then with an apologetic look for her mistress, handed the damning title over to Glain's father.

He methodically flipped through the volume. With every page he assessed, his white eyebrows drew closer and closer together until they formed a harsh, angry line.

Through his agonizing scrutiny, Glain stood stiffly at the center of the marble foyer and took care to keep her gaze concentrated beyond her silent father's shoulder. All the while, mortification spread through her. At having her selected book read. At having it done in this public way, by her father, and with her family servants there to witness.

The duke picked his head up. "What nonsense is this?" He didn't allow her a word edgewise. "What are you reading?"

Her tongue went heavy in her mouth. Her face burned hot. *Oh god.* This was so much worse than she could have ever imagined. "I stumbled upon it —"

"Stumbled upon it *where?*" he demanded.

And from the point where her gaze remained, just above his shoulder, Glain caught her sister at the top of the stairwell that overlooked the foyer. Opal gripped the railing and pleaded silently with her eyes.

"I...Lady Westmorland." The lie slipped out easily, and she discreetly crossed her fingers.

The Duke of Wellington's favored niece and notorious for her political judgment, the lady was afforded the respect of the peerage because of her connections and head for political affairs.

"Lady Westmorland," he muttered. "I should have expected as much."

Just as *Glain* expected, he'd not challenge the powerful peeress.

"Perhaps this is why you're unwed after two Seasons," he snapped, waving one of the copies at her.

Glain kept motionless, her gaze forward. She knew precisely why she was unwed after two Seasons. Because she'd wished it that way and done everything in her power to fashion herself as an icy princess too cold to touch or approach.

Her father gave a look to a nearby footman.

The young, crimson-clad servant hastened over. "Dispose of this," the duke said in clipped, steely tones.

Glain bit the inside of her cheek to keep from crying out.

The footman collected the book chosen for her by Abaddon, and as he rushed off, she felt the overwhelming urge to weep.

She, however, didn't cry.

And she certainly didn't show those signs of weakness the duke so despised in his presence.

Her sister caught her eyes. "I'm so sorry," she mouthed.

Glain managed a small smile.

When the servant had gone, the duke returned his full focus to Glain. "I was looking for you and this is what you were doing? How you occupy your time?" Fury flashed in his eyes. "Do not let it happen again. You have more important matters to see to."

She flexed her fingertips at her side, and drew them into slight, tight balls attempting to drive the tension from them, fighting for composure, fighting for an icy calm to rival his. "What matters would you have me see to, Your Grace."

"I want invitations sent for a private dinner with the Prince of Chernihiv."

"I'll see to it." That loftiest of men, still present in London despite the winter, *would* be one of the few guests the duke would entertain.

Without another word of acknowledgment, the duke stalked off.

Glain remained there, her arms empty of her books, and more miserable than she'd ever been before at the prospect of planning an intimate dinner party for a royal and wishing she could return to a time just twenty minutes earlier with Abaddon Grimoire.

CHAPTER 6

She was back. Sneaking about, and doing so as poorly as she'd done the first time he'd caught her in his circulating library.

It was a clear violation of the promise he'd made the lady's sister, and yet, breach of agreement or not, the last thing he'd ever do was send away a patron.

Not as a matter of business—though he was known as being a shrewd businessman—but because he knew firsthand what it was to be denied books. As the illiterate boy from the streets taken in by the empathetic, altruistic former owner, Abaddon had resolved to see that anyone and everyone who wished to consume those books could and would.

He'd not cared whether his patrons were men, women, or children, and he'd certainly not cared what station they belonged to.

It was why, the moment he'd been stacking shelves at the back and caught sight of her hurrying inside, he'd not ordered her gone, reminding her she wasn't allowed to be here without her elder sister's appreciation.

Her elder sister. Lady Glain, who'd kissed with an abandon and heat he'd never expected of her.

And the memory of her fire and passion, filled him with a familiar rush of desire. She may be ice on the outside, but had proven to be all honeyed warmth on the inside.

"Aren't you going to ask me what I'm doing here?"

That perturbed child's voice slashed across those wicked rememberings, bringing Abaddon back to the moment.

Clad in trousers as she'd been the first time she'd stepped foot inside the library, the girl had her hands on her hips, and scowled impressively up at him.

The better question was why she was here when he expected her sister. Her sister who'd not showed for their latest appointment. After he'd kissed her—that embrace, a fiery conflagration that would leave the lady burned and likely never to return—he'd thought it doubtful she'd find her way back. Even so, there was a wealth of disappointment.

"Did you hear me, Mr. Grim? I was speaking to you?"

Forcing his head out of the clouds, he grinned. "Ah, you want to be seen this time."

"Yes," she said with the direct honesty only an innocent child was capable of. "And it has taken you long enough to notice me."

Oh, he'd noticed her.

He'd simply not addressed her.

"You know your sister doesn't want you here."

"Yes." She gave a wave of her hand. "That doesn't matter."

"The lure of the books is a powerful one."

"I'm not here about your books," she said, no-nonsense. "Not this time." She returned the book she'd been reading to the shelf. "I'm here about my sister...about Glain."

He hooded his eyes. Glain who'd reneged on their agreement. "Oh?"

"She wanted to be here."

Abaddon snorted and resumed tucking the books in his arm onto their proper place on the shelves. "That I highly doubt."

"She did," the girl insisted, with an adamancy fueled by the conviction in those two words. "You must believe me." Opal touched a hand to his arm, staying his efforts. "She wanted to come here, and I never thought she would, because my sister is really, really, really proper."

When it came to the flawless princess who'd entered his library two days ago, that might be one hundred 'propers' short of accurate.

"And I always judge her for it, Mr. Grim," Opal went on in a quiet whisper. "But I saw when she returned home...she was holding a book close, the way only someone who loves a book does. She wanted to read it."

Why did it not surprise him in the least that the girl had both overheard his arrangement with Glain and discovered Glain had shown up as promised for their first meeting? The king's army would be better served if it had people like Opal among their ranks.

Opal's eyes grew even more solemn. "She *wanted* to come back. She *did*."

"But she didn't," he said as gently as he was able. Offering smooth reassurances wasn't something that came natural to him, that deficit a product left over from his days on the streets.

"I know. But there is a reason for it, and I know she will keep her end of your arrangement. It's just she's ever so busy..."

Abaddon stared at her, waiting for her to continue, to explain what it was that kept her elder sister away.

"My sister is planning a dinner party for a prince."

And there it was. The lady was too busy planning a formal affair, for royalty. Royalty hobnobbing with royalty.

"Ah, plans for the lady to wed a prince?"

"I expect that is it, exactly," Opal answered. "He's very important."

As the girl went on with a lengthy list about the gentleman in question, Abaddon shook his head. It was to be expected. In fact, it fit with everything he'd have thought about a lofty one like Glain Carmichael.

Glain was the last manner of woman he should want, and the

world she belonged to, even farther from where he had any wish to be. Far from it. Why, then, did the idea of the fiery beauty who'd come undone in his arms wed to some pencil-mustached prince make him want to gnash his teeth?

Because that fire had given him a glimpse of who she could have been had she been any other woman, born to any other station but the one she belonged to.

Hers was a world he wanted no part of.

Not that there was really a question of whether he would or could be part of that world. That was, beyond the services he offered and provided to the ladies and gentlemen unafraid to enlighten their minds.

Opal tugged on his sleeve, calling his attention away from his thoughts and back to her.

"It's not her fault," she repeated, her enormous eyes rounded and filled with sadness.

The girl desperately wished to see more in her sister. She wanted her to be more than she was. And perhaps that was why he managed to release his annoyance and anger.

"I kept your stack for when you came back," he shared, and in an instant, the sadness vanished, replaced instead with a dazzling joy.

"Indeed?"

She sprung into step beside him as he guided her away from the wide front window where she'd be on display and over to the safer, secluded spot tucked in the corner of the room. A place where she could read and do so without prying eyes or the criticism of people who'd unfairly judge her for the simple sin of reading.

Nay, the station of lords and ladies was one he'd never understand, and one he didn't want to bother trying.

Let them have their princes and fancy dinners.

Unbidden, however, came an unwanted image of a strikingly beautiful Glain with some high-in-the-instep prince from a far-flung land.

"Here," he said, pulling out the chair for Glain's younger sister, picking up the choice he'd made with her in mind. "Have you read this one?" He turned it over.

"*The Mysteries of Udolpho,*" Opal moved her lips silently. She lifted eager eyes to his once more. "Have you?"

"Want to know the truth?"

Wide-eyed, she nodded.

"I've read nearly every book inside this library."

She howled with laughter. "Go on with you."

Abaddon pressed a hand to his heart and made a cross there. "I would never jest about books," he said with enough solemnity to that vow, he managed to quiet her boisterous explosion of mirth.

"Come on, now," Opal whispered, this time more reverently.

"How else could I help patrons know where to find the books they are seeking? Or whether it would suit their interests?"

"Why not let them find them, themselves?" she asked curiously.

"Sometimes," he explained, leaning in, "people are so used to being told what to read that they don't explore anything beyond those types of books. Those people need help opening their eyes to the truth that there's more out there."

"Like my sister," she said. Reaching inside the sack slung over her right shoulder, she fished out a small, familiar copy.

He skimmed the title. *A Vindication of the Rights of Women.*

"I saved this," Opal said.

Saved it. His jaw hardened. "Did you?" He should have expected—

"My father discovered her with it," the girl explained, so suddenly, so unexpectedly, Abaddon's head came flying up with a force to wrench the muscles along his neck. "I told you she wanted to read it. I know because when the duke berated her for reading such books, and took it away, Glain looked like she was going to weep."

With every word of the tragic scene she painted, a vise squeezed at his chest, until it was near impossible to get a pain-free breath in through his constricted lungs. It was somehow easier when he'd despised Glain for being a lofty sort who thought herself too good for the books here, than in knowing the truth—that she was in fact a woman who wished to read but was caught like some tragic butterfly tucked under a glass, her movements restricted, her flight stifled by the barriers wrapped around her.

"Do you know what I've learned, Mr. Grim?" Opal asked through the tumult of his thoughts.

He could only manage to shake his head.

"I've learned that the covers of books are quite unimpressive. Some are marbled leather. Some are speckled. Some old. Many have gold lettering. But they're all the same, and yet..." She fanned the pages of the copy of *The Mysteries of Udolpho*. "It would be deuced unfair, and tragic even if one assumed all the contents within those pages were the same when there's so very much more to them...if one just looks."

There's so very much more to them...if one just looks.

He smiled wistfully. "How did you get so wise?"

A slow, impish smile dimpled both her plump cheeks. "I read."

He chuckled. "Clever girl."

She beamed under that slight praise, and with all she'd imparted, the window she'd opened to her and her sister's world, he wondered how sparse words of approval and affection had been conferred. He'd wager not at all. That glimpse Opal had given had also revealed precisely how and why Lady Glain Carmichael had become the woman she had.

"Will you read?" he invited, motioning to the book she held in her fingers.

Her smile widened. "I would be happy to, Mr. Grim."

With that, Opal proceeded to read the book he'd provided her. How comfortable she was with it. How happy the reading of a simple story made her. And he wondered what Glain had been like before she'd been so shaped and molded by the heartless, cruel duke Opal had described. More, he wondered who she would be if she managed to break free of him and those constraints built by the gilded cage of Polite Society.

And dangerously, inexplicably, he had an urge to be the one who helped her.

CHAPTER 7

When Opal's governess reported her charge missing again, Glain knew precisely where to locate her sister.

After the day and a half of planning a tedious dinner party for the duke's latest, most important guest, Glain welcomed the opportunity of escape. And if she were being honest with herself, she relished coming to the Chetham's Subscription Library again.

*And seeing him...*A voice taunted at the back of her mind.

For yes, she could be honest with herself in that. She'd wanted to see *him*. She...liked Mr. Abaddon Grimoire.

It wouldn't make sense to most, but it made all the sense in the world to her.

She liked how he didn't treat her with deference and unfailing politeness for the simple reason of her birthright as a duke's daughter.

She liked that he challenged her both in the form of questioning and in the books he'd selected that would expand her mind and learning.

She appreciated that he was honest when even the smiles of the people in the world she'd been born to were false.

Nothing, however, could have prepared her for the sight of Abaddon as he was now, laughing and conversing with her sister.

Every other word of her enthusiastic sister's chatter drifted over...

"...and Emily is always crying...but I don't dislike her for it...because..."

On the other hand, Abaddon's deep baritone was so low as to be hushed and largely lost to Glain so that she only heard the occasional question posed. "...how does the author use...?"

"Oh, well, I think it is very clear," Opal said matter of factly with all the confidence in her opinion most gentlemen fresh from university displayed. "Everything about the setting is ominous. The buildings are soaring. The passageways dark and mysterious and..."

Abaddon leaned in towards Glain's sister, and Glain found herself leaning forward, too, in a bid to hear whatever he'd say next.

Only, she couldn't, and she mourned the loss of all the words he spoke.

For she also knew he didn't speak with the same judgment and condescension Glain's own father had shown about the books he'd found her with. And she knew for the simple reasons that Abaddon posed questions about the book they discussed, and her sister answered with ease and relaxedness. Nay, this was no condescending lecture.

He sat there so comfortably at a tiny round oak table entirely too small for his six feet, four-inch physique, chatting comfortably with a young girl about books that fascinated her. Nor did Abaddon judge Opal for her interests or seek to steer her to books that were safer topics and considered more suitable for a young lady. Rather, they conversed freely, animatedly, over a handful of leather volumes, and whatever questions he posed had Opal chattering like a magpie. Her cheeks bright. Her eyes sparkling as they'd never been at home.

And God help Glain, in that moment she fell more than a little in love with Abaddon Grimoire.

In a world, where noblemen—fathers, older brothers, and

husbands—didn't have the time or inclination to bother with their daughters, sisters, and wives, Abaddon saw them.

Not just women, a young girl.

Her eyes slid shut under the powerful wave of emotion that crested within her breast.

As a child, Glain herself had been even more invisible than she was now. Her father certainly hadn't a use for her. She'd not even minded so much. She'd simply thought that was the way of the world and had instead relished every moment spent with her free-spirted, loving mother. Then her mother had died giving birth to Flint, and Glain had become a solitary, lonely child, grateful for the brother and sister.

Two children whom the duke also hadn't given a jot about beyond the fact he'd at last had an heir.

Glain opened her eyes, drinking once more of the sight of Abaddon and Opal.

Her sister's lips moved a mile a moment. Her cheeks were flushed with happy color, and Glain's throat worked under the force of emotion.

She fell in love with him for being a man who not only didn't seek to restrict a girl's or woman's growth, but who treated them as equals in every way.

She fell in love with him for not thinking himself too important to bother with a girl.

It hardly mattered that he'd proven harsh and unforgiving in his opinion of Glain herself. After all, he wasn't wrong. He saw what the world saw and made the assumption she'd wanted the world to make —that she was some duke's privileged, pampered daughter. And not interested in being more than that.

Oh, how she wished though that he saw...her.

He'd given her those books.

He'd read her and rightly deduced that she both needed and wanted books that would challenge her and more, ones that would make her challenge the existing order.

"Glain!" Opal's happy shout filtered around the room, and Glain cringed at having been caught watching them.

Abaddon slid an inscrutable look her way, and Glain tried to make something out of that piercing gaze.

Wood scraped loudly upon wood, as Opal shoved back her chair, hopped to her feet, and raced over to join Glain. "I am ever so happy you came, after all!" She threw herself at Glain and nearly knocked them both off balance with that hug.

Some great shift had occurred between her and her sister. What had changed?

Stiffening, Glain awkwardly returned that half-embrace, feeling Abaddon's eyes upon them still.

"You can't keep rushing off without an escort, poppet," she gently chided, stroking the top of her sister's head in the same manner her mother had Glain's. Her sister, however, had never known their mother. "It's not safe."

"Mr. Grim will ensure no harm befalls me."

"Yes, I believe that." Glain lifted her gaze from her sister and looked to Abaddon. His opaque gaze revealed nothing of his inner thoughts. Unnerved by the unswerving intensity of those cobalt irises, she glanced down at Opal once more. "However, anything could happen to you on your way to and from the library."

"It won't," Opal said in an instant, with all the confidence only a child who'd remained untouched by the pain and suffering of life knew. And this, here, was alternately Glain's greatest accomplishment and her greatest failing.

Glain met Abbadon's gaze once more. "Wait for me in the carriage, Opal," she quietly directed.

And surprise of greatest surprises, Opal gathered up her books, held them to her chest, and with her head down, headed for the door.

The tinny belly jingled and Glain's maid waiting there escorted the recalcitrant girl from the library, closing the door behind them with a quiet click, leaving Glain and Abaddon alone.

She tensed, bracing for the barrage of insults and a verbal affront from him.

"Nothing to say?" she asked, angling her chin up a fraction

"You came back."

"To claim my sister." *And* because she'd wanted to come.

"You wanted to come," he predicted, his slightly graveled murmuring entrancing for the coarseness of it—tones that made him very real, in ways she'd never known men *could* be real, and it unsteadied her.

Glain fought her way through the dazed sensation in her head. She glanced down at the open book, and to give her shaking fingers purpose, she picked up the small volume, turned it over to read the title. "And I see you have my sister reading more of these horror stories." *I want to read them...I want to read these stories, too...* a voice in her head silently wept.

"We had an agreement," she said sharply, setting the copy down hard and quickly. It hit the tabletop with a soft thump. "Do you always fail to honor your pledges, Abaddon?" She wanted a fight. Spoiled for one.

Only he didn't comply.

Rather, his powerful gaze remained vague, impossible to make anything out of.

"The way I see it, your failure to honor the terms we'd set allowed me some greater freedoms on my end," he said quietly.

Glain bit the inside of her cheek. Where was Abbadon's vitriol? Why wasn't he coldly mocking or jeering this time?

The fight went out of her. "Thank you for being patient with her," she said. Unable to meet his eyes, Glain trained her gaze just beyond his shoulder. *And me...thank you for being patient with me.* Those, however, were the words she couldn't bring herself to speak, deserved though, they may be.

Abaddon inclined his head. "You don't need to thank me for that. She's a clever girl, with a head for learning, and a strength of character that will serve her well in life."

And it was certainly just one of Glain's many failings that she found herself envying her sister for the praise heaped upon her by this man.

"She is," she murmured, and there was a small amount of self-pride there, too. For all the ways in which Glain was a shadow of a person, she'd managed to protect her sister far longer than anyone had protected her.

"She's like you," Abaddon said, yanking her back from her musings, and a laugh exploded from her lips before she registered the somber set to his harsh, angular features.

Glain peered at his face. "You're serious." Surely not. Only, she didn't take him as one who jested freely.

"Deadly so," he said. "You've not been afraid to go toe-to-toe with me."

She dampened her mouth. "I wanted to return," she found herself confiding, knowing she should be horrified. "I just...had other obligations I was required to see to."

"I know."

He knew? Warmth spiraled through her whole being. Why was he being so nice?

"Here." He reached behind him and then slid closer, and her breath hitched as he extended a hand.

Cold leather penetrated her palms that in her haste she'd failed to cover with gloves.

She read the title, and relief so palpable, so beautiful and lifelike and strong slammed into her. The force of those emotions rolling together weighted her eyes shut.

Her father had burned them.

"You have another copy," she said, her voice clogged and thick with something that felt very much like tears. Which was of course, impossible. She didn't cry. And certainly not with relief, and certainly not over books.

"No," he murmured, grazing a finger down the curve of her cheek, the callused pad of his two middle fingers a seductive caress that obliterated all possibility of rational thought, as she felt only that ragged little brush. It brought her eyes weighted shut, and muddled her thoughts and her senses, so that she could only feel...and think of the kiss she'd known in this very room. "That's the one I gave you."

It took a moment for that handful of murmured words to penetrate the haze his quixotic touch had wrought, and then it did.

...That's the one I gave you...

As in the copy. As in...

"Your sister rescued it," he confirmed.

Rescued it. Which meant...

Glain's entire body tensed, and her eyes came flying open, and she at last registered the look in his. The glimmer she'd taken as desire, she now saw for what it really was.

Oh, God.

Pity. It radiated from his eyes, searing her in a different way, and she recoiled, retreating from that sentiment, and for her startling lapse in composure and control of her senses. "I don't need your pity, sir," she hissed, swatting the hand reaching towards her once more.

"I don't pity you."

"*Liar.*

"I understand you more, Glain," he murmured, striding over, and she realized she'd backed away from him, and he slowly edged out that space. Not threatening, but also direct.

"I'm not some complex puzzle, Mr. Grimoire," she said tightly, between clenched teeth. "I'm not a scientific study for you to try and make sense of."

"I've never been one for puzzles," he murmured. "But I somehow seem to make all number of exceptions where you're concerned, darling."

Darling.

That endearment rolled together with his words knocked loose the remainder of the argument on her lips, and it flew from her head.

She was just a woman. But no one had seen that. Not before him. And likely never again, after.

Her lips trembled. "Here, now," he murmured, tracing the pad of his thumb along that quivering flesh.

Glain's breath caught. The earth stopped spinning, and yet she found herself dizzy like she'd spun in a thousand fast-moving circles, dazed by that soft, mesmerizing touch.

He let his arm fall, and she silently, secretly cried out for the loss.

Only, he did not retreat.

His gaze lingered on the flesh he'd so gently stroked with his finger.

He was so close, his mouth so near hers, all she need do was stretch up on tiptoe and their lips would meet.

She trailed the tip of her tongue over that flesh which prickled with the memory of the feel of that first...and last...kiss.

Abaddon leaned down slowly, allowing her to move, to flee, to retreat, but God help her she couldn't. Nor did she wish to. Her lids grew heavy, as she stretched up, towards him, towards the kiss she craved.

And then their lips touched. Her breathy moan mingled with his low, guttural groan. That sound rumbled within his chest, and moved through her and once again, she surrendered herself to this man's embrace.

He slanted his mouth over hers with an ardency of one who wished to devour her, and she matched him hunger for hunger.

Gripping the front of his soft wool jacket to keep herself steady, she pulled him nearer.

With the pad of the same thumb that first kindled the flames of her desire, he pressed along the curve of her jaw, delicately prodding, wordlessly urging her to open for him, and Glain did. She let her lips part and let him inside, and whimpered the instant his tongue touched hers.

He tasted faintly of mint and honey—an unexpectedly sweet taste for a man so hard and powerful—and it liquefied her. She lashed her tongue against his, swirling her flesh around his, in a bid to consume him and that sweetness.

Abaddon sank his fingers into her hips, kneading the flesh, then slipped his palms under her buttocks, cupping her.

The life drained from her limbs and she went weak in the knees, but he simply caught her, and edged her back, guiding her to rest on the edge of the small oak table.

Of their own volition, her legs slipped open, the fabric of her dress crunching in a shamefully hedonistic rustle that should have recalled where she was and stopped her. Instead, she found the ache between her legs throbbed all the more, and she was incapable of centering herself on anything other than that ache that was both terrible and wonderful all at the same time.

Abaddon gently nipped at her tongue. He was a primitive beast marking her, and she returned that light bite in kind.

He growled his approval, and Glain thrilled at it—and in this, a powerful awareness of her femininity. She reveled in her desire and in this glorious man's hunger for her. In a world where people disdained her, looking upon her as the aloof, frosty figure she'd deliberately fashioned herself into, Abaddon saw a woman capable of passion and desire.

He palmed her breasts, and a low moan spilled from her lips that sound lost to his kiss, before he drew his mouth away.

She whimpered at the loss, but he merely shifted his attentions, touching his lips to the shell of her ear, flicking that flesh with the tip of his tongue then moving onward in his quest.

He placed his lips against her neck, touching them to the place where her pulse pounded for him and his embrace.

Abaddon lightly suckled and nipped at that spot, and on a shuddery sigh, she tangled her fingers in his unfashionably long golden strands and held him close.

She'd never believed she was capable of this because she had come to see in herself what the whole world did. Only to find, she *was* capable of great emotion and fire and burning, and that she wanted all of it.

She wanted to live life as fully as this embrace. She wanted to know love and passion and—

And she never could.

Glain wrenched back, recoiling from that truth and this embrace she ached to continue. She wept inside and railed at the impossibility of what she'd wanted.

"Stop," she rasped, and even as he instantly ended that kiss, Glain shoved him.

Despite her ineffectual push against his broad, powerful physique, he straightened so very casually...as if they'd not just been making love with their mouths, and took several steps away from her.

Glain jumped up. Her skirts fell noisily about her ankles and to give her hands something to do, to give herself a purposeful task so she didn't have to meet Abaddon's eyes, she frantically patted at the front of her dress.

The bell at the front of the library jingled announcing a patron, and Glain lifted a frantic stare to Abaddon, needing him to retreat lest they be seen standing so closely together. Yet, with the speed of a London pickpocket who'd filched her reticule outside the theatre one night, years earlier, Abaddon had already moved,

Glain kept her head down and headed for the door.

"My lady," Abaddon called. "You're not going to want to forget your book." He pointed to the volume she'd thought her father had burned, the one Opal rescued and returned.

And the only reason she grabbed it was so the dark-eyed patron now giving her a curious look didn't wonder at her empty hands.

Throwing her shoulders back and tilting her chin, Glain marched from the library with her head held high and not a single word more for Abaddon Grimoire.

CHAPTER 8

Abaddon didn't have too much of a problem with the nobility.

Yes, he thought they were hoity-toity, self-important snobs, but he also had seen enough of those men and women come through the door of this library to know they were to be pitied more than anything.

Gilded birds, the lot of them, trapped in cages, with their wings clipped, and no hope of flight or escape.

He'd seen enough and had enough experiences with them to also know their world was the last one he wished to belong to.

That those people weren't the kind he cared to rub shoulders with— aside from his dealings with the ones eager to fill their minds with knowledge or escape in the pages of the books he offered.

That was, with the exception of the Duke of Strathearn, his greatest sponsor, and the latest gentleman to enter his shop.

And now the exception includes a certain lady who kisses like a temptress,

"A quiet day," the duke remarked. Tugging free his gloves, Strathearn stuffed them inside the front of his fine woolen cloak and cast an interested look out the window. "That is with the exception of... that one."

He followed the other man's pointed stare to where Glain, her cheeks red from either her blush or the cold of the winter air, moved with purposeful steps towards the black lacquered carriage waiting across the street.

Abaddon grunted. "You know, winters in London are quieter. To be expected there aren't as many patrons," he said, hoping that was enough to throw the other man off wherever this questioning was likely going.

Alas, his attempts proved in vain.

"I don't recall seeing Lady Diamond here before," Strathearn remarked.

"You know her?" Abaddon asked, that uncharacteristically impulsive question slipping out before he could call it back, and he silently cursed himself that lapse as his closest and only friend turned that sudden, entirely-too-interested focus back on Abaddon.

"Indeed. Our fathers were close as only two powerful dukes who took themselves and their stations too seriously could be."

Of course, the duke would know a fellow duke's daughter. Those two would move in the same circles. And it also meant, Strathearn had known Glain since she'd been a girl. "Played together as children, did you?" Feigning casualness, Abaddon forced a drollness into his tone, attempting to pull more information from the other man about what Glain had been like as a girl.

The other man scoffed. "Hardly. She was a child, ten years my junior. My recollections of her largely include a silent, sullen girl too self-important to speak, even when spoken to. Her aloofness as a child, however, is nothing compared to the glacial woman she's become. Now she's Polite Society's greatest Diamond, just as her Christian name suggests, as glitteringly beautiful as that precious stone, but as cold and unfeeling as it, too." The other man's lips tipped up in a derisive smile. "Her reputation as an ice princess precedes her."

Ice princess?

The frigid moniker given the lady hardly matched the passionate creature who'd come undone in Abaddon's arms not once, but twice now. No wonder she'd been cross when he called her princess. A woman who lifted into his kiss and whose hips moved rhythmically while he stroked his tongue against her, and—

Abaddon took a slow, steadying breath, pushing back those desirous musings.

"You seem to have a lot of questions about the lady," the duke remarked, steepling his fingers, and studying Abaddon over the top of them.

"She's a new patron." The fib slipped smoothly from his tongue as only a boy, who'd lived and lied in the streets of East London could manage. Determined to put an end to the discussion, he proceeded to gather up the books Glain's sister had been reading, stacking them in a neat pile to put them away for when she returned. "It's my business to know about the people who enter my library." His arms full, Abaddon headed for the front.

He'd first met Strathearn seven years earlier, when the man had inherited his late father's title and obscene amounts of wealth and come to Abaddon's circulating library with an offer of some twenty-thousand pounds to renovate the building and update the volumes by some two thousand books. From that moment on, the two had become unlikely friends. That friendship, however, did not mean Abaddon wanted or intended to talk about the desirous Lady Glain.

After he'd set aside Opal's books, Abaddon returned to where Strathearn, standing precisely as he'd left him, stared at him with a concerned look.

"What?" Abaddon asked impatiently.

"You'd do well to avoid that one, Grimoire."

"What would you have me do?" he snapped. "Turn her out of my library?" It was a vow he'd made, something he'd sworn never to do. Now, the other man would expect Abaddon do that to Glain?

"You can't forbid her from entering," his friend allowed. "No doubt she'd attempt to ruin you—would have her father do so—for that slight."

His friend spoke of Glain's father, that nobleman who'd confiscated her book? Something told Abaddon Strathearn knew even less about the lady than Abaddon himself, did.

"Just steer clear of her, as much as you're able, Grimoire. All of Polite Society does. Ladies and gentlemen alike."

He drew back in surprise. A duke's daughter, refined in every way, one who advised on rules of decorum, was shunned?

"There's such a thing as lords and ladies too aloof for even Polite Society," the duke explained, following Abaddon's train of thought. "She is one of them. Gentlemen have courted her, only to be coldly mocked as they did. She is known for having a lofty opinion of herself."

Annoyance rolled through him. "Perhaps those men are just bitter, attempting to save face." He'd seen enough gents with inflated heads, who wouldn't take well to rejection.

"Possibly," Strathearn allowed. "I thought as much, too, once."

Something hovered unspoken in his friend's words but as real as if it had been uttered.

An unpleasant sensation roiled in his gut. "You courted the lady," he said, his voice, rougher than usual. An image of the regal, basically royal pair together set his teeth on edge.

"Not at all." A light flush filled the duke's sharp cheeks. "In my case, I attempted nothing more than a dance with the lady. When I attempted to speak with her through the set, she looked away, appearing bored, and told me if I was searching for shared interests, not to bother, as there was absolutely nothing either of us had in common, except our link to a dukedom and in that, she was right. We are *nothing* alike."

The duke dropped an arm around Abaddon's shoulders. "And you, dear friend, will do well to remember that. A lady as cold and unfeeling and heartless as that one is also one who'd ruin you and your business, for nothing more than the pleasure it would bring her in doing so."

As if he considered the matter put to rest, Strathearn gave Abaddon a light thump on the back, and headed off to inspect the latest shipment of books he'd personally funded.

Tension rippled through Abaddon's frame as he clenched and unclenched his jaw. That harsh assessment Strathearn had leveled at Glain, somehow grated as much as the idea of the lady with the other man.

It didn't matter that he'd been similar in his first and even his *second* opinion of her. The uncaring, unfeeling, cold woman described by Strathearn was inconsistent with the one who looked after her younger sister and brother with a greater care than even a governess would—or in this, case, had.

Glain had proven to be a woman with protective layers about her, and he found himself wanting to peel each one back, to discover who she really was inside, this lady who desperately longed for the freedom of reading books, but who feared doing so.

Abaddon knew one thing definitively—despite his friend's warnings, Abaddon had no intention of ending the arrangement he'd made with Glain, and he had every intention of finding out for himself more about the enigmatic beauty.

CHAPTER 9

In Glain's nineteen years, she'd been a favored guest of the king, dining in the palace alongside him and some of the greatest dignitaries in the world. She'd attended famed performances given at both Covent Garden Theatre and the Theatre Royal of Drury Lane.

Never once in all Glain's attendance at those extravagant affairs had she felt the eager thrill of anticipation that she did the following morning as she made the short walk from her carriage to Abaddon's circulating library.

She'd never met anyone like him in her entire life.

In fact, she'd never known there could be anyone like him.

As she reached the narrow front stoop, she paused, schooling her features and calming her heart.

Or attempting to, anyway.

He was just a man.

A powerful, virile, quixotic man.

No, those reminders meant to steady her didn't help.

How could they? How, when he'd kissed her with so much passion that her lips and body still burned with the remembrance of the feel of him.

She—

The door opened, jarring her from her desirous musings, and a blush burned up her body as one of Abaddon's patrons beat a hasty berth around her. Glain came crashing back to the moment.

Enough. You are not some silly, pathetic creature with her head stuck up in the clouds. You are reasonable and rational and unmoved by everything.

She gave her head a slight, clearing shake, and entered the shop.

After she'd drawn the door shut behind her, she pushed the hood of her cloak back just enough so that she might take a look around.

Busier than it had been, all her previous times visiting combined, the circulating library buzzed with patrons, perusing shelves, and sitting at the tables throughout the room. She moved her gaze past all of those lords and ladies, many whose fine dress gave away their station. The men and women were so absorbed in whatever books they read that they didn't so much as spare her a glance.

And then Glain found him with her gaze.

Her eyes landed and locked on Abaddon. With his arms filled with a piled of books, he moved between the shelves his arms. Stacked against his broad chest as they were, the volumes looked impossibly small.

Just like that, her heart jumped and kept at a dangerously fast pace, and her mind, body, and soul recalled her and Abaddon's latest embrace.

As if he felt her stare, Abaddon paused, looking her way.

Glain shot a hand up, giving a slight, bold wave that would have scandalized her father, and shocked society.

But she didn't care. Something in being here and being with him freed her in ways she'd never been in her entire life.

He—

Abaddon inclined his head in return, then casually proceeded with those books he carried. He set them down on a gentleman's table. The two men, dissimilar in every way: Abaddon, broadly muscled, chiseled of stone, and bearing a look of one cut from the same cloth as the all-powerful god, Zeus. The other tall, but slender to the point of painfully so, and with a crop of black Byron-esque curls, artfully and deliberately arranged.

Abaddon's presence commanded. He finished up with his patron, and she felt her pulse skitter to a too-fast beat. She held her breath in anticipation.

Now, he'd come see her.

Now, he'd—

Now, he turned on his heel and headed down another aisle.

She wrinkled her nose. Her cheeks warmed by a thousand degrees, and she forced the hand still hanging mid-air back to her side.

It was not a familiar way she found herself—him not looking at her. Him not seeing her.

That's how the entire world treated her.

But all those other people, she'd sought to dissuade from noticing her or talking to her. For the world, she'd donned that frosty façade so that she might remain unmarried and stay with her younger siblings.

Abaddon on the other hand, for him she'd let her guard down and let herself be as approachable as she could be. That was, as approach-able as she could make herself be.

Abaddon who was so very indifferent to Glain.

With all the grace and aplomb, she could muster still, Glain marched through the library, heading for that table tucked in the corner where she'd found Abaddon reading with her sister. Unlike yesterday when there'd been a number of volumes littering that small oak table, today it was empty.

Unlike before, he'd not pulled volumes he thought she might like to read, ones he'd set there to challenge her, and for her to challenge herself. Which was fine. Or really, it should be. She didn't need him picking books for her. She was more than capable of seeing to the task herself.

Oddly, that left her bereft.

For, she'd found she rather liked knowing he'd thought of her and picked books with her specifically in mind. Because it had meant he'd been thinking about her.

Just as she'd been incapable of thinking about anything other than him and his kiss. *Their* kiss.

To give herself a purposeful task, Glain unfasted the clasp at her throat, and shrugged out of her cloak. Close to where her table rested, several hooks hung bare upon the wall, and she availed herself of one of them.

Glain headed off in search of a book. Only as she moved along the increasingly familiar aisles, she found her gaze not perusing the many gold-leafed titles but searching instead for him.

Stop it.

Stop it.

Stop it, this instant.

Those commands were a deliberate mantra, she played over and over in her head.

Without seeing the title, Glain tugged out a book positioned at eye-level and peered through the peephole she'd made.

And then promptly wished she hadn't.

Her gaze locked on Abaddon and a pretty young woman with plump cheeks, and an equally pleasingly plump form—voluptuous in every way that Glain— painfully thin—was not.

He was speaking, giving that lady several books. Only as the young woman collected each one he handed over, her eyes weren't on the titles but rather the dashing man who'd personally selected them for her.

Glain's teeth set together hard, clanking so noisily it was a wonder the duo didn't hear her.

But then, why should they? They would have to be engrossed in anything other than one another and their blasted conversation to have noted the fact that Glain stood watching them, a vicious, insidious poison-filled jealousy channeling through her veins.

Why *shouldn't* Abaddon note the petite, full-figured woman?

With her midnight black curls, and wide green eyes, and ample curves, she was a sight.

Unlike Glain who who'd perfected icy, aloof indifference and sharp, disdainful glares, the other woman smiled freely. Damn if a different emotion other than jealousy didn't form in that wad in her throat. And if she didn't know better and if she were actually capable of the sentiment, something that felt like tears.

A low rumble: Abaddon's laugh, filled the aisles.

Something he said, a low murmured response he gave the lady elicited a little giggle and a brighter blush, and Glain could not help it.

She growled.

A low, primal, primitive, raw growl climbed her tight throat and lodged there.

Abaddon's gaze crashed and clashed with hers, noting her noticing him and Lady Perfection.

Heart thumping, Glain swiftly jammed the book onto the shelf.

Mayhap he'd not seen her. Perhaps he'd merely been searching for another book for his perfectly lovely patron. After all, Glain had arrived this morning, expecting it was going to be entirely different between her and Abaddon. How could it not? There'd been a seismic shift forged by his embraces. He'd shaken her and her world. He'd left her hot and burning, and longing for more—longing to see him.

Abaddon, on the other hand, hadn't even looked at her. Throughout her time here, patrons had come and then gone, until only a handful remained, and still he didn't visit her.

She stared blankly at the books that sat between her and Abaddon. That stack proved a blessed screen that saved her from seeing him and the latest woman he offered his assistance to.

In fact, he'd helped those two other patrons more than Glain, whom he'd hardly noticed, at all.

One a young dandy for whom he'd dropped that stack of books on a table.

The other, a striking beauty who made little attempt to conceal her interest.

Glain compressed her lips into a firm line. Good, let him entertain Lady Beautiful. That meant he wasn't bothering her.

"Have a good look?"

She gasped and spun about so quickly, her skirts snapped noisily at her ankles. Glain grasped the shelf to keep herself on her feet.

Abaddon stood at the end of the aisle with his arms crossed in that lazy negligent pose that put his heavily muscled chest on full display, only heightening his masculine appeal.

He strode toward her with those languid, panther-like steps that dried up all the moisture in her mouth.

And then his words registered.

The crooked grin on his hard lips indicated he'd noticed her scrutiny.

She gasped. "I most certainly was *not* looking at you," she said on a furious whisper the moment he reached her. "Why should I care one way or the other if you were helping the young lady?" *She didn't.* "I didn't,"

His opaque gaze glittered...with amusement? "I meant, did you have a good look at the books," he drawled.

Glain rocked back on her heels. "At the books," she repeated dumbly.

Abaddon nodded and pointed to the objects in question. She followed his gesture, and instantly recoiled, drawing her toes tight in her satin slippers.

That was what he'd been talking about.

"Y-Yes," she said, the words emerging in a high-pitched squeak she didn't recognize as her own voice. "I...I had a great look. A very good one." Great was better than good. "Great," she repeated her earlier clarifier. "Just... great," she muttered.

That glint in his dark blue eyes gleamed all the brighter, and he leaned down. "Noticing me and one of my patrons, were you?" he murmured, amusement lacing his deep baritone, and her cheeks burned hot with another blush.

"I...was not. At least, not intentionally," she mumbled.

He grinned.

His smile was that of a cat who swallowed the canary and chased it down with a bowl of fresh cream.

And damned if she didn't wish she were that ill-fated bird, so she could be free of this exchange, and his knowing eyes.

She'd noticed him.

No, she'd not just noticed him, she'd been watching him with a lady, and by the way she bristled and flushed, she'd not liked it, one bit.

There was a masculine thrill of satisfaction at the fact she'd been...jealous.

"Have a problem seeing me with another woman, is it?" he asked, and the lady's blush burned several shades brighter.

"Absolutely not. At all." She slashed her gloved palms down towards the wood floor. "At. All."

"I believe you already said that, darling," he drawled.

If possible, she went an even brighter shade of crimson, her cheeks burning bright enough it was a wonder she didn't catch fire.

"Because it bore repeating. It's hardly my concern which patrons you spend your time with."

He schooled his features. "In which case, if you'll excuse me. The lady still required—"

"No, she doesn't. She's leaving," she exclaimed, pointing at the lady in question, just as the young woman swept outside, along with the last of the library patrons, until he and Glain were alone.

"So you didn't care I was assisting a pretty young lady?"

She gritted her teeth loud enough that they clinked noisily together. "*Was* she pretty?"

"Oh, I think we'd say she is."

Glain pursed her lips.

Bringing her shoulders back, the lady donned an indifferent and icy don't-approach-me look he wagered she used with lords and ladies alike at *ton* events. "What you do is not my business, Mr. Grimoire," she said quietly. "The only reason I may have—"

"Did," he corrected with all the insolence only he could manage.

"Noticed you, was because we entered into an agreement with one another, and as such, it is my expectation that as I am honoring my commitment you will honor yours, and make yourself available to me."

Abaddon preened. "So you noticed me, did you?"

"As I said, it was hard not to notice, as we have an agreement, and you should have been helping me, as our time together is limited."

The lady spoke the way only a peeress could.

Insolent. Rude. Filled with a knowledge of her own self-importance.

At their first meeting, he had judged her mightily for it.

Since that day, however, a great shift had occurred in how he viewed her.

"Why are you looking at me like that?" she demanded, stealing a glance about. "Go," she ordered. "Find me something to read."

Her eyes were faintly pleading, directly belying the command of her words.

Abaddon remained rooted there, contemplating her still. "Do you know what I think, Glain?" he murmured quietly.

She tensed, but did not shake her head, so he continued without her invitation to do so.

"I believe you like being here. I believe your being here has only a small thing to do with the agreement we made, and everything to do with the fact you want to be here, Glain."

Her eyes flew wide, her golden eyebrows shooting to her hairline.

"And I also believe," he said, leaning in close, "that you like me."

The long, graceful column of her throat worked, and he expected she'd deny his last claim.

But she didn't. Instead, her gaze slid away from his, and to a point beyond his shoulder.

Intrigued and filled with more than a little masculine triumph at her unspoken admission, he brushed a finger down the curve of her jaw. "You don't deny it."

"Why would I?" she asked tightly as he guided her gaze back to his. She still, however, directed her words to a point above his brow. "I...do like you. I do like being here, that is," she said on a rush.

"You don't have to act like that, you know," he murmured, moving his caress higher, brushing his fingers along her sharp, chiseled cheekbone. "Haughty, cold. Unfeeling."

She stiffened, and then pulled away. "I *am* haughty, cold, and unfeeling," she said on a furious whisper.

"A woman who burns hot like you is anything but." He stroked the pad of his thumb along her slightly fuller lower lip, and rubbed, setting that pouting flesh a'tremble. "A woman who kisses like you do, Glain, has fire inside, and is far more than the silk-stocking ordering me and everyone about."

Glain drew back like he'd struck her. Her cheeks paled.

"You don't know anything of it," she spoke in hushed tones, laced with fury, and then in a clear indication she intended to say nothing else of it, spun on her heel, and marched, in the opposite direction, to the end of the aisle.

He easily overtook her long strides with his even longer ones.

Catching her gently but firmly by the arm, he steered her through the doorway located at the very end of the row.

He closed the door behind them, shutting them away in his private offices. The click of that door drowned out the lady's gasp.

"What do you think you are doing?" she demanded on a furious whisper. "This is hardly proper."

"Well, it's hard to have a proper conversation in the middle of the library."

"I'm not looking to have a proper conversation."

"An improper one, then," he said, keeping his features deadpan.

"Not an improper one, eith—" Her words abruptly cut off, and she wrinkled her nose in that endearing way of hers. "You're teasing."

He also suspected that two days ago she wouldn't have been able to spot whether a person was teasing her. He suspected even more that no one ever had teased her.

"Do you know what I think, Glain?"

She tensed, and for a long moment said absolutely nothing, and for an even longer one, she didn't so much as twitch a muscle or blink. And he waited.

Because he also knew she wanted to know...that eventually she'd give him the go-ahead to continue.

And then ever so faintly, but still discernable, she shook her head.

Abaddon continued. "I think you're the most flawless lady, I've ever seen walk into my library. And if I were one who rubbed shoulders with your sort, in ballrooms and dining rooms, then I bet you'd be the most flawless lady I met there, too. But no one is as perfect as you let on that you are. No one is that cold. No one is that icy and unapproachable."

"I a-m," Her voice caught slightly.

"You are, but it's by design, so I'm left with the question of...why?"

"Because I'm some puzzle," she gritted out. "Some mystery that you'd seek to solve. Well, I've told you before, I'm not a mystery to make sense of. Let me spare you once more the disillusion that I'm anything more than precisely what you've taken me for." She made to step around him, but he slid into her path, blocking her way.

"No, that isn't it, Glain," he said quietly.

"Then, what is it?" she cried softly, modulated even in frustrated fury, as only she could be.

"Because like I said, I suspect you like me...and I like you, too."

Her lips parted, and her jaw slackened, and she wore the same look of wonderment as someone who'd first caught glimpse of new, foreign lands. And then, her entire body jerked, as she drew up into herself. "No one likes me."

"I don't think anyone really knows you."

I don't think anyone really knows you.

She wanted to tell him to shut the hell up, in just that, rude, unrestrained way, too.

She wanted to tell him that he knew absolutely nothing about what he said.

Only...he did.

And he was right.

And she was torn in equal parts, wanting to both flee as fast and far away from him and this place and continue running never to return, and wanting to stay here with him forever, in this moment, where there was truth, and at last a person who saw her, who saw more than the shallow, snobbish lady she let herself be.

"I am precisely what you take me for, Abaddon," she finally brought herself to say. "I'm nothing more than that." Her voice sounded tired to her own ears.

And she was.

Tired to her soul of being alone and being cold and she didn't want to be this way, and yet, she had to, and she also now knew no other way.

He cupped her cheek in a tender touch, his large palm rough and callused, and she leaned into him.

"No, you're not," he said, with a conviction he shouldn't possess, for Glain herself didn't even have that confidence about herself in those spoken words. "There's so much more to you. The façade you present to the world, is not who you truly are inside. The question is...why?"

She stood there, so close she was nearly in Abaddon's embrace, so close, but not close enough. She wanted to be in his arms, because in his arms, she felt...alive. She felt like a real person with warm blood flowing in her veins and believed, in those instances, that he might be right. That she was somehow more.

"I was not always this way." She hardly recognized her whisper as quiet and small as it was, and she wanted to run from that admission, hide herself away before she spoke freely about herself. For she didn't speak about herself. She was the Ice Princess, immune from pain and disdain and cold looks.

Only, Abaddon stared at her with a quiet patience, in a way that made her want to open herself to someone.

Nay, she wanted to open herself to him, let him in.

"I was very much like Opal." Her gaze grew distant and her smile wistful as she recalled herself of long ago. "I was even more wild than my sister. There wasn't a tree too tall to scale, or a lake too wide I could not swim...and naked, at that." She closed her eyes briefly, the recollection so vivid, of her sluicing through the chilled waters so swiftly, she'd ceased to feel the cold, and had only been invigorated. "I read everything. Absolutely everything. My mother handpicked my governess..."

"One of those stern sorts who sought to transform you?" he predicted after Glain's long stretch of silence.

"Anything but," she said, smiling as she recalled that equally passionate instructor. She had formed the closest of friendship with the woman. Despite the difference in years between them, they'd been kindred souls lashing out at the constraints imposed upon them.

"She encouraged me to think and to do more than just sketch and curtsy. I was never freer than I was with Mrs. Burton."

A coldness rushed in. Glain interlocked her fingers and stared at the fine leather that encased those digits. "Until my father finally took note. He discovered me and my mother and Mrs. Burton engaged in a snowball fight." Her chest tightened, the same way it had from racing around that long ago day, in the frigid winter air. "Duke's daughters did not run, and they did not laugh and smile obscenely. They were proper and polite and prim and groomed for but one purpose, making advantageous marriages," she repeated each word by rote.

"It was the last snowball I threw," she said, and sucked in a shuddery breath. "And it was also the last I saw of my mother. After that, he exiled her to one of his country properties, and only he visited her, and then he did so with the express intention of getting more children on her. Periodically, a wet nurse would return with a new babe. Opal and Flint. There was another between their births, but he was sickly and feeble, and died not long after he'd taken his first breath."

Glain struggled to speak through a pain that would always be there. "My mother died giving life to Flint."

"Oh, Glain," he said softly, and she found comfort in that gentle offering of his support.

"My mother was lionhearted," she said. "Like my sister." Unlike the person Glain had shaped herself into. "Eventually, he crushed my mother. But my sister does not realize what can happen, what *will* happen, if she conducts herself in a way the duke doesn't approve of," she said, willing him to understand. "And I...I needed to protect her and Flint."

His eyes fixed on her face. "What are you saying?" The gentleness in that question threatened to undo her.

Glain hesitated, before turning over that great secret she'd carried. "I know what I am. I know my birthright and dowry and," she grimaced, "how I look make me an object that many men would seek to possess, and if they did...if they do...then I won't be there to protect my brother and sister. They will be on their own."

He stared intently at her. Then understanding dawned in his eyes. "You presented yourself as a woman people feared being around."

She hesitated, and then slowly nodded. "Sometimes I wonder that it was so easy. I am his daughter, after all. How else to explain how I was able to make myself a woman men wouldn't consider marrying, and a person other women didn't wish to call friend?"

When she finished, she waited for the rush of discomfort and nervousness that came in revealing the most intimate parts about her life to another.

Only, it didn't come.

Rather, it felt so very good to share of herself—to let another soul in.

CHAPTER 10

If a person had asked Abaddon just days ago about Lady Glain, he'd have said there was nothing more than what existed on the surface, and if there was somehow anything more, then he'd no wish to look closer to figure out.

And he'd have been as wrong as every other person who'd ever judged her.

What a fool he'd been.

Sometimes I wonder that it was so easy. I am his daughter, after all. How else to explain how I was able to make myself a woman men wouldn't consider marrying, and a person other women didn't wish to call friend....

She'd known so much hurt and pain at her father's hands.

Was it a wonder Glain had shaped herself into a distant figure, one who shut out the rest of the world, and kept people out, and kept herself from feeling?

Abaddon carefully measured his words. "Glain, your father is a cruel bastard who hurt you, your siblings, and your mother. He isn't a man who'd think about protecting Opal and Flint. The fact that you did means you're nothing like him," he said quietly. Her chin quavered, and she dropped her gaze to her gleaming leather boots. Needing her to hear him, to see him, and all the truths he spoke, Abaddon guided her chin up until her gaze met his. "You are nothing like him," he repeated for a second time, willing her to understand that. To believe it. "In any way."

And then a lone tear wound down her cheek: a singular fat, crystalline drop that took a meandering path. Followed quickly by another. And another.

Surprise lit Glain's eyes, and she drew back slightly, touching a finger to one of those tears. "I'm crying," she whispered. And then, a beautiful, exuberant, fulsome laugh spilled from her lips. "I'm crying," she said in a joy-tinged echo. Gripping him by the front of his jacket, she brought herself up onto tiptoes to meet his gaze. "I'm crying."

"Glain?" he asked, concernedly. "Are you all right?"

"I am! Better than I've been in *so* long. I buried away all my emotions and built an armor inside to protect myself, only I forgot how wonderful it is to just *feel*."

She laughed all the harder, and the happiness emanating from her person enveloped him in such a warmth and reciprocal joy, he wanted the feeling to continue forever. He wanted to be consumed whole by this nameless sensation, one he'd never, ever felt before.

Then, stepping out of his arms, Glain danced a happy little jig around the now-empty library, laughing all the while as she did, and he found himself joining in. His mirth mixed and melded with hers.

"Come on," he finally said, taking her gently by the hand, and her merriment ebbed.

"Where are we going?" she puzzled aloud as Abaddon led her back to the library.

He fetched her cloak from the hook and helped her into it.

Abaddon paused only long enough to grab up his thick wool cloak, and toss it around his shoulders, before collecting her fingers once more, and guiding her on.

Glain puzzled her brow. "What are you doing?" She adjusted her stride, hurrying to keep up. "Are you throwing me out?" her query emerged breathless and harried.

His heart tugged. "We," he gently corrected her. "What are we doing, you mean? And no, I'm not throwing you out. Why would I throw you out?"

Some of the tension eased from her narrow frame, and he felt the way her fingers softened in his. "Because of my father," she said. "Because I reminded you how powerful he is, and how he would not tolerate me being here in your library. That he would ruin you the same way he did her."

From the corner of his eye, he caught the way she scrabbled with her lower lip, and Abaddon slowed his steps, ceasing the flight he'd set them on, and he looked squarely at her.

"I'm not afraid of your father, Glain," he said gently, but with an intentional firmness underlying that pronouncement.

"You should be." She slipped her fingers from his, and hugged herself in a sad, lonely little embrace, and he mourned that transformation, wanting to bring them back to just moments ago when joy had transformed her. "He is *not* a good man, Abaddon. He is powerful and uses that power to shape the world, bending it and people to fit his will and..." Her tone grew increasingly frenzied. "And he could destroy your library if he so wished it, and you...he could—"

"Shh," he said gently, touching a finger against her lips, staying that frantic flow. "I'm not afraid of him," he repeated. "I've dealt with uglier, meaner, more heartless monsters during my days on the streets."

Her gaze grew stricken. "I didn't know you lived on the streets," she whispered. "What you must think of me complaining about my comfortable life as a duke's d-daughter." Her voice broke, and she turned her gaze from his.

"Hey now," he said gruffly. Cupping her cheek and angling her face, he guided her eyes back to his. "There are different kinds of hardships, and what you endured, having a father separate you from your mother, witnessing how he treated her..." *Like a goddamned broodmare.* Rage spiraled once more, and he took a slow breath, fighting hard for control. When he trusted himself to again speak, without fury shaking his tones, he continued. "You were hurt emotionally by the man who should have done everything in his power to protect you from pain. And that, Glain? That's no small pain. It's no less significant because it's different than the suffering I knew. It's just as real and profound and hard."

Her mouth trembled, and a glassy sheen filled her eyes.

A pained groan escaped him. "Don't cry."

She blinked wildly. "I don't c-cry. " And she didn't. Those tears remained trapped in her eyes. "The d-duke said they are signs of weakness."

Never more had Abaddon wanted to find a man and thrash him within an inch of his rotted life.

Wordlessly, he tugged Glain into his arms, pressing her slender fame against his chest, and he just held her. He held her as she desperately needed to be held.

She was soft and quiet through that silent embrace.

Only when he felt the tension ebb once more did he free her. "Come," he said gruffly, catching her by the hand once more, and leading them outside.

A gust of cool winter air stole the air from his lungs and stung his nostrils.

"Where a-are we going?" she asked, her voice trembling from the cold, and her breath stirred a soft cloud of white.

"You'll see."

They continued north along the silent, empty London streets covered by the latest dusting of snow, until the cobblestones gave rise to a wooded knoll in the distance.

Glain slowed her steps. "What is this place?" she whispered, her voice filled with a reverent awe.

He stared on at the lands ahead, recalling the same wonderment he'd felt as a boy when he'd first looked upon them. "Finsbury Park.

That there," he pointed to the source of her amazement. "Those are the last remains of the old Hornsey Wood," he said, leading her onward to that almost mythical forestland, until they stopped before a pair of towering oaks their enormous branches twisted and blanketed in snow, giving them a look of old wizened scepters tasked with watching over this enchanted land.

He untangled their fingers, and instantly felt the loss and coldness which came from that separation.

And yet, she stared transfixed by the winter wonderland around them.

"It is...magnificent," she whispered, that exhalation inordinately loud in the December quiet. Transfixed, Abaddon drank in the sight of her.

The cold had left her creamy white cheeks stained with endearing cherry red circles. Their walk had loosened the lady's hood and the winter wind had tugged free several golden tendrils, those wispy, flyaway strands softening her. "Magnificent," he murmured softly.

Her. She was magnificent. Beauty and grace personified. And he wanted nothing more than to erase the sadness from her eyes and chase it away with a smile.

In his life Abaddon had faced any number of dangers. None of them seemed greater than his falling for this woman before him.

Magnificent...

Glain's heart thumped wildly.

For when Abaddon had spoken in a husky baritone, she could almost believe he was talking about her.

Her gaze locked with his heated one. The intensity of his piercing blue eyes speared her, robbing her lungs of breath. Hopelessly, she stared back at him.

Abaddon drifted closer, and her body swayed toward his. Her

eyes slid shut, as her mind and soul both replayed their previous embraces, and she longed for another of his kisses, the ones made of magic that drove away all the sadness and misery that had been her life these past thirteen years and filled her with lightness and joy.

The snow crunched under his booted footfall, and even with her eyes closed, she felt him draw nearer, because her body ran so in tune with his, she didn't need to see him.

He—

Something hit her lightly, right where her heartbeat pounded, and Glain cocked her head, registering that slight chill.

Her eyes flew open, and she looked from the smattering of a shattered snowball upon her chest over to Abaddon.

Abaddon's eyes which glittered, not with desire, but merriment.

Glain's brow climbed. "Did you just hit me with—?"

A second snowball hit her square in the chest, leaving more white flakes upon the emerald, green velvet.

"A snowball," Abaddon drawled, passing another missile he held back and forth between his strong hands, like a juggler she'd once observed at the Royal Circus. "Why, yes, I did."

This time, she was prepared for it.

With a breathless laugh, she dove out of the way just as he launched that snowball at her, diving for cover behind a tree. "You dastard." Her breathless laugh took the teeth from her words. "You cannot just go abou—eek—" She ducked behind the enormous trunk. His latest snowball struck the center of the tree with a sharp *thwack*.

"Are you coming out?"

"That depends," she called.

"On?"

"On whether or not you intend to stop pelting me with snow."

"Fine," he vowed.

Lifting her chin, Glain stepped out from behind her cover.

Thwack.

A third missile struck her in the shoulder, drawing a gasp from her lips, as she ducked behind the enormous, gnarled trunk once more.

"Abaddon Grimoire, did you just...lie to me?" she charged.

"All is fair in love and war, darling."

Even as she knew he referred to the latter, her heart raced all the more. "I don't throw snowballs."

"That's a shame."

She wrinkled her nose. "And why is that?"

"Because it means you're going to find yourself trammeled with snowballs, then," he drawled, his voice drifting closer, confirming he was nearer.

And this time, her heart beat hard for altogether different reasons. With a delicious joy stealing through her, she dove quickly from her hiding spot and headed for another nearby oak.

This time, Abaddon's snowball sailed ineffectually over her shoulder, as she dropped behind the trunk of the tree. "Duke's daughters do not have snowball fights," she called in her haughtiest tones, even as she squatted and silently as possible assembled a snowball. The skill came back to her as if a lifetime hadn't passed since she'd last played so in the snow with her mother.

"Seems you're at a disadvantage, then, darling," he teased.

Surging to her feet, she charged forward.

Abaddon's eyes flared with surprise, and she delighted in that moment of shock.

She tossed her snowballs in quick succession knocking the hat square from his head so that remnants of the projectile rained down on his blonde hair, and shoulders, and pelted him square in his chest.

He glanced down and stared silently for a long while at the mark made on the black wool fabric of his cloak, then slowly he picked his gaze up. "Oh, this is war, Glain Carmichael."

With a breathless laugh, she dashed off, taking shelter behind another tree.

And as she and Abaddon raced about like two children, playing in the snow, time melted away, and Glain surrendered fully to the moment—until he caught her with another snowball to her chest.

Breathless with laughter, she collapsed on her back. The cold of the frigid snow penetrated her garments, but she didn't care. She felt only this great, full joy so very powerful within her.

And it was because of this man.

She angled her head and studied him as he joined her on the ground. Their shoulders touched. Their hips kissed.

"This was s-splendid," she said softly.

"Yes." His eyes locked briefly with hers, before he closed them. "It was."

And once more, even as she knew he was talking about the moment they'd shared, it felt so very much like he spoke of her.

With his eyes closed as they were, she studied him. She'd never known anyone like him. A man who dealt in books, and didn't seek to stifle what a woman read, but rather who encouraged her to expand her mind and grow...and who also played as freely as a child in the snow.

She loved him for it.

She...loved him.

Glain froze. Her heart ceased to beat.

Loved him? What was this? She couldn't love him. It wasn't possible. She knew him but a handful of days. He was practically a stranger.

He was also a stranger who'd challenged her more than she'd ever been challenged in her nineteen years. He was someone with whom she'd shared more of herself than anyone. He listened to her and spoke with her and encouraged her to read and be free in her thoughts and with her opinions.

And you're just confusing your appreciation with him for something more...

That's all it was. She sought to reassure herself of that.

Abaddon's quiet voice slashed through her frenzied musings. "What is it?"

She gasped and looked over to find his hooded stare upon her. "Nothing," she blurted. "I...it is nothing. I was just thinking." *About the fact that I'm falling head over toes in love with you.* "How did you find this place?" She'd wondered this since they'd first come upon the park, and also the topic felt far safer to discuss than her burgeoning feelings for him.

He flipped onto his side. Propping himself up on an elbow, Abaddon rested his cheek in his hand so he could face her. "I discovered it by chance when I was a boy, picking pockets. I'd snagged a purse, and the gentleman noticed and called for the constable. I never ran as fast in all my life. I ran through the streets and kept on running until my lungs hurt and my legs were numb. And when I stopped..." With his spare hand, he gestured to the area around them. "I reached this place."

A wistful grin tugged at his hard lips, softening him in a way she'd never before seen him, and also in a way she'd have not thought possible. The sight of that smile did the strangest things to her heart's rhythm.

"I thought for a moment, I'd run so fast I'd carried myself back to some long-lost time, where trees grew, and grass covered the earth..."

The image he painted was so strong, so vivid, she could practically see a younger, smaller version of Abaddon Grimoire in her mind. She imagined him as he'd been. And she hated so much for him that his life had been filled with such strife and uncertainty that he'd been reduced to picking pockets in order to survive.

Abaddon shifted closer, drawing her back from her own thoughts, and returning her to this present moment with him. "But then as I headed closer, I noticed a tavern, and well, then I knew I was stuck still in regular old England."

Her gaze went to the inviting smoke emanating from the chimney. There were people inside that large, stone establishment. She should be concerned with the possibility of discovery and yet...she couldn't care.

For just like that, she was reminded all over again how very shallow she and her entire existence had been, of the comforts she'd enjoyed while he had struggled so. Glain turned onto her side, matching his movements so they faced one another.

She moved her eyes over the chiseled planes of his beloved face, lingering her attention on the faint crescent moon scar at the upper portion of his right cheek, and the faint stubble that formed a day's worth of growth on his unshaved cheeks.

"I am so sorry, Abaddon," she said softly, suddenly wishing she had noticed people before him, and not because of him.

Abaddon shrugged. "I survived."

"But that doesn't mean it was easy to do so. And people of privilege, people like myself had a responsibility to notice and do something. Instead, they...I...we, remained oblivious to your suffering."

"You had your own suffering to contend with, Glain," he murmured, running a finger along her chilled cheek.

Only his touch, was warm, and the heat of that slight caress chased away the cold.

Her lashes fluttered, as she leaned in, just as he did.

They froze, their mouths separated by nothing more than a hairsbreadth. Reality fought them both for a foothold.

"I've done any number of dangerous things in my life, but somehow this need to be with you, Glain," he said quietly. "This seems like the greatest danger I've ever faced."

She dampened her mouth. "Because I'm a duke's daughter." She well understood those reservations, that fear.

He ran his thumb over her lower lip, as was his way, in a touch she'd forever associate with this man.

"On the contrary, darling. Because I want you," he said bluntly, drawing a gasp from her lips. "And I know nothing good could ever come of it for either of us." He leaned close, and she leaned nearer, so close she felt the warm sough of his breath fan her lips. "But even so, I'm hopeless to stop—"

Glain kissed the remainder of the words from his lips.

He stilled for a moment, and then he met her kiss in kind.

His lips moved in time to hers, devouring that flesh, and then parting them, he slipped his tongue inside.

A desperate whimper escaped her as he kissed her like a man who wished to consume, and she ached to be consumed by him.

He rolled onto his back and drew her atop him, trading the chill of the frozen earth floor for the warmth of his heavily muscled chest. They never broke contact with their mouths, their kiss a fiery conflagration, a violent explosion of passion and hunger.

He lightly nipped at the tip of that flesh, and she suckled him in return.

Abaddon groaned and their bodies pressed as close as they were, she felt that rumble all the way through her.

And there was no winter cold.

Had there ever been cold of *any* kind? There was only this all-consuming, glorious heat that she felt low in her belly and wickedly between her legs where warmth pooled.

His tongue tangled with hers in a dance far more wicked than any waltz she'd danced.

Glain gripped the front of his cloak, wanting to crawl inside him.

She'd never be cold again. Not after this man. Not after this embrace. She was destined to be forever warm in—

Something cold and wet landed hard on her back, and she grunted.

Abaddon rolled her out of the way, just as another branch overhead shook, raining down a sizeable amount of snow.

They stared at the now bare branches responsible for that interruption, and Abaddon chuckled. "Come," he said, jumping fluidly to his feet. He stretched a hand out, tugging her up. "I have to get you back before you freeze."

Only, as she allowed him to lead her along, back through Finsbury Park, she found she wouldn't mind risking that cold just to be with him a moment longer.

CHAPTER 11

•

She came to the library every morning.

She'd taken to arriving prior to normal operating hours, and a large part of him believed—hoped, even—that her reason for doing so had to do with her wanting to be alone with him.

Sometimes she asked for his help selecting books.

Most times now she did not. Most times she fetched her own, filling her arms with volumes and bringing them to that same table... and then she'd call him over and speak to him.

Every time, excitement filled her voice and lit her eyes, as she spoke so quickly her words tumbled together, rolling as one long sentence that had the ability to make him laugh with her contagious enthusiasm.

He learned she loved the works of the Enlightened Thinkers—especially Mary Wollstonecraft.

He learned she also had a penchant for gothic novels, romantic in nature.

He knew when she spoke of either, her hands moved like little whirlwinds, as she gestured wildly.

This was one of those moments.

"Did you know that this only came to be," she lifted up the slender copy of the book he'd come to recognize as her favorite, "is because she was engaged in a war of words with Mr. Burke? She attacks not only hereditary privilege but also the words Mr. Burke uses to defend it."

Outside ice-tinged snowflakes pinged against the window.

"Burke didn't deny the existence of natural rights," he pointed out. "He simply thought they were too abstract to be applied to societies."

She drew back. "Surely you aren't defending Mr. Burke?"

Had he condemned Old King George and vowed a revolution, Glain couldn't have sounded more shocked and horrified.

Seated opposite her, Abaddon leaned in. "You sound like a regular ole' revolutionary, Glain."

"But you have to admit, there's merit to everything Miss Wollstonecraft says," she went on, and it didn't escape his notice that she didn't deny those claims. She didn't allow him a word edgewise.

"At first, when Miss Wollstonecraft published anonymously, everyone took her seriously. But the moment they printed her name in publication, people called her ideas emotional, and impassioned. Every analysis I've read of her works calls her incoherent and illogical, and yet, I cannot think of anyone who makes more sense than she."

Glain did. This woman right here. Being with her made more sense in the world than anything.

She continued, wholly oblivious to the thoughts spinning through his head. "She—"

Abaddon leaned in and kissed her.

And then, as if it were more natural than breathing or completing that unfinished though, she kissed him back. He moved his mouth against hers, drinking of her. She sighed softly, and he slipped inside to taste of her, too. Their tongues met.

"I want you, darling," he whispered hoarsely between kisses, needing her to know so she understood his want, and so that she had the sense to halt all of this—stop when he was too much a coward and selfish bastard to break this connection.

Abaddon kissed a path down the curve of her cheek. He reached that soft, sensitive skin of her neck that he'd come to learn drove her wild when he worshipped. "You should go."

Glain's head fell back, and she groaned low and long and wonderful. "I want to stay." She paused, angling away until their gazes met. "I want to stay here...with you."

He searched her face, attempting to understand what she was saying. Did he merely imagine what he wanted her to be asking?

Not breaking contact with his eyes, Glain took his hand, and guided it to her breast, placing it over that organ that thumped and pounded wildly—for him. And his own matched and then rivaled her heart's rhythm.

And he was lost.

Surrendering on a groan, Abaddon stood caught Glain up in his arms, and carried her through the library to his offices. All the while, he kissed her. She whimpered and moaned, and he devoured the breathy sounds of desire that escaped her.

He let them inside to his private office, headed to the small cot at the far back corner of the room, then he laid her down.

"Do y-you live here?" she panted against his mouth. She sounded more intrigued and relieved than horrified.

His lips twitched. "No, darling. I've in a townhouse." Not on the fine end of Mayfair where she and her sort lived, but on a respectable enough side. "On days I work longer, I occasionally take to staying the night." He slipped his tongue inside her mouth, swirling the flesh with hers.

"W-Well, I am very glad you have a bed," she breathed between each glide of flesh.

She chatted as much while making love as she did when conversing about books. It was an endearing detail about her, and a new discovery of her, too. And he found he yearned for all those intimate details of what made Glain who she was. He knew she snorted when she laughed and he knew the books that made her smile widest, but he wanted to know all there was to know about her: whether she snored when she slept or how she took her tea.

He froze.

His heart thumped frantically for a different reason.

A reason that had nothing to do with this hungering to make love to her, and everything to do with the even more intimate yearning he had for her.

Dazed, Glain's lashes fluttered wildly. "Am I doing it w-wrong?"

Her hesitant question filled with such doubt, it chased away the panic clamoring in his mind.

He groaned. "You're doing everything right, love." Drowning out the voices jeering at him for loving where he oughtn't, Abaddon surrendered to the moment.

Their lips met again, and this time, as he kissed her, he reached between them, working her modest neckline down, baring her skin to his gaze and worship.

Abaddon paused only long enough to drink in the sight of her, filling his palms with the gently rounded, silken flesh.

Under his scrutiny, her chest rose and fell harder and faster.

He brushed the pads of his thumbs over the pebbled pink tips. "You are magnificent," he said huskily, his breath pitching faster, too.

Glain sank her teeth into her lower lip and moaned low and long. Her head fell back as she reflexively pressed herself against his touch.

Emboldened, Abaddon drew the peak of her right breast into his mouth, suckling deeply of her.

A shuddery gasp exploded from her lips, as she arched up. Tangling her fingers in his hair, she clasped him close, holding him in place. "Mmmm."

That incoherent dissolution of her speech sent the heat of his hunger spiraling, and he growled his approval.

He worshiped that flesh, only pausing to switch his attentions to the previously neglected breast.

Glain moaned. Her hips moved with an increasing franticness as she pressed herself to the hard ridge of his arousal.

Abaddon edged her skirts and chemise up higher, then higher, and with every swath of skin exposed, he caressed his fingertips along that silken soft flesh. Her calves were surprisingly muscled as if she were secretly a Spartan warrioress who raced about wild lands. He moved his quest higher, sinking his fingers into her supple hip.

"Abaddon," she groaned, the pace of her gyrations grew.

He slipped a hand between her legs, cupping her center, and Glain went suddenly, absolutely still.

Abaddon paused and lifted his gaze, determining whether she wished to stop. "Tell me what you want, love," he murmured, his voice hoarse and desperate to his own ears. "Do you want me to stop?" Even as he asked it, he started to withdraw from the thatch of silken golden curls that covered her mound.

Glain laid her fingers over his, anchoring him in place, keeping him there.

Her eyes locked with his. "Do *not* stop." Hers was a command of a queen, and he was more than content to spend the rest of his days as her subject, answering her desires.

He teased the entryway of her femininity, sliding his fingers through her damp curls, and then slowly, slid a digit inside her.

Glain stiffened, and then with a sharp hiss, she moved her hips once more, lifting wildly into his touch. "You're so wet for me," he praised, and she whimpered, the thrusting of her hips grew increasingly frenzied. His shaft ached, and he wanted to slip a knee between her thighs, part her, and plunge inside the only place he wished to be.

But even more than that, he wanted her pleasure.

He plunged another finger inside her wet, warm sheath. She cried out, that incoherent echo of her desire ratcheting around the room.

Sweat dotted his brow.

His body throbbed, his shaft aching from the need to make love to her in every way, but he continued to tend her hungering—stroking her over and over again. Inside and out. Slow and then fast, and then slow, once more. Until Glain was rocking her hips from side to side, gyrating against his touch.

Then sliding down her body, he lowered his mouth between her legs.

She gasped and pushed herself up onto her elbows. "Wh-What are you doing?"

He paused, looking up at her. "Do you trust me?"

She parted her legs in answer, in invitation, and then leant a breathless confirmation. "I do."

Abaddon scooped under her buttocks, filling his hands with that voluptuous flesh. Then he guided her higher and lowered his mouth.

The scent of her—all desire and pure woman—flooded his senses, and he stroked his tongue over her warm, wet flesh, suckling of the little nub, lapping of her.

"Abaddon," she gasped. Then as if his kiss had sapped her of all energy, she collapsed on the small bed and tangled her fingers in his hair, guiding him, riding his tongue.

In the past, sex had been sex.

It had always been nothing more than a physical need to tend, as basic as eating or drinking.

But that had been before Glain. With her, with this woman, all that mattered was her pleasure.

Glain who curved her fingers sharply in his scalp, tensing and relaxing, as she urged him on, and then guided him on, pressing him deeper when she yearned for it, and edging him back when the sensation became too much.

She was close.

He felt it in the frantic, disjointed thrusting of her hips, and knew by the tension in her body. "Come for me," he coaxed.

He increased his strokes, and then her entire body stiffened, and a wicked little curse exploded from her lips as he slipped his tongue inside her tight sheath once more.

"Abaddon," she screamed, his name a prayer and a plea, and she ground herself against his mouth, over and over, and he continued to drink of her, draining every last drop of her desire, until she collapsed, sated.

His heart thundered in his own ears, and his cock throbbed, aching for more. Aching for all of her.

Instead, he gently lowered her skirts and joined her on the narrow cot.

A soft, sated smile teased at her lips. "That was magnificent," she said, her voice still breathless, her breathing still quickened.

"*You* are magnificent," he said, tugging her against him, and she went, resting her cheek against his chest.

"I never knew anything could be like that," she said softly, stroking her fingers up and down, back and forth, over the place where his heart still pounded for her. She paused, and slowly lifted her gaze to his. "Like the books."

He flashed an uneven smile. "Either that's the greatest compliment for books in the history of compliments, or an indication that my efforts in lovemaking are lacking."

Her lips twitched, and a light blush filled her cheeks. "Hardly. They're different types of wonderful, but both splendorous." Her eyes, locked with his, grew serious. "I just never knew I could feel passion, or that I could love books the way I do. And you," she pressed her palm firmly against his chest, emphasizing her words. "You opened my eyes to all of it, and I can never repay you."

He caught her hand and raised it to his mouth. "I don't want repayment," he murmured, pressing a kiss against the seam of her wrist. *You. I want...you...*

And God help him, that terrified the everlasting hell out of him. The last thing he knew anything about, and the last thing he wished to be part of, was Polite Society.

Glain's eyes darkened. She ran her gaze searchingly over his face. "What is it, Abaddon?"

And he found himself unnerved in a new way: by her awareness of the tumult running through him.

"We should get you straightened up," he said, too much a coward to talk to her about the thoughts knocking around his brain. "The library will open soon, and...I'd not see you ruined."

Disappointment lit her expressive blue irises.

The moment suddenly stilted when it had never been so between them—not even at their first tense meeting. Abaddon and Glain presented their backs to one another, each of them straightening their garments.

When they'd finished, they faced one another once more.

And all the breath in his body lodged somewhere in his chest at the sight of her.

Her cheeks were flushed a shade of cherry red, much the way they had when they'd frolicked in the snow. The sapphire and emerald peacock hair combs tucked in her hair had become loosened, releasing several golden strands that hung enchantingly about her shoulders.

"What is it?" she asked, patting her face. "Do I look a fright?"

"You look..." *Perfect. Breathtaking.* "Just fine," he murmured those safer words. "Just a couple of hairs out of place." He proceeded to straighten those fine jeweled pieces in her hair, worth more than anything he'd owned for the first twenty years of his life, and still finer than anything he'd worn or possessed in his entire twenty-seven years. A tangible, material reminder of the different worlds they belonged to.

They headed from his offices, just as the tinny bell at the front door jingled announcing his latest patron.

Glain stopped abruptly, as her gaze landed on the figure framed in the doorway.

Abaddon followed her stare.

He silently cursed.

The Duke of Strathearn moved his gaze between Abaddon and Glain before ultimately settling on the lady. "Good day, Lady Diamond," he greeted, with an aloof chill Abaddon had never recalled of the other man in all the years he'd known him. "Mr. Grimoire," his friend said, not taking his focus off Glain.

A blush climbed up Glain's prominent cheekbones, and she dropped a queenly curtsy. "Your Grace," she returned in clipped tones to rival the duke before them, and also not ones Abaddon had heard in so very long from her. "Mr. Grimoire, I thank you for your assistance." She made a show of gathering up some of her books and tucking them into her satchel.

Avoiding his eyes, she hastened around Strathearn, making a graceful beeline for the door.

His friend didn't waste any time. "What are you doing?" he asked, the moment Glain had gone.

"I think it should be clear," Abaddon said with a grunt. "I'm working." To demonstrate as much, he proceeded to collect the two books Glain had left behind. He stacked them, putting them away for when she returned tomorrow.

"You know that isn't what I'm talking about."

Of course, as a notorious rogue, with a reputation for charming actresses and widows alike, Strathearn would have recognized the wrinkles in Glain's gown.

"I'm talking about the lady. Nothing can come of that," his friend said matter-of-factly. "Her sort? They'll only break your heart."

Her sort. "And what sort exactly is that?" he asked, infusing a steely warning there.

"A pompous lady," Strathearn said bluntly. "One who is icy and cold and—"

"You don't know her," he said tightly.

"Actually, I do. I know both her type, and the lady herself."

That reminder set Abaddon's teeth on edge for a host of reasons.

His friend persisted. "She'll take her pleasure with a man outside her station, but—"

"Have a care," Abaddon warned in soft, steely tones that managed to briefly silence the other man.

"Think, man. Even if she did want a respectable future with you, would you want with one her? One that requires you to be part of Polite Society? Not on the fringe of the ton, dealing in books, but dancing attendance on lords and attending balls and—"

He saw his own horror reflected back in the other man's eyes.

"Precisely," Strathearn said. "You don't need her sort in your life. As it is, her father has her pegged for a prince's wife."

A prince's wife. She'd be royalty in *every* way.

And Abaddon found himself wanting to hiss and snarl like a wounded beast, and then hunt down the man who'd be the better match for her.

The duke rested a hand on his sleeve. "You need to let this go."

His friend was right.

Abaddon needed to let *her* go.

And even understanding that truth, knowing he and Glain were two people born to two vastly different universes, he found himself secretly wishing there could be a future with her.

CHAPTER 12

The moment Glain exited Abaddon's library, Glain wanted to turn and run.

She'd believed there couldn't be anything worse than being discovered by the Duke of Strathearn, until she hastened from the library, and found her father with his hands clasped behind his back, standing beside his black lacquer carriage.

The Duke of Devonshire lingered his hawk-eyed gaze on her slightly mussed tresses then he moved his focus to her face.

Cold and horror of the moment lent her teeth a noisy chatter, and Glain prayed the duke attributed the winter's chill to the color in her cheeks.

And then he locked his focus on her mouth, her swollen mouth. Her lips felt full and heavy from Abaddon's kiss...ten minutes? ten years? a lifetime ago?

She wanted to flee back inside and into Abaddon's arms, and away from this moment.

Alas, the decision was made for her—stolen from her.

"Get inside, Diamond," her father ordered.

Glain remained rooted to the pavement, wanting to tell him to go to hell, wanting to tell him even more explicitly what he could do with his ducal commands.

"Unless you want me to see this bloody library closed forever, I said get in," he said in a voice, his fury tightly controlled.

Glain sprang into movement. Resisting the urge to steal one last glance at Abaddon's circulating library, she accepted the driver's help, allowing him to hand her inside.

The duke joined her a moment later.

Glain made a show of staring out the window at the passing streets.

He knows.

From the moment she'd spied him there, she just knew. The Duke of Devonshire had gathered there'd been more of Glain's meetings with Abaddon. She'd seen it in his eyes.

Her father didn't again speak until the carriage lurched into motion. "Where is your maid?"

She kept herself motionless, refusing to tremble under his icy stare. "I was just finishing up and sent her on to my carriage." The lie slipped out surprisingly smooth and easy, considering the tumult inside.

This was bad. This was dire, indeed.

For her. But worse for Abaddon.

And for your time together.

As if sensing the lie, knowing one when he heard one, even one that had been effectively delivered, her father narrowed a sharp stare on her, and she remained still through this latest scrutiny.

"Let me see it, Diamond."

It took a moment to register he spoke to her. Because in these past weeks with Abaddon, she'd ceased to be Diamond and had come alive as only Glain, a woman capable of laughing and smiling and knowing love...

And also unfortunately, knowing great hurt.

"I said, let me see it," he barked, and she jumped at that unexpected loss of control.

With trembling fingers, she turned over her bag.

He tipped it over unceremoniously and her books tumbled to the floor of the carriage. Her precious volumes, hand selected by Abaddon who'd come to know so very well precisely what she loved to read, lay in a sad, sorry heap between her and her father's feet.

The copy of her Mary Wollstonecraft lay open on its spine, putting the title on full display. Never had Glain felt more exposed, more vulnerable than she did in this moment.

Her father grabbed his cane, and as if he were Perseus dealing with Medusa's serpent locks, he jabbed at the leather volume. "What do you think you're *doing*, Diamond?"

"They are just books," she said dumbly, wishing she had a greater defense than those words, particularly as they were so very much more to her.

"Just books?" he echoed. "Just *books*?" His voice climbed, and she felt her pulse rise, too, for the duke never showed such displays of emotion. He never showed *any*.

Bending down, Glain hastily returned the titles to her satchel. Her fingers trembled so mightily, she fumbled with that simple task.

As if recalling himself, the duke sucked in a slow, noisy breath through his flared hawkish nose.

He slapped the tip of his cane down on the lone title she'd not managed to tuck away from his wrathful stare.

And then he reached for that leather volume and took it from her. He robbed Glain of that beloved book, with the same ease all mercenary fathers and leaders everywhere, snatched rights and freedoms from their daughters and wives.

Glain wanted to rail. To snap and hiss like an angry cat. She yearned to rip that cherished copy from his fingers, shove the door open, jump from the fast-moving carriage, and run as fast and as far away as she could to another place and another time where no one sought to keep a woman from reading whatever book she so wished.

"Look at me, Glain," her father ordered, a frost to match the winter's day coated that demand.

Damn him. Damn him and his orders and his bullying her and her sister and brother, and their mother whom he'd banished from their lives.

For the first time ever, Glain met his gaze squarely, and glared at this man who'd sired her, with a lifetime's worth of hate.

He narrowed his eyes. "Do you think I can't take one look at you and know you've been conducting yourself like a wanton?"

Oh god. In an instant, she faltered, drawing back sharply into herself. Of course, she'd known he suspected but something in his speaking it aloud made it all the worse. "I've always known you had your mother's streak in you," he said crisply, snapping off his gloves. He beat those fine leather articles together. "Wicked in every way, she was."

And Glain knew she should be measured, she knew riling him was the absolute last thing she should do, and dropping her eyes, and being demure the first and only thing. But as he droned on, a harsh soliloquy on the woman who'd given her life, Glain's rage kindled like a slow-building ember that fanned, and grew, into a blazing conflagration of fury. "Your mother—"

"My mother was not wicked. She loved to read and explore topics men are free to study. She challenged me to do the same. She was a *good* woman," she said sharply, relishing in the way his brow flared with shock. "The very best."

He sputtered. "Your mother was fortunate I was magnanimous and did not see her shut away for what she did."

"What she *did?*" she repeated. "What did she do other than teach me to laugh and love and live? And for that, you *did* send her away. Not to a hospital but to a place in the country." Where he'd only ever visited the duchess until he'd managed to get an heir on her, in a final pregnancy which had taken her life.

"Your mother had outrageous thoughts about a woman's place."

He may as well have called Glain's mother a faithless whore for the vitriol contained within his words.

"I'll not have my daughter conduct herself in that same manner."

He glared at her. "You are done with that bookshop that caters to all manner of riffraff."

"*Library. It is a circulating library* and its doors are open to all people, regardless of station."

"Precisely. It is—"

"It is as the world should be, Your Grace." One where a person's lineage, nor gender, mattered. Where people were all welcome and united in a shared love of literature.

Rage tightened his features. "You are done with that man. Am I clear?"

He couldn't be clearer, and yet...

"No," she said, in this continued show of defiance, the first she'd ever displayed against the duke and his dictates.

His eyebrows climbed.

Who knew how very exhilarating a show of rebellion in fact, was? Her euphoria lasted but a moment.

"I will see him ruined, Glain," he said, almost bored sounding. "If *that* is what you wish."

Her lungs constricted. Moments ago, she'd have sworn there could be no greater pain than when her mother had been ripped from her life, and the duke had begun his full oppression of Glain. But this? Knowing Abaddon would suffer at her father's hands gutted her inside. She'd spare Abaddon every pain if she could.

Even if it meant the death of every happiness that came in just being with him.

She bit the inside of her cheek hard, scrabbling with that flesh, wanting to cry and rail and shout. In the end, she knew that would only add to her father's fury, and that she risked Abaddon's paying an even higher price.

The interminable carriage ride ended, and she made herself sit still, until the door had been opened for her, and a footman reached a hand inside to assist her down.

"Glain?" her father asked, staying her.

She glanced back.

The duke held a gloved palm out, his meaning clear.

Glain looked between that hated ducal hand and the satchel. He'd deny her not only seeing a man whom she desperately loved, but he'd assert himself even in interfering with what she chose to read?

"Now," he demanded.

She tugged her satchel close. "No," she said quietly. "You may determine where I go and don't go, but I'll not allow you to dictate what books I read."

His snowy-white eyebrows snapped together in a line as shock stamped his features.

He quickly found himself. "Very well," he said matter-of-factly, but she was not fooled by that uncharacteristic blasé response to her show of defiance. "You can enjoy your titillating, trashy books. I will take my displeasure to the bookshop owner peddling—"

Glain slapped her satchel in his hand.

"Very good, Diamond," he said coolly. "Very good. That is all."

That is all.

How casual he was about stealing literature from her, how matter of fact he was about exerting control over her. Hatred burned in her veins, threatening to set her afire from within.

"Damn you and your efforts to stamp out joy," she said tightly.

She yanked her attention away from this man whom she so despised.

The footman held his fingers out once more, and this time she took them, ignoring the pitying glimmer in the servant's eyes.

She made a slow, purposeful march up the stone steps, sailed through the front door, and climbed the stairs, feeling her father's eyes upon her the whole way.

Only when she reached the hall, did she let her shoulders sag, and with a silent sob, Glain took flight, racing as fast as her legs could carry her. She yearned to to run away from this place, and her father, and the threats he'd made, and from the pain of having her relationship with Abaddon severed...and the misery of not even having the freedom to read whatever books she wished to read.

Glain stumbled into her chambers. The moment she was inside, she collapsed against the solid oak panel of the closed-door borrowing support where she could.

Her chest and shoulders heaved, as she fought to breathe through the pain of it all. She'd believed all men were like her father. That they all sought to control and prevent a woman from having any freedom to exercise her thoughts and mind.

Until she'd met Abaddon. He'd not only challenged her to think more broadly but to explore philosophers and authors whom she'd never, ever thought to read, because she'd not known those works could make her feel as they had: her mind free and at the same time whirring with the magic of newly discovered ideas and thoughts she'd never before considered, because of her previous ignorance. Abaddon had introduced her to thinkers and theories that made her see the world and her place in it, in a whole new way—which was no doubt why, weaker men wished to bury those books and starve women of the possibilities presented on those pages, so that they never hungered for more.

After all, one could not know the sweetness of chocolate without having tasted it upon their tongue.

Abaddon didn't seek to oppress Glain but rather, encouraged her to find her voice, and speak it freely. He had debated with her, and talked with her, and for the first time, since her mother had been ripped from her life, she'd felt free to share parts of herself with another person.

Tears welled in her eyes, and this time, she didn't fight them. This time, she welcomed the freedom that came in simply feeling and surrendering to her pain at the inequity that was a woman's life. At losing her books.

At losing Abaddon.

A tortured moan slipped from her lips, and she hugged her arms close, tightly around her middle, squeezing herself in a bid to tamp out some of this misery.

Her efforts proved futile.

She would never stop wanting him nor loving him. Because yes, she did love him. She didn't even fight that realization. She—

A hesitant knock sounded at her door, and she straightened. Her father.

"Glain?" her sister ventured, and some of the tenson left her.

She smoothed her shaking palms over her face. "Enter."

The panel opened, and her brother and sister stepped forward hesitantly. When Opal closed the door, she looked at Glain. "I..." Her words faded. "You're crying," she whispered, and their brother blanched, tugging sharply at his cravat. "I...I've never seen you cry."

Yes, because she'd buried away all emotion.

No more.

Her father might control her in so many ways, but he'd not have this hold over her, too.

Flint looked over his little shoulder at the door covetously and grunted when Opal grabbed him by the arm and jerked him forward. "What is that for?" he demanded.

"You look like you want to leave."

"I don't want to leave," he groused, shifting back and forth on his feet. "I'm Glain's brother. It's my responsibility to protect her."

No, it was her responsibility to protect them, and that was what she'd been doing all these years, and she'd never stop.

She reached out, grabbed them both, and pulled them into her arms. Opal and Flint immediately folded theirs about Glain.

"Whaffsthatfor," her brother's muffled response came buried against the fabric of her dress.

"I was wrong," Glain whispered, drawing them closer, clinging to them. *About so much.* "I...Mr. Grimoire, and his library..." She made herself release them from her arms but placed her hands upon her sister's little shoulders. Glain crouched slightly so she could look the smaller girl in the eyes. "I want you to continue going there. I will...protect you." She might not be able to return but her sister could...and more importantly, her sister would. Glain looked over at Flint. "I'll protect both of you." Soon enough he'd return to Eton but until he did, and while he was here, she'd look after him, too.

"Hey, now," he said gruffly. "That's my job."

"Our job," Opal shot back, tossing a glare her brother's way.

"It's not," Glain said gently, touched and grateful for that evidence of their love.

Opal drew back. She passed a stricken gaze over Glain's face. "But what about *you*?"

She forced a smile, the gesture feeling strained on her muscles. "I saw everything I needed to see," she lied. "It was enough." *It would never be enough.*

Fire lit Opal's eyes. "I don't believe that. I believe you care very much about the library and Mr. Grimoire. In fact, I believe you've fallen in love with him."

Her sister's words hit Glain squarely in the chest, and she recoiled from hearing another person—her sister—speak them aloud. Something in that made it more real, and hearing this particular someone say it aloud only reinforced how impossible it was to love Abaddon, as nothing more could come of that relationship.

The fight and life drained from her being, and Glain slid slowly onto the floor, borrowing support from the door panel.

Opal hesitated, and then joined her on the floor, with a reluctant Flint sliding onto the other side of Glain.

"You...don't deny it," Opal ventured tentatively.

It wasn't a question, and even if it had been Glain didn't have the emotional energy to answer.

Opal rested her head upon Glain's shoulder, and Glain closed her eyes, angling her head towards her sister's. Alas, her sister hadn't ever been comfortable or content with silence. "You should marry him, you know."

A sharp, pained laugh exploded from Glain's lips.

"What?" Opal said defensively. "You should." The girl looked to their brother. "Isn't that right, Flint?"

"Quite. He makes you happy and there's nothing more important than—"

"You and Opal are more important. And if I marry I won't be here with you."

Her sister proved relentless. "But we don't want you to be here just because of us. Isn't that right, Flint?"

The boy nodded. "Certainly not."

"See," Opal said earnestly. "We don't want you to not marry the man you love—"

"It's done, Opal," she said with a gentle insistence. "It's done," she repeated as much for herself as for her sister and brother.

It was done.

The memory of the books she'd read and the time she'd spent with Abaddon would have to be enough.

CHAPTER 13

She'd stopped coming.

She'd sent around a polite enough note, thanking him for the time he'd spent elucidating her as to the nature of his establishment, and the enjoyable time she'd spent there—not with him, specifically—and had assured him that she'd seen all she'd needed to see.

And just like that, their time together was done. Sealed by nothing more than a respectful note of six sentences, and the swooping, elegant inked letters that had made up her name.

Abaddon should have expected she would. From the first moment he'd met Lady Glain, he'd known their time together was limited, and that she was not the sort to enter this establishment. She'd been, in short, everything he'd expected of a pompous lady.

But in the weeks they'd known one another, she'd proven...so much more.

And mayhap that was what made her sudden disappearance from his life all the more agonizing.

It had been easier to think of her as a shallow, self-important lady who peered down her haughty nose at people outside of her station and books she deemed unworthy of her attention.

It was an entirely different thing to have discovered she'd only built and presented that masterful façade to the world, so that she could protect her younger siblings. That underneath the sheen of ice the whole world—himself, at first, included, saw—was a fiery, passionate woman, possessed of a keen wit and intellect. A woman who devoured books like a starving man did bread.

Seated at the front table she'd made her own for all those times she'd come here, Abaddon re-read a note he'd already committed to memory.

It was for the best.

As Strathearn had pointed out, Glain belonged to a whole different stratum, and it was absolutely a world Abaddon had no wish to be part of. He was more than content to run his circulating library, procuring nothing more than books for both commoners and those people who were Glain's social equals. He didn't want to attend fancy dinners with them—lord knew he'd hated the lessons Strathearn had provided before those events Abaddon was forced to drag himself to with the express intent of procuring greater funds and sponsors among that ruling elite.

And he certainly didn't want to attend balls or any of it.

Abaddon traced a fingertip over the swoopy letters that made up her name.

The thing of it was...he would have done it, and he would have done it all gladly if it had meant she was in his life.

"You look like hell."

He glanced up.

At some point, Strathearn had entered.

"Didn't even hear the bell," his friend drawled. "I think that's a first." He helped himself to a seat, and turning the spindly oak chair around, he straddled it. His gaze fell to the note, and belatedly Abaddon picked up the small sheet, folding it and tucked it inside his jacket. "Never thought I'd see you this way."

"What way?" he asked surlily. But he couldn't help it. He was angry and miserable and spoiling for a fight.

"Besotted by a woman." His friend gave his head a wry shake. "At that, a woman like Lady Diamond."

He slapped a palm on the table and the books Glain had left behind, jumped. The books he refused to move because then it would mean all of her and all of her time here was at an end. "What do you know of it, Strathearn?" he hissed. "You see what the whole world sees, but sometimes there is more to a person."

As he spoke, his voice grew more booming, filling with fury. "If Mr. Baughan had taken me for nothing more than a street thief, even now I'd be stealing, dead, or worse." He paused, taking several deep breaths to rein in his temper. "And there was...*is* more to her."

Surprise glinted in Strathearn's eyes, and his friend sharpened a knowing look on Abaddon's normally ascetic face.

The fight went out of Abaddon. "And her name is Glain," he finished tiredly, running a hand over his brow. "Her name is Glain."

His friend beat his hat against his thigh. "Do you want to talk about it?"

"There's nothing to talk about."

And yet, Abaddon spoke, the words tumbling forth about the time he'd spent with Glain, and how desperately and hopelessly and helplessly in love he'd fallen with her. He shared with him the time he'd spent talking with Glain about books and philosophers, and his hungering for more with her.

When he'd finished, Abaddon removed her note, and read it once more. "Who the hell thought I'd find myself this way?"

From the corner of his eye, he caught the twitch of his friend's mouth. "Certainly not I." He paused. "Have you...thought about... speaking with the lady? Telling her how you feel? If she is the woman you take her to be—"

"She is."

"Then, she will want a future with you, Abaddon," his friend quietly finished over that interruption.

The bell announced a new patron and his friend glanced over, and Abaddon followed the other man's gaze.

His heart jumped, and he braced, waited with bated breath for the woman to follow in behind that familiar pair, a young girl and boy.

But Lady Opal and Lord Flint merely drew the door shut and headed over. He and Strathearn made to stand, but like a duke he'd one day be, the boy waved them back.

"No need for any of that," Opal said, availing herself to a chair, and spinning it around, she straddled it the way the duke beside her did. She nudged her chin his way. "I'm disappointed in you."

The duke touched a hand to his chest. "I daresay that's the first I've—"

"Stuff it. As I obviously don't know you, I'm speaking to him."

"Sorry," Flint silently mouthed to the other gentleman, but Strathearn merely waved his hand in a like manner the boy had done moments ago.

Opal took in that exchange, and eyed the duke warily, before looking to Abaddon. "Is he a friend?"

Abaddon inclined his head. "He is. The Duke of Strath—"

"Don't care for introductions," she cut him off. —Strathearn's lips twitched.— "I just want to make sure he's not some pompous fellow whose going to take exception if I call you out in front of him. I don't need him trying to shut down your library."

"And...you intend to call me out?" Abaddon hazarded, feeling the first stirrings of anything other than misery these past days.

"I sure as hell do," she snapped.

"*We* sure as hell do," Glain's brother corrected.

"You did not come," Opal continued.

He stared at her.

She threw her hands up. "To see my sister."

"Was she...expecting me?" His heart kicked up its beat.

Opal narrowed her eyes into thin, dangerous slits. "*I* was expecting you."

There was a rush of disappointment. "Expecting me to..."

"To offer for her." Exasperation sent her voice climbing, and a patron at the opposite end of the library looked over and frowned.

Abaddon inclined his head in apologies, before returning his focus to Glain's sister. "Has she...given some indication that she," *wanted*, "expected that?" he ventured, with a calm he didn't feel.

The girl actually growled.

Lord Flint caught her by the arm.

And then the anger seeped from her taut little features. "I expected it," she said again, this time, softly, sadly. "Because she was so very happy every time she came from seeing you, and she laughed and read books and her eyes were so bright that I could only believe she loved you and that you loved her in return."

Every word was a dagger dragged over his heart because he wanted everything Glain's sister spoke of to be true.

And yet...

"Your sister and I came together because of an arrangement," he said carefully. "And that arrangement ended."

Opal's frown deepened, and she looked over to Strathearn.

The duke shrugged. "Don't look here. I told him he should go to the lady."

The girl grunted. "Didn't think I much liked dukes, but I might make an exception for you."

Strathearn inclined his head. "I'm honored—"

"Don't make more of it than it is. I said I *might* make an exception. You're still a duke." Dismissing him, Opal looked to Abaddon. "My sister cannot come here," she said, her voice earnest. "I overheard it from the housekeeper who heard it from one of the maids who is sweet with one of the footmen, that my father told her that he would shut down your library and ruin you if she continued coming here."

His chest tightened, and so much rage blackened his vision it was briefly blinding. "What?" he whispered.

Flint nodded. "And she cried, Mr. Grim. She *cried*," Glain's sister repeated for good measure.

Oh. God. That was why she'd ceased coming around. Because her bastard of a father had intimidated her into doing so. Abaddon balled his hands into painful fists, wanting to throttle the man for hurting Glain as he had.

"And he took her books." Fury burned bright in the little girl's blue eyes, eyes that were so very much her sister's. "Her books, Mr. Grim. Her books. He handed them over to another footman to burn but that footman gave them to another footman who gave them to his sweetheart who is friendly with Glain's maid, who in turn gave them to Glain..." He sought to follow that lengthy chain of individuals. "And I have snuck into her room, when she is sleeping, and I find her with her books tucked under her pillow—"

A tortured groan escaped him, drowning out the rest of Opal's words. Abaddon surged to his feet.

"Where are you going?" she demanded.

"I..." It occurred to him he didn't even know where Glain lived.

Strathearn cleared his throat. "If I may?" He provided the address.

Flint's eyes clouded with confusion. "That's where we live."

For the first time since she'd stormed the library that day, Opal's eyes brightened with something other than the deserved fury. "It is! He is going for her!" She looked happily to Abaddon. "You're going for her!"

Abaddon clenched his jaw. He was going for her, and he'd be damned ten times to Sunday if he left without having her in his life.

Strathearn jumped to his feet. "My carriage awaits."

CHAPTER 14

Surprisingly, the prince was *not* the pompous person Glain had expected him to be.

He'd conducted himself with distinction during battles with Napoleon. He continued to serve as a diplomat and did not think anything of talking about those topics with her, a woman.

He was handsome, with a tall, slender frame, pleasing face, and clever mustache.

But none of it mattered.

He was not Abaddon.

He didn't speak about books and literature or ask for her opinion. Rather, he spoke about himself and his accomplishments, and seemed just as content speaking to her father as he did, her.

At that particular moment, the prince sat across from the duke, both men speaking about matters of horseflesh.

As they did, she welcomed the reprieve from having to be polite and pretend to be interested in him and whatever he spoke about.

Her gaze drifted over to the window. The curtains had been drawn back which placed the grey London sky on display. Then she saw it. A single flake. So faint, she may as well have imagined it. So small she blinked but when she opened her eyes again and looked, there was another. And another.

As the men's conversation droned on, her mind drifted to another day not so very long ago, but also one that may as well have been a lifetime past...to the time she and Abaddon had frolicked in the fields of snow, hurling snowball as their laughter had echoed on the still winter air.

She registered the frantic flurry of footfalls and looked up, just as the door was drawn open, and the family butler revealed the quartet behind him.

Her gaze bypassed the duke and her siblings for the tall, powerful man whose presence commanded greater than any mere title could.

Her heart tripled its beat. "Abaddon," she whispered, his name emerging noiseless.

A smile twinkled in the old butler's eyes. "A Mr. Grimoire to see Lady Diamond," the butler announced in his slightly nasally tones.

"What is the meaning of this?" her father demanded, surging to his feet. "We are entertaining."

Abaddon stepped into the room. "You forgot something, Glain," he called, easily overpowering her father's lofty tirade. Reaching inside his jacket as he came forward, he stopped before her, and withdrew a book.

She stared dumbly at the title she'd left behind that day. "Oh," she said, deflated.

His gaze locked with hers. "And you forgot something else...me."

His quiet pronouncement slammed into her, and incapable of words, she shot her eyes up to meet his.

Abaddon sank onto a knee beside her.

"Get away from her this instant!" her father shouted. Thumping a fist on the arm of the chair, he thundered for footmen.

Abaddon ignored him. "Every day since you've been gone, I've missed you," he said quietly, stroking her cheek. Closing her eyes, Glain leaned into that bold, familiar, and magical touch. "I've missed your smile and debating you. I've missed watching you scour shelves, and...and...I miss the way you dog-ear your pages." He paused, and she opened her eyes. "I love you, Glain, and I want to spend every day of our lives continuing to make you smile and finding out everything there is to know about you."

Her chest quickened and tears filled her eyes. "You love me," she whispered.

"And it is my hope that you can one day love me—"

"I love you," she rasped, launching herself at Abaddon

Abaddon, who easily caught her, and kept on his feet, holding her close.

Opal and Flint let out a triumphant cheer, clapping wildly.

"Footmen!" her father bellowed and then looked frantically to the prince. "You must forgive me. This upstart has no place—"

"It seems the couple is in love," the prince said, with a smile in his voice.

Her father seethed, turning his wrath back on Glain and Abaddon. "I'll see you destroyed."

"Actually, you won't," Abaddon's friend intoned from the doorway. "Mr. Grimoire has enough powerful patrons that your word will have no impact, one way or the other. I've as much if not more influence than you because I'm not a bastard about my title." He spoke with a haughty cool that only a duke could manage, and one to rival her father's.

"Strathearn," Glain's father muttered. "I see you turned out *nothing* like your father."

"Thank God, for *that*." The younger duke flicked an imagined speck of lint from his shoulder. "It is interesting you should mention my late father. I'd be remiss if I failed to mention, thanks to he and his journals, I've a substantial bit of information that serves as a reminder to me."

Her father peered at the other, formidable man. "Oh? And what reminder is that?"

The Duke of Strathearn locked his gaze with the older nobleman's and smiled. "Not *all* of us are as illustrious as they may seem.

Lady Diamond marrying Mr. Grimoire, and your younger children being free to visit whatever circulating library they so choose would really be no grand scandal in the scheme of...say, *other* things."

Glain's father blanched. He cast a frantic look at the frowning prince, and then returned his attention to the duke. "Are you *th-threatening* me?"

"I wouldn't dare." Strathearn inclined his head. The feigned levity vanished, as his eyes hardened. "I trust, given the circumstances, I won't *need* to threaten you."

His meaning remained clear.

The Duke of Devonshire cursed roundly.

Opal clapped her hands happily. "You're definitely moving up in my estimation, Duke," the girl praised.

Strathearn shot her a wink.

Abaddon rested his brow against Glain's, drawing her attention back to him.

"I'm not a prince," he said quietly, caressing her cheek once more. "I'm not a lord. I'm nothing more than the owner of a circulating library with a modest townhouse and even more modest wealth—"

"None of that matters," she interrupted, her voice breaking.

He continued over her interruption. "—asking you to marry—?"

Glain kissed the remainder of the proposal from his lips, and he returned that kiss.

Ignoring more of her father's blustering, Abaddon drew back and grinned. "Is that a 'yes', darling?"

"That is a yes," she murmured, and a giddy laugh spilled from Glain's lips, as he kissed her and, in his arms, she at last found herself...*home.*

MORE HAPPILY EVER AFTERS!

Be sure and check out the latest installments from Christi Caldwell's bestselling Heart of a Duke series!

Defying the Duke

Bookish and spirited, Lady Lettie Brookfield is firmly on the shelf. The last thing she wants, however, is to spend the rest of her days as an unmarried sister, dependent upon her family's charity. Accepting she won't have a love match, she finds herself coming around to the idea of marrying the only suitor she's ever had...that is until she's suddenly reunited with her brother's former best friend, the brooding, formally charming, Anthony, Duke of Granville.

To Marry Her Marquess

Lady Caroline and Wynn are thrust together by Caroline's matchmaking mother but Wynn has obligations to his family. Will responsibilities and duties guide Wynn and Caroline? Or can they give love a chance...*together.*

The Devil and the Debutante

In order to save his gaming empire, head proprietor Rex DuMond has no choice but to pursue Lady Faith Brookfield, an innocent debutante, for the secrets she holds. Can true love ever be born in treachery and deceit? Accustomed to a world where the house always wins, Rex must wager all he owns on the greatest gamble of all...love.

Devil by Daylight

Coming to the world of Heart of a Duke, the romance between *Miss Honoria Fairfax and Tormund Stone, the Earl of Rockford!*

ABOUT THE AUTHOR

Christi Caldwell is the USA Today bestselling author of the Sinful Brides series and the Heart of a Duke series. She blames novelist Judith McNaught for luring her into the world of historical romance. When Christi was at the University of Connecticut, she began writing her own tales of love—ones where even the most perfect heroes and heroines had imperfections. She learned to enjoy torturing her couples before they earned their well-deserved happily ever after. Christi lives in Charlotte, North Carolina, where she spends her time writing, baking, and being a mommy to the most inspiring little boy and empathetic, spirited girls who, with their mischievous twin antics, offer an endless source of story ideas!

Printed in Great Britain
by Amazon

16673141R00169